D1335361

SLOW DOWN ARTHUR, STICK TO THIRTY

Harland Miller was born in Yorkshire in 1964, and now lives in north London. He has been in a band, printed T-shirts for bands such as The Fall, Bauhaus and the Jam, and worked as a model and escort. He now continues his work as an artist.

SLOW DOWN ARTHUR, STICK TO THIRTY

HARLAND MILLER

Fourth Estate • *London*

FOR AVA

First published in Great Britain in 2000 by

Fourth Estate Limited

6 Salem Road

London W2 4BU

www.4thestate.co.uk

Copyright © Harland Miller 2000

10 9 8 7 6 5 4 3 2 1

p.32: 'Born To Be Wild' lyrics and music by Steppenwolf © Music Sales; p.4: 'Isis' music by Bob Dylan, lyrics by Bob Dylan and Jaques Levy © 1975 Ram's Horn Music/Special Rider Music; p.118: 'Gonna Make You A Star' lyrics and music by David Essex © Music Sales; p130: 'I Die You Die' lyrics and music by Gary Newman © Music Sales; pp.231, 233: 'I Am What I Am' lyrics and music by Jerry Herman, Hayward © EMI Music Publishing Ltd; pp.234–5, 237: 'Les Toros' lyrics and music by Jaques Brel © Pouchenel Editions Musique; p.245: 'DJ' lyrics and music by David Bowie, Carlos Alomar and Brian Eno © 1993 Tintoretto Music/EMI Music Publishing Ltd/EG Music Ltd/Warner Chappell Music Ltd. Reproduced by permission of International Music Publications; 'Repetition' lyrics and music by David Bowie and Brian Eno © EMI Music Publishing Ltd/Westbury Music/Music Sales; p.251: 'Boys Keep Swinging' lyrics and music by David Bowie and Brian Eno © EMI Music Publishing Ltd/Westbury Music Sales; 'Move On' lyrics and music by David Bowie © EMI Music Publishing Ltd/Westbury Music/Music Sales. *Every effort has been made to locate and contact all relevant copyright holders; where errors or omissions occur please contact the publishers so this can be rectified in future editions.*

The right of Harland Miller to be identified as the author of this work has been asserted by him in accordance with the Copyright, Design and Patents Act 1988. A catalogue record for this book is available from the British Library.

ISBN 1-84115-282-X

All rights reserved. No part of this publication may be reproduced, transmitted, or stored in a retrieval system, in any form or by any means, without permission in writing from Fourth Estate Limited.

Typeset in Plantin/Frutiger by MATS, Southend-on-Sea, Essex
Printed in Great Britain by Clays Ltd, St. Ives plc

CONTENTS

PROLOGUE   7

PART I   21

PART II   109

PART III   191

PART IV   215

EPILOGUE   241

It was thus rather the exacting nature of my aspirations, than any particular degradation in my faults, that made me what I was.

If I could rightly be said to be either it was only because I was radically both.

Robert Louis Stevenson
THE STRANGE CASE OF
DR JEKYLL AND MR HYDE

PROLOGUE

CAMDEN TOWN, SPRING 1987

'Sorry, s'cuse, ahh, yeah, it's run out *again*.'

The woman at the benefit office hands me another pen.

NAME: William Glov . . . I write, then cross it out and put Nick Barrel instead.

DATE OF BIRTH: 11/11/63

ADDRESS: 2 Hugh Charlton House, Davis Street, Camden Town

FULL POSTCODE: NW1 5RH

My eyes scan down to the next question.

TELL US ABOUT YOU AND YOUR PARTNER (continue on an extra sheet of paper if necessary). I make the shape of the words on my lips, *You* and *your* partner.

ARE YOU AND YOUR PARTNER IN LEGAL CUSTODY? ARE YOU OR YOUR PARTNER MENTALLY ILL?

The Indian woman who's given me the pen leans over the desk and touches my elbow.

'Are you all right?'

'Ugh!' I flinch, making her jump.

'Are you all right?' she asks again. 'You feeling OK?'

'Oh yeah,' I say, realising I've been off staring at the words at the top of the form for what's clearly been an inappropriate length of time. I look down. With her blue biro I've unconsciously speckled the form with a series of dots and desultory sweeps.

'If you like,' she says, eyeing the form from upside down, 'I can give you another one. Take it home with you, post it to us when you've completed it. Here!' She thrusts a clean B1 and an addressed envelope at me.

'Thank you,' I say, standing up.

'Excuse me!' she calls out sharply as I turn to go.

'Yeah?'

'My pen!'

I hold out the biro but deftly withdraw it as she makes to take it from me. '*Our* pen!' I say, handing it to her.

Back at Hugh Charlton House I shove open the door to Baz's flat, compressing the growing arc of junk mail to the skirting. I don't bother to check if there's anything for me, because nobody bar Baz Barrel knows I'm here. I go into the bedroom and throw myself down on the mattress. After a bit I take out the folded B1 and absently leaf through it before tossing it to one side. It's dark in the room. Tiny beams of sunlight filter through a constellation of pinpricks in the blackout blinds, picking out dizzying swirls of dust. In my head I hear a voice begin to ask questions about my life, posing them in the same impersonal and inquisitorial language of the DHSS: Tell us about everything. How did you reach this point, do you think? Why are you so fucked up? *Are* you in fact fucked up? Begin with your past, your family and friends. How do you feel about them now? How have they affected you, do you think? Mention aspirations, dreams, nightmares, neuroses, phobias. And the mental illness? Perhaps you can skip. What was it Doctor Slater said – 'Consider the pluses in your life, do whatever you feel like doing. If you feel like having an ice cream, well, go ahead and have one.' Mention good times, there *must* have been some good times. Just sit right down and begin. (Continue on an extra sheet of paper if necessary.)

I light a Sir Nige and pick up the snowstorm. The submerged city swarms with fake snow, each flake the size of a newspaper buoyed on the wind. I replace the perspex dome on the bedside table and bring my giant's face up close to the plastic ruins. They look like broken teeth dropped in formaldehyde. Through swirling Sir Nige smoke the storm plays itself out. Sir Nige? That old slang catches me by surprise. I haven't used it in ages.

On the speaker cabinet serving as a bedside table, the emptiness of the room is borne back to me in the shiny surface of one or two of my few salvaged belongings: a digital alarm clock, a silver cigarette lighter, shades of the Elvis Presley Las Vegas era, purchased a few nights back with petrol.

'Just the petrol?' the attendant had asked.

'And these,' I'd said, plucking them from a revolving display.

I'd put them on to hide the puffiness round my eyes. I never thought I'd cry, real tears, splitting up with Susan – my partner as the DHSS would say. But as I'd driven away from her that night, it was such a relief to let go, and the visceral knot in my stomach began to work itself out through the gear change and the acceleration. At a reckless speed on the Westway I'd wound down the window and let the breeze dry all the wetness on my face. Then, like some hellraiser in a western, I'd shouted out indecipherable articulations of emotion. All lost in the rush of the wind and the overtaking traffic. Momentarily, I'd felt much better.

For a couple of days after that I'd been washed up in my Renault: drinking, not eating much, driving occasionally, tuning the radio in and out. At night I'd fall asleep to a frequency I pictured as an erratic luminous squiggle on a hospital monitor, all-night Radio Luxembourg – 'Looking good, feeling fine.'

It was near Kew Gardens one morning that I was woken by a tapping on the window. Blearily I'd opened my eyes to find a dark face pressing through the condensation on the glass. I banged my knee on the steering wheel and felt the same panic

I had every morning when I woke not knowing where the hell I was. Through the pain I heard a familiar greeting.

'Hey, Billy – Kid, dude. It's me, Baz.'

'Jesus, Baz.'

I made to get out of the car. I hadn't seen Baz for a year or more but there he was, still smiling, the way he was the last time I saw him. He made to give me a big hug, but as I emerged unshaven and shivering on to the dewy morning verge, he seemed to change his mind and pointed at the car saying: 'Heh, heh, ah says to Maria ah sez, hey babe, I recognise that old fuckin wreck anywhere.' He laughed at that and clapped me on the shoulder.

Then he introduced me to his new girlfriend. She was Dutch and beautiful with long blonde hair and inquisitive blue eyes. 'I've heard lots about you,' she said. Her eyes seemed to be searching for some swatch of detail to match the mental picture she'd formed of me.

'Oh yeah,' I said.

They were dressed for a fashionable stroll through Kew. Maria in particular looked amazing. It was only while in her radiance you might say (if you were that type of romantic guy) that I'd begun to feel the full extent of my own degradation.

'You look rough as houses, pal,' said Baz cheerfully.

I inflated myself and at the top of my breath let out a short 'yuh'. I explained that I'd split with Susan and all, hence living in the car. He didn't seem too bothered. Truth being, he'd never liked her that much.

'It's your lucky day,' he said, diving into his pocket. 'I've moved in with Maria now.' He flashed her a cosy smile which she, in acknowledgement of his insensitivity towards my circumstances, gave demurely back to me. I felt like the little shoeblack in the very morbid Victorian poem my grandad used to recite at Christmas: 'As I walked slowly down the street but a few days ago, I came across a little shoeblack shivering in the snow,' and if he could get beyond this without being told to shut up by my gran, he'd tell us how the little shoeblack looked up at the man and asked, '"Can I clean your boots, sir, please?"' And how the gentleman placed his foot upon the block muttering, '"Very well, but, boy, be quick, for I'm expected by my fireside," and at these words you should have seen how bitterly he cried.'

'So – here!' said Baz, holding up the keys to his empty council flat in Camden Town. ''S all yours, dude. Oh, thes a snag,' he added, withdrawing the keys the way I was subsequently to snatch back the pen from the lady at the DHSS. 'Due to a complicated sub-letting clause, you have to pretend to be my brother – Nick.'

'But your brother's *black*!' I said, catching the keys.

'Yeah well, you'll have to work round that. If anyone asks say, uhmm . . .' he snapped his fingers, 'say you're adopted.'

Two abrupt raps at the door make me tense up a moment before I catch the papery fall of mail on the mat, and the whistle of the postman making his way back along the landing.

I'm still not used to the noises Baz's flat makes. The other night a banging woke me and I lay there in the dark listening to the water rushing around the plumbing. It was a good few seconds before I remembered where I was. In the Renault I'd wake up and think for a moment I was in bed with Susan. Here in Baz's flat I still sleep in the foetal position, imagining, I suppose, I'm curled on the back seat of that car.

I stretch out and cast around, luxuriating in all this space. Next to the Elvis shades is a diary with a marbled cover. I pick it up and flick through. Certain words snag my memory like barbs. Did that really happen? I bring my knees up under the duvet and, resting the diary on the feathered lectern, sift the pages that are already crisp with age. The blue ink and pink lines have run like litmus tests.

My sleepy gaze drifts over the faces in a photograph that's slipped out of the diary's pages. The row of faces is blanched out in the cheap flash. Hazel's eyes are mutant red in the vampy whiteness of her face. I stare at her a while, wondering if she'll animate into some kind of fantasy I can jerk off to. As her modelling career has taken off, she's begun to appear on billboards all around town. This photograph here only seems to illustrate how far apart we've grown, and the vague stirring I'd felt abruptly disappears. Next to her is Purdcake, with his shades and make-up and mujahedin scarf with little bobbles on. The last time I'd seen him he'd been slumped unconscious in the corner of a pub, his cigarette burning a hole in his expensive top.

At the end of the row, slightly apart, lost in this kind of amber burn-out of the last exposure, is Ziggy. A special guy, a guy I'd really loved. Ziggy Hero, a David Bowie impersonator from Halifax, or interpreter as he would have had it. I haven't thought about him in a long while.

The snowflakes have settled among the crudely replicated ruins of the old Roman city where I come from – Eboracum. E-bor-a-cum. Eee-bor-ahh-cum. I pick up the souvenir and peer into it, like old Foster Kane whispering the name of his childhood love, going back in time through fake plastic snow to real snow and shouts and a sleigh in flames. 'I wonder what did he mean – Rosebud?' 'I guess we'll never know, Mac.' I reach for the ashtray and am clenched with the memory of that day, on a trip with the school – I thieved the snowstorm back when I was what, ten? Eleven?

'An ancestral trek . . .' Mr Fletcher was saying, striding up and down the aisle of the school bus, '. . . to study the remains that distinguish our city as having been the first capital of Britain, as it was in . . .' He blathered on as the rain slated against the noughts and crosses on the misted windows. I lost him in AD something or other.

14

'Game,' hissed Ovo in my ear, drawing a winning line through three Os.

'YOU TWO! Glover, Ovodicci!'

'Yes, sir.'

'Are you listening, boys?'

'Yes, sir.'

'Yes, sir, yes, sir!' he mimicked, his chest heaving in exasperation. 'Always the same faces, isn't it? All right then, well, get your coats on.' He swung round. 'Everyone get their coats on or I'll have all your mothers ringing me up.'

The rain was coming down like the great flood had begun and we ran for the shelter of a wooden gift shack as if it was the ark. On the door it said *Schoolchildren two at a time*. Strangely enough I *hadn't* thought of stealing anything but that sign was out and out provocation. *I* didn't need a souvenir of Eboracum, I'd grown up there and like old Ultravox, what was it? – Vienna – it meant nothing to me. That cracked me up, oh Vienna, fucking ridiculous. For me, these temple gardens were just a convenient short cut home. The canal, which ran right by them, went all the way back to my estate. It wasn't necessarily quicker, but it was more interesting than traipsing through the streets. I liked nosying into the guesthouses that backed down to the towpath, especially at those teatime moments between lights going on and curtains being drawn. And so on and on, through the concentric spread of suburbia until I came to the sprawl of the unfinished Ashtree estates with their dormant bulldozers and, here and there, foundation trenches sectioned off with coils of barbed wire, lending the muddy land the air of battle. Wispy smoke rose from the distant factories. My dad crossed this place every day, over the top on his bike, an old gas-mask bag for his flask and sandwiches slung across his back. He worked at one of the chocolate factories making Black Magic.

It was him I was thinking of inside the gift shop as I picked up a tankard from the shelf above me. My nicking technique was to browse, casual as hell, and not create suspicion by continually looking all around, as Ovo was now doing. I would locate the staff in a reflective surface such as the copper beer tankard now in my hand. While I examined the tankard like a prospective purchaser I was actually using it to monitor the shop assistants. I remember it was etched with the Yorkshireman's advice to his son:

See all, hear all, say nowt.
Eat all, sup all, pay nowt.
And if ever tha does owt for nowt,
Make sure tha does it for tha sen.

I replaced the tankard and slipped the snowstorm into my pocket. Only the shop assistant saw me, or I fancied she had, so to disguise the way the snowstorm bulged against my groin, I thrust my hand into my pocket over its hard dome. It was slippy with sweat. My heart galloped as I headed for the door which was about a thousand miles away just two steps ahead. I was getting hot in my kagoule. I didn't realise how hot till a tourist came through the door, holding it open for me, and I felt the draught on my face.

'Thanks,' I said.

'Yur're welcome.'

I shot down the rickety wooden stairs and pell-mell into the drenched bushes, pushing through like old Papillon on the run till I came out under the shelter of what was left of an imperial stone parapet. Taking the snowstorm out of my pocket I quickly worked off the shop sticker, noticing as I did so, five, six feet away, hidden from general view behind some fallen pillars, a young couple, office clerks by the look of them. The girl's legs in taupe stockings were waving insect-like above the column that had once held up the temple, the very replica of which I held in my hand. As my own panting subsided inside the noisy crinkling of my kagoule hood, I heard their moans and saw in the bloke's press-up position, a tremulous echo of the old Roman pillar itself. Removing my hood I caught their panting better, much better. Then I felt breath on my neck. I spun round in a panic to find Daniel Ovodicci and Simon Knight right behind me.

Ovo's face was a mask of glee. Si (pronounced sigh) whispered breathily, 'If ah fall ovur now, mi knob might snap.'

We watched in silence as the scene played itself out. Quite quickly it was over, like the storm which had settled in my hand. The man collapsed and lay on top of the girl and for a while there was no sound except the rain. Finally, he got up and respectfully dogged out while she squatted down on her haunches. She hugged her knees with her knickers round her ankles and the sound of her piss was lost in the rain. When she finished she stood up and, pulling her hem down side to side, went over to join him. He lit a cigarette which they passed back and forth and then they both got under his mac and made a run for it.

On the coach, as we pulled away from the ruins, I experienced a pronounced detachment from Si and Ovo, from everything in fact, including myself. A tiredness came over me and my eyes seemed to slip back in my head. I became aware of my reflection in the coach window ghosting through the temple ruins and out into the town. Down Fulman Row we stopped outside Hillard's supermarket where my face hovered momentarily above a checkout girl like old Randall & Hopkirk Deceased. And then we were off again, weaving through the streets, through the railway offices, past an usherette smoking outside the ABC.

Back home, despite the pandemonium of teatime, I was still feeling strangely detached. After the plates were cleared, it was Dad's habit to scrape back his chair and read out loud from the *Evening Echo*. It was the way he thought the head of the house should behave. Normally this was all just so much more Vienna to me but tonight, shuddering from the wooden rub of chair leg on lino, I found myself sort of nedding what he was saying. He had to raise his voice as the rain redoubled in intensity against the window.

'"Plumber's mate!"' he said, scanning us to make sure we were paying attention. '"Harry Martindale was installing central heating in the cellars beneath the Treasurer's House when he suddenly heard the muffled sound of a trumpet some distance away. Soon afterwards the sound was repeated, this time much closer. Harry spun round to find himself confronted by the bizarre sight of a horse's head appearing through the cellar wall. Understandably terrified, he retreated into a far corner and watched speechless as the ghostly horse and its rider emerged from the solid brickwork. Behind the horse came a troop of Roman soldiers marching dejectedly, two abreast, carrying swords and spears. The men were unshaven and wearing dirty green tunics with kilt-like skirts. Even more strangely, the soldiers' lower legs appeared to have been cut off and they were marching across the cellar floor on their knees. Local archaeologists have known for some time that the Treasurer's House lies on the route of the old Roman road out of the city, and excavations have revealed that the old road is approximately knee-deep below the cellar floor. Although the troop's clothes which Harry described don't at first tally with the popular image of Roman soldiers, experts have confirmed that his description matches the uniforms worn by auxiliaries stationed in Eboracum towards the latter part of the Roman occupation. It has been suggested by psychic researchers that the cellar ghosts are perhaps a shattered patrol which perished at the hands of savage Picts during the collapse of Roman Britain."' A pause, then, 'Utter . . .' he folded the *Echo* to swat a fly, 'BUNKUM!'

My little sister Stacey looked scared. A forgotten chunk of fish finger was cooling on her fork. 'Ad rather break me arm than see a gurst,' she said.

Dad snorted and scraped the squashed fly into the coke

scuttle. 'Ad rather see undred ghosts than break me little finger,' he said.

The photograph on the front page that night was of a woman, her face smeared with the black strike of the bluebottle's entrails. She was Wilma McCann, a prostitute from Leeds, the first victim of the serial killer later dubbed the Yorkshire Ripper. I always felt squeamish when I saw people's faces spotted with grease from chips, or trodden over with footmarks to save the rug, that sort of thing. Mum looked at the squashed fly and made a face. Then, brushing hair across Stacey's forehead, she said, 'There's no such things as ghosts, hen, 'n' even if the were, they can't harm you.'

Just then the kettle began to whistle. 'Chinaman in the kitchen,' said Dad, lifting the tired old joke over his *Echo*.

'Boy-ling,' replied Stacey, with the time-honoured response. 'Boy-ling-boy-ling.'

I got up to turn the kettle off. Outside, the black night had made the kitchen window mirror-like. I saw myself reflected there beneath the bare bulb that hung above the cooker and, for a second, I thought of those Roman soldiers marching out along the main drag, a journey I too would one day make.

PART I

A COMPLETE REST

In a city of approximate dates then, let's say it was the autumn of 1980, which would make me what? Coming up seventeen. Let's also, for the sake of some sketchy anonymity, keep referring to this city by its old Roman name – Eboracum.

I'm returning there now, after six months convalescing in Scotland. When I left I'd not known exactly when I'd be back. I'd had this sort of break-down, truth be told, but as my condition hadn't been properly diagnosed, there was no real prognosis. Slater, our family GP, had listened to my symptoms while oscillating thoughtfully in his chair and making vague circles round his temples with his cigarette. Unconsciously, he seemed to be implying these mental illnesses could go round and round the brain, perhaps interminably. 'Just don't rush things,' he said magnanimously. He lowered his cigarette and, clearing his throat in a bluff rasp, began to make smaller circles out in front of him. 'Just take it easy,' he said, brushing ash from his sleeve, 'you'll get there in the end.' His languid reassurance reminded me of an actor playing the part of a small-town doctor. It was the way he blew smoke down his nose and punctuated my explanation with perpetual hmms. 'Hmm,' he'd said, leaning back, 'Go on, go on.'

'Uhmm . . . well,' I began, wondering why I couldn't now reel off the confident monologue of symptoms I'd breathily rehearsed in his waiting room. 'It's like . . . uhmm, a kind of disorientation. Like I have to turn my head very *slow-leeee*, cos if I move it too *quick* . . .' I turned to look at his examining couch. 'It's like I get dizzy, I can still see your image, but it's like a ghost image.' My hands made a hasty outline of his head and shoulders in the smoke. 'It fades so quickly, though, I can't really see it but I uhmm . . . sort of sense it. Then when it's gone, then I can focus on what I'm looking at. Your couch! I see it now.'

'Hmm,' he said, and snuffling lifted a line of verse into the air, something about dead souls leaving the bodies of dead sailors. His raised arm disturbed the thick drift of smoke.

'Sorry?' I said.

He repeated the line, ' *"The souls did from their bodies fly, they fled to bliss or woe."* "Ancient Mariner",' he said, snuffling again, '"Rime of."'

'Oh,' I said. I'd no idea what he was talking about, but the upward thrust of his arm had suggested to me a tennis player tossing up a ball to serve. My eyes traced those souls ascending to the nicotine-yellowed rose on his ceiling, and down the electric cord to a shabby lampshade under which the Ancient Mariner was still amusing itself on Doc Slater's purple lips.

'It's a lot like one of those stage-by-stage diagrams,' I said, returning the idea he'd put in motion. 'Of how to send down an ace in tennis, or strike a golf ball correctly. You know, when you see the racket or club tracking through space 'n' that. Every still's frozen for a second then it fades.' I served a phantom ball in slow-mo through the smoke and made a 'Duh duh duh duh' sound that suggested itself as accompaniment to the movement.

'Hmm, I see,' said Doc Slater. 'A visual trail, interesting.' He smoked on in absent consideration of this. 'And the collapse?'

'The collapse?'

'You said you'd collapsed.'

'Yeah, yeah, I did. That's right, in the snow. Uhmm . . . well. It was while waiting to cross at the top of Windmill Place. I saw Eric waiting on the other side. It was snowing heavily and when I waved to him he didn't see me.'

'And Eric is?'

'Sorry, Eric Marshall – my first employer when I left school, he's got a small graphics studio and he'd taken me on as a junior, a lackey really. I didn't stay long but I never forgot him. You couldn't really – he was about six foot five, used to be a goalie for Huddersfield Town but he had a car crash. Lost his eye bit like Gordon Banks and had to have a false one that was really kindov uhh . . . conspicuous. Anyway, like I say, I waved to him but he still didn't seem to see me, so I crossed the road holding out me hand to greet him, and I met him in the middle and had to virtually grab him and I say "Hi, Eric" and everything, and I was like pumping his hand and sort of forcing him gently back over to his side of the road so that we could stand and chat for a bit, and – I don't know when it was exactly – he slipped and p'rhaps it was then, through some sort of rush of expression on his part I saw that he wasn't Eric at all. He was only about five foot nine for a start, maybe even shorter, and he had a full head of hair and . . . and he had *two* eyes.'

'And how did you react?'

'What?'

'When you realised it wasn't your former employer.'

'Oh I uhmm . . . mumbled apologies or something and walked off and I was feeling really . . . really odd.'

'I see.' Doc Slater leant forward and made a note. 'And then you passed out?'

'Yeah 's right. I woke up lying in the snow with someone shaking me and saying are you OK.'

'Hmm.' Slater asked me about drugs and if I'd been taking any. I said I hadn't and though I don't think he believed me, he didn't push it more than to suggest that prolonged use of certain drugs – they sounded strange as he tripped them off – 'LSD, marijuana . . .' he nodded over his glasses, '. . . and such, can sometimes produce similar effects.' Deferring to his subtlety, I said that of course I'd tried all those things in the past, like the next person, but I wasn't taking any now, which was all more or less true.

'Oh . . . kay. Oh . . . kaaaay. Er . . . anything worrying you at the moment? No? Nothing at all? No girlfriend problems? OK.

Good. . . . Hmmm, and you're a *graphic* artist you say.' He took a pull on his fag. 'You know, my brother's a sculptor.' And as though to emphasise this he began shaping his ash on the side of the ashtray. 'I think the artistic temperament can sometimes be brittle, you know, perhaps you've been overdoing things, hmm? You say where you work is quite a stressful environment.'

I told him about my job designing T-shirts for New Wave bands and such, and poring over a prescription pad he lingered with amusement over the phrase 'Neeewaaave'. Doc Slater was quite a cool guy with his cigarettes and purple lips, his whisky flask sliding back into the drawer as I came through the door. I made a mental note to check out 'The Rime of the Ancient Mariner' sometime.

'Oh . . . kaaay,' he said. 'I don't think it's anything to worry about really. I think you're probably just overtired. What you need is a complete rest.'

THE LUMBERJACK YEARS (EVEN THOUGH THEY WERE ONLY MONTHS)

'Overtired,' shrieked my mum, exactly as I'd anticipated. 'Well, that's a laugh – how can you be overtired when you don't do anything?'

Doc Slater's assumption that it was within my means to just 'get away from it all' was another cause of mirthless laughter round the tea table. Finally, however, the family rallied round and my malady was strung out down the phone lines, as far as Uncle William in Scotland. Uncle William whom I was named after. He worked for the Scottish Forestry as a lumberjack basically. Surprisingly, it was he – he who never normally came up with anything, not even a card at Christmas – who suggested his old forester's cabin in the woods.

I'd been up there once before to my aunt Cathy's funeral, and I must have politely said I liked his spot or something because my dad reminded me of it when he said he'd fixed it up for me to be a Man o' the Trees.

'Man o' the Trees?' I repeated dubiously.

'Correct, laddy,' said Dad, doing a couple of neck exercises.

Despite sounding like a secret handshake society, the Brotherhood of the Bell or something, the Men o' the Trees was an organisation of older men who simply loved trees. My uncle was one of them. He picked me up from the bus stop in Ballinluig in his open-top Land-Rover. 'The cabin came wi the joab,' he shouted as we bumped along a cinder road into the forest. 'S wee aye used ta live wee yer aunt Car-thy bifor she deed, son.'

Proffering me inside the cabin, his right arm became irritably caught up in a cobweb. 'Kud do wi ah wee dust maybe. Bah' fits quiet yur need'n, son – yu'll sut-unlee find it here.'

VIBRATION REMEDY AND DEATH

In the tradition of days following days and turning into weeks, six months slid by. The Rest Cure proved a surprising success. At the beginning I thought I'd come to the worst possible place on earth for my condition. On the first day, every tree in the forest – and there were many – multiplied six, seven times over, each one ghosting its neighbour in a perpetual shifting medley like the DTs. On the second day, Uncle gave me a chain-saw to cut myself firewood. That night, when I stood with one foot on the log pile and pulled the saw into life, I had the sensation that for the first time in ages I was seeing things the way they were. When I'd finished sawing, a burning smell of metal, petrol and wood filled my nostrils and seemed to penetrate the two frontal spheres behind my eyes. I was inspired to consider how I felt. Silence surged back, and I dared to imagine that I was just the teeniest weeniest bit better.

After a while, a few weeks, these dusk-filled moments at the wood pile became that cherished time of the day when I would reflect on things. I'd say to myself, Well, kid, you've been here, what – nearly a month now. How do you feel?

Better, better, came the answer.

It was around this time that I began the diary from which I'm reconstructing these events.

93,000,000 MILES AND 6 FEET AWAY

Conversely, while I was improving, Uncle was overdoing things, loading himself to the gunwales with work, Catholic guilt I think. Nobody knew about his secret visits to a prostitute in Pitlochry, that was all revealed later. Similarly, nobody knew about his heart condition, so his death came out the blue – though I don't believe I could be held in any way responsible for 'bringing it on' as was the unspoken notion among his side of the family. The way they all spoke to me at the funeral – suspicious and stand-offish – I was shocked, really shocked. Each in their own way said something to the effect of, 'So, you were the last person to see him then, Billy.' To which I steadily and patiently answered, 'No, that was the woman whose house he stopped into for a glass of water on the way home.' Then I'd pause, screw my face up at the sky and say, 'Ooh, a good hour or so after he left me.'

They'd turned out their lips and walked away. Nothing in their minds had changed and I was weary of the wake. I sensed a traditional Glover send-off in the Leaping Salmon.

FROM THE PINE-SCENTED WOODS OF BALLINLUIG TO THE TOILETS OF THE TRAVELLER'S REST

My uncle's death provided the perfect juncture for my departure from the wood and after the wake I returned to Eboracum with my family. On the coach, my mother, sitting next to me, said, 'Well now, mado, how you feeling?'

'Much better.'

'And what you aiming to do now?'

'Well, like I say, I feel better so . . .' I broke off to indicate my physical presence on the coach, '. . . as you see, I'm coming home.'

'Home.'

'Yeah.'

'You mean *home* home.' She looked vexed.

'Well, yeah. Just till I get another place, like. If that's OK.' I acted a little hurt.

'Of course,' said my mum, all up in arms, 'it's yur home, you can come here anytime you like, I told you that.' Then she added, a little suspiciously, 'And what you gunna *do* at home?'

'I dunno,' I said. 'I hadn't thought about it. Become a man o' the dole I spose.'

'Well, that's not funny.' She scowled and then remembering something said, 'Oh, and you know I've turned your room into a sewing room.'

I looked at her. 'But you don't sew.'

'I aim to start.'

The weather had filthied up the coach window and by Tyneside the border snow had turned to sleet. As we crossed into North Yorkshire this was sieved into an imperceptible drizzle, visible only in the halos of street lights.

Lifting my head from the coach window I viewed Eboracum through a complex and many-stranded pattern, left by my hair in the condensation. I didn't wipe it for a better view, preferring, as we turned into the terminus, a softer focus. Back in the city of my birth. A sudden braking shot us all forward. 'Oh, God, save us,' cried Mum, slapping back into her seat like a crash dummy. 'Look at that nit.'

I OUGHT TO BEGIN TO HAPPEN

Outside, in the rain, skipping back on to the path, an unusually dressed figure was hastily regaining the cool stride he'd been forced to abandon as the coach had nearly run him down. As it was, it had splashed him with skeins of rainwater from the puddled entrance to the terminus. I saw just exactly how this had occurred. The traffic had stopped to let the big coach swing in and the jaywalker dude had casually crossed in front of the coach, giving Keith, the driver (I'd caught his name on his lapel), no option but to brake hard and shoot us all out of our seats. As we resumed our turn into the depot, I craned my neck and pressed my cheek against the cold pane to try and catch another glimpse of his face. But he was gone, tailing away, a troop of Queen Anne's schoolgirls in tow, their distinctive green uniforms rucked about in truant-style. He himself was wearing a grey fedora hat, tilted forward at a funicular angle that suggested those cliff lifts used by spies in forties cinema. He looked like he thought he was in *The Third Man* or something, waltzing through Vienna, a fantasy, I imagined, that prospered under what little the wide brim of his hat allowed him to register of his surroundings. The Wallace Arnold Bus Garage, Hillard's super-market, the Traveller's Rest. As the coach driver shouted at him, he casually lit a Sir Nige and extinguished the match with two pronounced shakes of his wrist which seemed in part to answer him back. His drenched mac was slung loose about his shoulders in the manner of a poet. But most noticeable of all, like I say, was this group of four or five Queen Anne's schoolgirls who were following him – green pleated skirts and long white socks, a touch greyed with rain. The way they thronged about him was something the coach driver would never, ever, ever, understand.

'Flamin pansy,' breathed my uncle John, dusting his knees. He'd risen to retrieve his coat from the overhead and been slung down the aisle.

The ripple of anger the flamin pansy engendered among my assembled relatives in the coach cut straight through the six wooded months and back to a little café on Wollman Row, the Centurion, which was run by Ovo's old man. I'd seen the mystery guy in there one time when I was with Ovo and my cousin Kitty Petch. I remember that as he'd entered the café there'd been a similar wave of dissent. Myself, Ovo and Kitty had all been swimming and were drying off over afternoon tea when he'd looked over at our table, more at Kitty really. Sensing it, she'd become self-conscious and, flicking back her wet hair, she lost the drift of what she was saying. Ovo, who'd been trying it on with Kitty all day, said irritably, ''S aw right, you can be normal again now, he's fucked off.' She glared at Ovo and then upset her spoon in his direction, spilling tea all over him. 'Ahuooow fuck,' he cried, scraping back his chair and wiping a light spray of tea from his face. While he was doing so she sneaked a quick glance back. He'd gone to join a crowd of beatniks in the back booth from where a black kid had half stood and waved a cowboy hat at him, making a big thing of looking at his watch and saying, 'Nice bit of time-keeping, dude.'

But of course he'd waited, they'd all waited. And would have waited a sight longer. Because this was Ziggy Hero, or rather, as I didn't know who it was at the time, it was the character I came to know as Ziggy Hero. He was from somewhere outside of Halifax, I was later to discover. Though I'd have to say his likeness to Bowie wasn't that striking, the undeniable truth was he sounded *exactly* like him. Eerily so. And he acted like him too. He had all the moves down cold, and rarely let the attitude slip. He obviously practised and had a large repertoire of gestures to hand, gleaned from every scrap that came his way: books, films, magazines, music papers, records, LPs, EPs, singles, rare imported bootlegs, et cetera. Through all of this I fancy a kind of merger had taken place, a kind of fusion between the outfits run up to the hum of the Singer sewing machine and the mimed image in the full-length bedroom mirror. Anyway, at the time of first seeing him I, Kid Glover, was sixteen, trying to make one coffee last for ever, and shortly about to collapse face down in the snow. He, Ziggy, was just someone older than me, *cooler* than me, at least Kitty seemed to think so, and on reflection I have to say she was probably right.

'Are you stoppin there all day,' said my aunt Sheila.

Around me, relations were busying themselves with coats and bags in the luggage racks overhead.

'We're just going to the Traveller's for one.'

'The Traveller's *Rest*?' I said. I was suddenly beset with the memory of its jukebox, Steppenwolf's *Get ch mo-der ruunin, lookin fur ad-vent-cher, or whad-ever cums maa waaaay.*

'Oh yes, it's bin dun up now,' said my aunt, ''s dead posh.'

When I'd left town the Traveller's wasn't posh. It was a biker pub, even though hardly any of the bikers who went there actually *owned* bikes; if they did they were usually in bits somewhere. 'Still being done up. Sell it you if you want, dead cheap, like.' Drugs were what united the clientele of the Traveller's. The casualties of every youth movement – Teds, mods, rockers, prog hippies, soulies, punks – had all wound up in that place and whatever they'd brightly begun as was over. I'd seen, even in my short life, fresh-faced kids from Hopwood Secondary go all out for notoriety – to be MAD Benny instead of just Ben and get the nod of approval from the Undead in the corner of the tap room. Crazy Dave, Wolf Child, arise Mad Benny of Bantum Drive.

While their images altered, their sobriquets stayed as odd reminders of what they'd once been into. Mad George the Mod still wore a thin tourniquet of fabric tortuously knotted under a button-down collar, two-tone with dirt and a tiny hole in the cheap weave where once a Who badge had stuck and left its mark. Now, if anything, Mad George looked more like someone's dad emerging from a bad day in William Hill, spaced out in the afternoon light, stumbling like a ghost, humanised by loss.

As I walked in that afternoon, I could tell straight away that the brewery had gone to some lengths to change its image. But despite the bright optimistic refurbishment aimed at the feel of an Olde Coaching Inn, I noticed in the smoky corner nearest the door, marking us as we came in, a belligerent core of the original clientele. It was ironic that no one at the Traveller's ever went anywhere, and any real tourists, just off the bus, who chanced to walk the four or five faltering steps into its murky acoustics, would usually walk straight back out. A safe distance up the street they might imagine the click of a pool break starting up the conversation again.

At the bar Uncle Ray was preparing a toast. 'Well – cheers then,' he said. 'Here's to old William.' With half-closed eyes they took down my dead uncle's memory in great gulps. Uncle Ray, down in one, let out a lengthy ahhhhh of satisfaction and ordered another round. 'By, that Scottish beer was ruuub-bish. Specially that stuff at wake.' He wiped his lips as though the taste of it still bothered him. 'Ah dun't know how you cud u stood it, Kid.'

'Didn't get out much,' I said.

'Ahh well – no.' He nodded, as though recalling his brother-in-law's near zealous sobriety. 'Nah, you wun't do,' he sighed, pressing his lips together and then parting them with a sorry smack. 'Silly oaf really,' he began, suppressing a belch, 'all that ab-stain-unce.' He liked to mispronounce long words did Uncle Ray.

'Hmmm,' I said. The barmaid smiled at me as she pulled a pint. I smiled back and she dropped her eyes to the pump. Uncle Ray caught me glancing at her tits and gave me a knowing wink, then bit his fist like an Italian, which kind of depressed me and made me think, Oh fuck, I'm just like him.

Mum, tottering back from the Ladies', bumped into my dad on his way to the Gents'.

'Oh, hello,' she said, squinting. 'I'm drunk, are you drunk?'

'Yes, I'm drunk.'

'Well, that's two of us then.' They carried on in their respective ways.

'So, Kidda,' said my aunt Sheila, 'what was it like up there then?'

I began to tell her but she broke in.

'And j'u mean t' say you slept in that bed where Cathy died?'

'Sheeeeila!'

'What?' She turned on my uncle. 'I'm only showin interest.'

Uncle Ray shook his head. 'Sa damn shame, int it, first Cathy then William. Spose you dint fancy stoppin after that, hey, Kid?'

Aunt Shee butted in again, covering my hand with hers. 'You thought it might be catchin, dint you, love.' She took a swift sip of gin and, in her hurry to speak, some leaked on to her chin. 'Mmmm,' her tongue came in pursuit. 'Happen it is 'n' all. Did you see state of John Willie in t' graveyard? Ah sez to im, "Hey, John Willie! Thou ought not bother goin home."'

'Sheeeeila – yu didn't.'

'Ah did as well.'

Aunt Shee was one of those people Mum said it was good to have around at funerals – stop everyone getting so miserable.

'And yur all better now, aren't you luv? What did you do wi yer days? Were you sawing down trees 'n' things? Ah bet he had you thrang, dint ee, old slave driver, and you there fut rest 'n' all. Still, best to be thrang than doin' nowt, hey?' I drifted off while my aunt gabbed on. 'Ah say – Kid. Best to be thrang.'

'Hmm . . . what – sorry?'

'Ah say, YOU FEEL RIGHT AS RAIN NOW, DEAR.'

'Oh yeah, no, I sawed down a few trees,' I said catching up with the conversation. The feel of the buzz-saw was in fact still alive in my hands and they began to shake a little, causing the surface of my pint to ripple across a black memory of the morning coffee I was drinking the day my uncle died.

VIBRATION WHITE FINGER

It was while finishing breakfast that my rickety table had begun to shake due to the arrival outside of Uncle William's ten-ton truck. On the back of the truck was *Sweet Estelle*, my uncle's killer you might say, if you were that type of dramatic guy. Uncle had told me the night before that he'd bought the wheelhouse of an old offshore trawler, from a boatyard in Egremont, 'To use as a kind of summer house-cum-shed, son. She'll be here in tha mornin, but ah'll no be here unfortunately.' He pointed vaguely to a spot twenty yards or so from the cabin door. 'Ha jus wan err set doon over there. I can leave it wi you, son?'

'You can rely on me, Uncle,' I assured him.

That same evening I was carefully separating the rain-soaked pages of a porno mag I'd found discarded in the wood when my uncle pounded furiously on the door. He was absolutely livid that *Sweet Estelle* was facing the wrong direction for the morning sun.

'Well, what direction should it face?' I called after him, hastily zipping up an old raincoat and following him out to where he was trying to manoeuvre it round all by himself. Reddening in the face, he became inarticulate with effort. I basically just assumed the frisk position, making occasional grunts that could have come from the story I'd just been reading in *Colour Climax* and were echoed disconcertingly by my uncle going, 'Ahhhh ugh ohhuw.' Eventually he stopped and slapped his palm angrily against the timber then turned his back flat to the wheelhouse and, exhausted, slid down into a sitting position. Rain lashed against the windows every bit as though we were out on the high seas. Inside, the ship's wheel moved back and forth in a ghostly fashion like it was trying to effect the turn on its own. I gave up my mock exertions and took a few steps back, raising my voice above the storm, 'WELL – I don't think we're gonna move 'er tonight, Uncle.' But I had a sense that my words had not been heard properly and were still floating about somewhere in the air. I looked over as though I might see them drift away into the trees and, with a questioning lift in my voice, repeated, *'Un-cle?* Asay! I don't think we're –'

His head was bent forward, his chin resting on his chest, legs splayed out in front, like one of the town drunks he abhorred so much. I sploshed noisily over to where he lay and, extending a helping hand, I gently touched the sole of his wellington with my muddy trainer. 'Uncle?' He didn't move. 'Hey, Unc, get ARP.' I laughed nervously at my bad Gestapo accent: *'Uncle Vilhelm?'* I broke off and swallowed back the rest of it. The forest moaned and the sound of rain redoubled in all the puddles around me. I found I was still holding out my hand to him. My heart began thumping and I actually remember thinking I'd rather be back inside leafing through porn again. I'm hardly proud of that. And perhaps it was in some form of spiritual admonishment that Uncle's arm began to lift slowly out of the mud. When his huge wet hand, slithering like Carrie's out of the grave, gripped my wrist, I freaked and felt a warm burst of urine against my inner thigh. All the fear held hitherto at bay rushed through me. I almost collapsed.

'God, Uncle I, I, I thought you were . . . but you're . . . What happened?'

'Not a wurd uv this, Billy,' he said shamefully, getting to his feet, 'no wurd to naybody, Billy . . . ju hear me, Billy? Ah say, ju hear me, son?' Hunkering over and rubbing his arm, he inhaled deeply. His eyes widened and he looked suddenly lost, scared. With his thumb and forefinger he pulled his cheeks into waxy folds. But he rallied and made a remarkable job of getting brusquely into his Land-Rover and, as I told all his relies, it was when he was halfway to Pitlochry that he stopped to knock on someone's door for a glass of water saying he wasn't feeling well, it was there he'd collapsed and died.

At the funeral some of the men o' the trees had come to pay respects and one of them had read aloud about how even the mightiest oak can be struck down in its prime and so on. About how trees and the stuff men make out of them, like the cross and the casket, how it brings us all closer to God. The woman who'd obliged Uncle with the water had sat in a pew at the back. *Sweet Estelle*, I'd thought. No one had talked to her and when I'd smiled over, Mum had frowned at me.

'Ahh well,' Uncle Ray shook his head and pressed his lips together, 'silly oaf really.' He turned to my aunt. 'Best get off, eh, Shee?'

'Good night, luvee.' She squeezed my hand. 'Luvlee to see yer back.'

'G'night, Aunt Shee. G'night, Uncle Ray.'

PLANET OF THE MATES

I watched them leave, getting stuck in the door with their luggage. One of the Undead got up and made a very big thing of holding it open for them. Aunt Shee thanked him diffidently and he swept an imaginary feathered hat to the floor, in a suave, threatening way, like he'd watched *A Clockwork Orange* too many times. Uncle Ray sent me a loud 'Cheerio, Kidda' that brought a series of unwelcome glances my way from Smoky Corner. One of the Undead half stood and seemed to hold up a hand to attract my attention. I tried to ignore him thinking, Oh, God, who the fuck's this? Then I heard my name, 'Mr Glov-uuur,' an arc of sound as though from a passing bicycle. 'KID GLOV-UUUR.' I looked up. Coming out of the smoke was Daniel Ovodicci, my old mate.

'Hey up, son,' he said, holding out his hand. 'I thought it were you but a thought you wuz in Scotland. What's wit black suit, someone pegged it?'

'Yeah,' I nodded. 'Good to see you, Daniel.' While we shook hands, I explained quickly that someone had, in fact, passed away.

'Oh,' he said listlessly.

His hand was clammy, the way it always was, and strangely effete, the way Uncle William's had been when I groped for his pulse. While we exchanged news I wiped my hand on a beer towel. 'No, I'm back,' I said.

'*Back* back.'

'Yeah, back back.'

'Oh, great! So, ow you doin then?' he asked again. He was speeding and asked me this about fifty times without seeming at all interested in the reply. Nodding like a boxer taking instruction, pulling at his nose and sniffing, he cut in suddenly with a magician's 'Duh duuuh' and bared his teeth at me, hissing between them as he did so.

'What j'u reckon?' He pointed at them aggressively. 'Nuw fugin cheef.'

'Oh, oh aye,' I said. 'I knew there was something different but I thought it was the, er,' I stroked my upper lip, 'Jason King tache, like.' His new teeth were in fact better than his old ones – which had been crooked tombstones smacked out one drunken night last summer. Huge tombstones, huge gap – I couldn't believe I hadn't noticed straight away.

WE ARE ALL OF US IN THE GUTTER, BUT SOME OF US ARE LOOKING DOWN THE DRAIN

It was while garden-hopping one night. Ovo had tripped headlong into a fishpond. He got up stunned, feeling gingerly at his tattered gums, wailing after me in shock. 'Son, ssson, odd on, av losssht me cheef.' He looked down tearfully into the pond and when the ripples settled saw his own reflection by the light of the moon. 'OHUW FUCKIN SHIT, *LUK* AT ME!' He slapped the surface of the water with the flat of his hand.

'Hey, hey! Daniel! Hey, calm it, man. Maybe you can find em,' I suggested.

He thought for a moment, and then suddenly looked hopeful. 'Yeah, mebbe yu're right,' he said, getting to work on his laces. 'Strike a light, willya.' While he took off his shoes and socks and rolled up his trousers, I fished about for a match. 'I reckon thiv sunk to bottom bi now,' he said.

'I reckon,' I said, and thought of them falling weightlessly through the aqua black.

He nodded, dipping his toe in. 'Phoo, fuck! It's freezin. Ahhh, wha's at?'

'Just a fish, man.'

'Strike that fuckin match, willya?'

In the harsh strikes of matches, I glimpsed his face and the thick red liquid oozing down his chin as he cursed and burbled about for his teeth. 'Fuckin, cuntin fish have ad em. Hopeless fuckin task.' He stumbled along the bottom. 'OUCH, bashtuds.' By now he was openly sobbing. I looked away while he took out his anger on some gnomes. 'Bashtuds bashtuds bashtuds.' He hopped about the rockery holding his foot. 'Ahhh FUCK!' Upstairs, a light came on and a sash window went rattling up. An angry vested torso appeared in the billowing nets.

'Wha's goin on down ther?'

'Away, Daniel,' I shouted, pulling him off the gnomes. 'Away, leave em now.' I meant his teeth. As we ran I noticed that he seemed to have a pink rose in his mouth. Eventually his bare feet slapped to a standstill on the path behind me. He flagged me to stop and while I got my breath back I watched Ovo coughing out the rose, which kept coming like a conjuror's trick – turning from a flower into a pair of women's pink panties. He'd whipped them off the washing line while I wasn't looking, and shoved them in his mouth to stem the flow of blood, the spread of which, in those flimsy folds, somehow gave it that hybrid impression. He later told me that after that he'd got a real thing about cramming panties in his mouth, and would spend his nights creeping around back gardens in search of them. He developed preferences too, passing over many styles till he found a pair he liked. He'd just unpeg them and stuff them in. One night he urged me to accompany him, saying it was a weeny cushty laugh for bezny chivers. How could I refuse? I'll for ever picture him soaked to the skin in some drenched shrubbery, his hair plastered down and his mouth horribly stuffed with knickers, his powerful binoculars trained on a shadow flickering across an upstairs bedroom window. His stuffed mouth conveying muffled excitement, his hand working himself off, coming quickly over a cloche. Then, wiping himself clean with the knickers, he'd carefully peg them back up. It was only a matter of time before he got caught. Thankfully I wasn't with him on that occasion. He was reluctant to talk about it, but the fantasy I keep is of him standing on tiptoes just returning the knickers to the line when the garden suddenly filled with arc lights and there's the law with a megaphone telling him to put his hands in the air. He made the *Evening Echo*, 'Son of local café owner . . .' Workmates had a little CB tag lined up for him, 'The Prowler'.

That sordid memory dissolved against the glistening optics of the Traveller's bar as Ovo closed his mouth. 'Yeah,' I said, 'they're a big improvement, them.' And then to change topic, 'How's Si, by the way?'

'He's here.'

'Where?' I periscoped round.

Ovo pulled at his nose, sniffed and whispered, 'Come wi me.' I followed him into the loos where I guessed there was some duff speed going down, scored from Undead Corner. He trod softly over to a row of cubicles in his kung fu slippers, lifting his voice cautiously over the top of one. 'Hel-lo – Mr Knight?'

There was a shuffling of feet, more than one pair, and a cubicle door opened. 'Away then,' hissed a voice from inside.

As I squeezed in after Ovo, Simon was surprised out of his hawk-like repose against the wall. 'Billy! Fuck-in *hell*!'

'Si,' I replied, adjusting my eyes to the cramped space. He was almost too close up to see.

'Hey, Billy, what the fuck are you doin . . . ?'

'Shhh.' There was another kid in the cubicle who I didn't know. He laid a finger on his lips. 'Shhh.' The door to the Men's had opened and two voices could be heard above the brief blast of pub noise.

'Yeah, ah mean ah like iz early stuff – fuckin outstanding – but am not s' keen on the new stuff.'

'Ah you not?'

'No am not.'

Ovo, who'd been handed a spliff, offered it to me. I took a drag. Not having seen them for so long, I felt a rush of sentiment – which I thought I saw mirrored in their own faces. I wanted to say something that would express how pleased I was to see them, but instead, in the enforced silence, we had to listen to the jokes the men at the urinals were reading.

'Patient: I can't go to work I feel sick.'

'Doctor: How sick do you feel?'

'Patient: Well, am in bed wi me mam and a wanna fuck me sister.'

There was laughter in between a tap going 'fshhh' on, 'fshhh' off. Two tugs on the metallic roller towel. Door opening again – Rod Stewart 'I am sailing' – closing slowly – 'home again . . .' Silence.

We all began talking at once.

'Hiya there, Si!'

'Billy! Ow the fuck –' He seemed not to believe I was there and kept sort of touching me, turning his touches into little punches. 'What's wi suit, someone die?' Now that I could speak freely, though, I couldn't think of how to express all those emotions and so I just sort of punched him back.

'What was that you were trying to tell me?' I said.

'Oh, just that . . .' What he'd been mouthing to me in the enforced silence was, They've – been – clamping – down – in – here – lately.

'Oh,' I said, absorbing the blow to my ego. I'd thought he'd been saying, S'been – crap – in – ere – without – you – lately.

At that point the kid who'd shushed us began making mechanical winding noises out the side of his mouth that corresponded to the pivotal movement of his arm as he prepared to jack up. I turned and looked at him, he was sweating profusely. He had long red hair with a full explorer's beard. Up close, just visible under the growth on his sweaty neck, was the faded tattoo SKINS scratched in blue ink.

'Hi there,' I said to him. 'I'm Billy.'

He nodded, 'Thh-deeb.'

'Deeb?' I said. 'Sorry? D'you say Deeb? Or wosit – Steve?'

He glared at me, up at me in fact, as he was quite short. I felt a light spray of his spittle.

'Ow many fuckin cunts d'you nur called fuckin Deeb – eh?'

'Sos, pal,' I said, shrugging and pirouetting an imaginary cotton bud round my ear.

He grunted at me, then turned his attention back to jacking up.

NEVER EASE UP ON WEIRDNESS

In the bar, my family had seated themselves on the elevated area where bands used to play. Gran was getting morose. Perhaps affected by the ghosts of pub rockers who used to play up on the old stage, she started to sing at an imaginary piano, stabbing the air with arpeggios like Jimmy Cagney. *'Oh, there's a man going round taking names and he's . . .'*

'Ahouw – someone get er to pipe down, willya,' shouted Dad. 'Asay there – pipe *down*, willya.'

Daniel and Simon clapped and Ovo, in a passable Freddie Mercury, shouted, 'Heh-heh, Gran! Thez a man goin round tekin names, I like it, I like it. Rock on.' The speed I'd done in the lav was gathering momentum in my bloodstream like a huge roller about to crash over me.

'Yu'll see it's changed in here a bit,' said Si. 'Still get good gear from that Fizzy Paul bloke, though.' He jerked his thumb towards the guy who'd held the door for my aunt. In Hell's Angel script across his shoulders it said FIZZY PAUL and under that, straddling his spine in the same gothic style, ALONE. I'd seen him around. Like many people I was later friendly with, I disliked him at first sight.

'Who's that then?' I asked.

'Dunno – thought you'd know him, he knows your man Purdey.'

'My man Purdey? I think not,' I said, shaking my head. 'Anyway, I don't know him,' adding casually, 'J'ever see Purdey knocking about still?'

'Nah, gettin too weird.'

'Whaz at?' Fizzy Paul had suddenly appeared at my shoulder out of nowhere. He'd only caught the end of the sentence and clapped Ovo on the arm. 'Never ease up on weirdness, pal,' he said.

'Hah! Yeah yeah,' chorused Si and Ovo, feeling obliged to

laugh, 'Yeah.' But when he was out of earshot, Si mumbled, 'Never ease up on weirdness.' He shook his head. 'Fuck's sake.'

Then Ovo said, 'But hey, son, what 'appund bitwin you an Purdcake anyroad? Thought you wuz meant t' be working for im doing T-shirts – next I ear yur off up to Scotland to be a lumberjack.'

I remember how he'd thought this was hilariously funny at the time and had slapped me on the back saying, 'Only fuckin Glover weighing two fuckin stone could think of being a lumberjack.' When he was on speed, however, Ovo didn't find things funny – merely acceptable or unacceptable – so he grinned falsely through his false teeth. The speed was taking its toll on his talk, weeding out words like the, a, but, in, and, if. I was getting pissed. I hadn't had a drink for six months and a sudden regurgitation of beer and hops fizzed into my oesophagus. I'd been fine more or less till the spliff and the speed in the loo but now perspiration prickled my back like coconut matting on a helter-skelter and I was aware I'd soon be making a move into paranoidsville.

'You what,' I said. The bar optics, the coaching murals, my own family, all took up the carousel.

'A say he's sound when you gerra know im like,' Ovo was saying.

'Steve, he's sound azuh pound like he iz he's fuckin sound. Iza right laf . . . lives wi us now . . . iz a bit touchy bout his speech diffi-culty though.'

'Yeah,' I cut in as firmly as possible. 'I noticed.'

'Anyway, any-way-zer.' Ovo began boxing out his words, his feet shuffling on the carpet swirls. I caught every fourth word or so. 'Nice t' see you . . . Yeah . . . No, chucked her . . . Yeah, still at th' Wigwam . . . come over, wi av a laugh sometimes.'

From the door Deeb called out, 'Si, Ovo, away. Coach is here.' They were on their way to Leeds to an all-night northern soul do.

Daniel looked round. 'Ah, we're off then.' He pulled at his nose. 'Right – see ya then, Billy.'

'Si . . . Ovo, away, will miss fuckin coach.'

As they came over to the door I looked up and took the restorative breath of a fell walker, calling back, 'Yeah, see ya.'

HALF AN ORPHAN

My brother Ray had split with his on-off bird Sue, so he was back sharing the sewing room with me again. One night he said her name in his sleep. Next morning I called Purdcake to ask if I could rent my old room back. He said, 'Uhm, no, well, Ziggy's using that room to rehearse in actually.'

I think this was the occasion the peripheral repetition of that oft-heard name finally lodged with me, but I was too cool to say anything like, Who's that then? So I said, 'Oh, no matter, thought I'd pop round anyway, collect some me stuff.' He told me to throw stones up at the window as the bell was fucked.

I got there round nine and rattled a handful of gravel against the pane. Fleetingly, he appeared behind the nets mouthing, Hang on a tick. He looked to have aged badly, his hair seemed to be a bit grey. He was only, what? Mid-twenties? I never really knew for sure. He was always vague about himself. What I did know was he'd been a student of something and was about to take his degree when he met James Derby, an older man with a passing resemblance to Dirk Bogarde. Derby wasn't his real name but he was so-called because of the brown derby hat he always wore. He was very suave and one day, with an even promise in his voice, he would say to Purdcake, 'What do you *really* want to do, Alex?' It was 1979, the height of New Wave, and Purdey came back at him with the idea of setting up a shop printing and selling New Wave T-shirts and badges and just about anything else that was faddish to do with being young and what-have-you.

For a song, James Derby unlocked the dusty door of Grimshaws's, an old family-run butcher's on the outskirts of town that had been closed for as long as anyone could remember. The shop was braced within old scaffolding and the traditional tiled façade was covered in a lasagne of peeling fly posters. A few months later, with T-shirts hanging on all the old meat hooks, Grimshaws's opened to the public. There wasn't exactly a stampede. Purdey made a sign – COME IN WE HAVE SPACE INVADERS – but perhaps the butcher's accoutrements still gleaming forth from the otherwise derelict building put people off. Is it a printer's? A minicab office? Is there a brothel upstairs? You saw these questions on the faces of those who slowed as they walked past, trying to peer in. By and by, though, the kids started to come in to play the Space Invaders, sniff the poppers bottle labelled Tester and listen to the music. Purdcake always had good music.

I met Alex Purdey one night in the Theatre bar, some several months prior to his shop's big opening day. He was sitting, staring at his hands like he'd just strangled someone and was appalled at what he'd done. His fingers were covered in printing ink. As I watched him from the next table, his expression changed to one I recognised as frustration – he was no artist and had realised that he badly needed someone to take over that side of things and I badly needed a job. I'd just missed my bus – I was *always* just missing my bus from that stop – and had gone for a cup of tea. I can't remember exactly how we got talking, but when I look back it always strikes me as being something like that Dylan record, *A man in the corner a-pproached me for a match, I knew raaard away he was not ord-in-aree . . . When I took up his offer I must ha bin maaaad.*

That was over a year ago now. I cupped a hand to the butcher's window. From the dim glow of the Space Invaders I could make out Bob Marley, A Clockwork Orange, Joy Division, Andy Warhol's banana for the Velvets. It hadn't changed much. It hadn't changed that much from when it was selling pies. Purdey couldn't be fucked with all that. I cringed at the memory of Purdey bringing an actor back from the Theatre bar who, on making out the meat hooks in the dark, said, 'Oh but how *brrr-illiant*, you've kept all the original fittings.' Purdey replying, 'Yes yes, it was my absolute idea that – I thought it gave a certain *free-son.*' This was around the time Purdey was letting me the small room at the top, before my collapse. I hadn't seen him since but could he have aged so much in six months? When he opened the door I saw that his hair wasn't grey but was powdered in a high rockabilly quiff. Following him upstairs I noticed he was wearing knee breeches and white socks. Sensing me looking, he said, like it bored him to death, 'It's my new look. A sort of a baroque-a-billy type thing.'

The long dark passage still smelt of fusty old packing trunks making the front room with its log fire always a pleasant outcome. Sitting at the far end of the room with his back to me watching television was undoubtedly this guy Ziggy Hero I'd seen about. He didn't turn round when I came in and when I said, 'Hiya,' he just sort of nodded and blew at a strand of orange hair that had flopped in front of his eyes. He was sitting down in a kind of method acting pose – leaning forward over the back of the chair, resting his chin on his arms. On the sofa there were three girls. I thought I recognised a couple of them from the other day outside the bus depot. They were smoking cigarettes and drinking cans of lager, making a big thing out of doing both. One of them seemed to be unbelievably beautiful and I found I was staring. She was lit by the flicker of television and I wondered if she could really be as beautiful as she seemed. Then she stood up and any doubts dissolved into the perfectly intersecting planes of her face. She really was gorgeous. She was tall with long black hair that swooped in front of her eyes.

Smoothing crisp crumbs from her skirt, she quietly asked Purdey for the toilet, lifting up the end of the question with a defiant flick of her hair as though it was nothing to her to say the word toilet.

'I have to change for work,' she told the other two. They looked back blankly, like the Ugly Sisters, who didn't have to do anything except eat crisps, drink and make a big thing of smoking cigarettes.

Of course I knew where the lav was, so I piped up, 'End of passage, first left, shu– sugar.' She glanced at Purdey who verified with a nod. I started tossing up a cigarette, watching it loop towards the ceiling. I did it a few times and, as she passed me, by fluke I *caught* it in my mouth. But she hadn't seen, nobody had, which was a bastard really. Lighting it, I threw the match on the fire, then crouching down I began to throw live ones in, getting a kick out of watching them flare up. What I couldn't have known just then was that earlier, after I'd got off the phone to Purdey, he'd replaced the receiver and announced to the room, 'Oh, there's this guy Kid Glover coming round. You won't have to mind him too much he's mad, you see, nuts, doo-lally.' He'd crossed his eyes and let his tongue loll out, slavering a little. 'No, seriously, he's just been recovering from some mental illness or other up in Scotland, he used to work for me.' (It was the tall Vampirella girl, Hazel, who'd just gone to change for work, who was later to report this to me.)

I tossed my last match into the fire and tried again to break the ice. Turning on my haunches I smiled broadly around the room, but no one was looking my way. Purds was busy in the kitchen and the two Ugly Sisters were still making a big thing of smoking and were almost totally enveloped in Sir Nige smoke. Ziggy had a Sir Nige on the go too, which I noted he made no attempt to smoke at all, content it seemed to just let the plumes drift up around him. On his wrist he wore a couple of silver bangles that, every now and then, caught the light from a nearby table lamp.

Though he didn't exactly express pleasure, in some intimate way I could tell that he was pleased. I wanted to break in on his reverie, say something to him, something along the lines of I'd seen him around, but it didn't seem much to say, so instead I stayed quiet. He was watching *The Man Who Fell to Earth* and he was concentrating hard on the screen. When Purdey brought in tea and set it down, we all just sat in silence and carried on watching the film. We were at the bit where Bowie's character, Mr Newton, is in the back of his limousine and he says to Arthur, his chauffeur, as he's driving along, like he's got a headache, 'Arthur, would you please slow down, it's making me feel dizzy, keep to thirty please.'

Mr Newton obviously didn't travel well. I only remember this bit because at that moment Ziggy suddenly jumped up and turned off the TV leaving just surprised static filling the room. I was surprised too, what with him being such an obvious big fan and all. I looked over at Purdcake who shrugged. I would have turned it back on but Ziggy looked as though he was nursing a headache himself. I didn't know what to do or say so I started chucking my moped keys up in the air and after a bit of this I said, 'I'm gonna get off then.' I looked down the passage towards the stairs. I wondered if I could expect to see the tall girl again before I left. I thought we might brush past each other in the hall.

'See ya then,' said Purdey.

'What?'

'See ya then, you said you were going.'

'Oh – yeah, yeah.' I bade a general 'See ya' all round. The two Ugly Sisters murmured 'Bye' and 'See ya,' and then each shot an accusing glance at the other.

Ziggy said nothing, but just as I was putting my helmet on, about to go out the door, he lifted his head from his hands and said, 'Hey, Arthur man. Stick to thirty, huh.'

'Stick to thirty,' I said, laughing to myself. What a nut.

'What's the big joke?' asked Mum, slicing Swiss roll.

'Oh, nothing,' I said, taking a swig of tea. 'Just something someone told me today.'

'Is it vulgar?'

'No.'

'Well, it sounds vulgar.'

'What, slow down, Arthur, stick . . .'

'Well, shush,' she stopped me. 'I don't want to know if it's vulgar.'

'It's not vulgar,' I said.

'What's all this?' said Dad, irritably scrunching the *Echo* into his lap. He glared over at me, then for the umpteenth time a voice in my head chimed in with his as he said, 'Whad av you dun to yer hair, lad?'

'Dyed it.' I sighed, feeling the leaden weight of my reply.

Mum biting into cake said, 'Well, you look a perfect fool.' She fingered crumbs back into her mouth and screwed up her eyes as though seeing me from afar. 'Like something from the mud flats.'

'Great Crested Grebe,' said Brother Ray, shovelling in Swiss roll and beginning his slightly sinister, Lurch-like laugh, spraying chocolate crumbs all over the place as he did so. 'U-hu u-hu u-hu.' Ray's a greaser with hair halfway down his back. He flicked at it effeminately, still laughing.

'Yes, that's it,' said Mum, leaning back. 'You look like a Great Crested Grebe.'

'Do I really?' I said.

From behind the *Echo*, Dad said, 'You want to get back to Slater, lad.'

A few days later, I went to look at a flat but it had gone, which was a bastard, really. On the way home I stopped in at MIND to look for a copy of the 'Ancient Mariner'. They didn't have one but my eye caught sight of a smart white suit and I was just trying it on with some powder-blue Italian shoes when this tall black kid came in wearing a cowboy hat. He ducked theatrically as the shop bell jangled, giving a jaunty greeting to the two old women slurping tea behind the till. They stopped gossiping and eyed him suspiciously. He was wearing a thin-lapelled leather jacket and heavily pleated pegs, he took off cool-looking shades and chewed one of the stems as he browsed. Then he picked up a large toy fire engine and, winding out the plastic ladders then winding them back, he said, 'Hmmmm, cool.' Tucking the engine under an arm he produced some pound notes, one of which he plucked from his fist with his teeth as he sauntered to the till.

I bent over to take off the Italian loafers. When I straightened up he was in front of me. Briskly, he produced a card and said, 'I've seen you about, haven't I? Dint you used to work at Grimshaws's?'

I shook my head.

'The Centurion café maybe? Any-waze, here – I wanna give you this. You've godda good face. Interesting structure.'

The card read:

Baz Barrel

Photography

Telephone 596843

'Y'ever dun modlin? Dun't madder if y'aint, if y'ever want your photograph taken, gimme a call – won't cost you anything just ring, yeah. You've godda good face.'

I'd got up too quickly and felt dizzy. By the time I came to my senses he was at the door, and as the bell jangled I called out, 'Righto . . . er . . . Baz.' He pointed the nibbled stem of his sunglasses at me. 'Good face,' he said again turning to go. Above loud tuts from behind the till he called out, 'Come over tomorrow if you want, there might be a few cool people stopping by.' He dialled the air. 'Call me – Ciao, dude!'

In the diminishing jingle-jangle of the bell, the old women went nattering over to the window where they positioned themselves behind an old mannequin draped in a kaftan. Drawing aside its sleeves like nets, their eyes pursued him up the street, muttering all the while between bites of Penguin and slurps of tea, what he could possibly want with a kid's fire engine.

In the changing room I was thinking over what he'd said. 'A few cool people stopping by.' While the two old bags were busy-bodying away about the Coloureds and how you can't trust them, I saw my chance and slipped back into the Italian shoes. I went through my old clothes, quickly transferring everything into the pockets of the old white Jaeger suit I was still wearing. Then taking a peep from the curtain, I headed confidently for the door.

'It's not that I'm prejudiced,' I heard one of them say as I yanked it open.

The bell jangled again, and they barely stopped yacking to bid me a curt 'Good day'.

'CIAO,' I called back.

Outside, I resisted the urge to belt off, but instead hastened up Skeldergate with the tell-tale stride of a guilty bastard who thinks the whole world knows he's just nicked something. Aware of nothing so much as this, I felt my exaggerated gait straining the delicate tendons round my groin as I made time.

Once lost down some back alleys, I began to feel bad about the theft. The fit of the shoes wasn't so good and I felt conspicuous in the white suit. No good'll come of this, I said to myself. Stealing from the mentally ill was bad, very bad, and I made a mental note to make large donations to their funds when I was rich. I saw myself caught in the *Echo*'s flash, handing over a large cheque to the MIND top brass. Heard the clamour of reporters: 'Thank you, Mr Glover. And again, Mr Glover. Over here, sir.'

'Gentlemen, gentlemen,' I held up my hands, 'call me Kid.'

Being the youngest of two brothers, someone had called me Kid once and it had stuck. It seemed to fit a self-made man, suggesting, as it once was meant – a bright young hope.

THE CRUMBS

Entering the kitchen that night, dressed in the height of MIND fashion, I thought how sallow my family appeared under the naked bulb. On the back of Brother Ray's cut-off was a newly and poorly rendered legend: *You've just eyeballed The Flying Tiger.* He was into CB, our Ray, and this was his tag, The Flying Tiger. Straddling his hunkered spine was a hyper-real rock chick, her clothes all ripped, her flesh freshly clawed. The red daubs of paint denoting blood were disturbing in their crudeness.

'I don't know that I care for that,' Mum was saying, frowning at Ray's back. He was bent over a copy of *Motorcycle News*, his jaws voraciously oscillating on an already bitten-down fingernail.

'Hmm,' was all he said, so Dad flicked him on the ear.

'Stop gnawing, lad!'

Ray, nursing his ear, glared at my dad, and made a motorbike rev-revving noise in his throat that transformed through gritted teeth into his opening words. 'Rurrgghhh-zup wi you, wart?'

'You – thas wot's up. Gnaw gnaw gnawing away every time I look at you, and don't call me wart.'

They began to strong-arm wrestle. The kettle began to whistle.

'Chinaman in d' kitchen,' screamed Stacey in delight.

Mum, getting up to turn the kettle off, was distracted by a mark on the wall and took an age to get over to the stove. 'What the devil's that?' she mumbled, frowning. Wetting a finger she began to worry at it.

'Boy-ling, boy-ling,' screamed Stacey, pulling at her eyes, making them go slitty.

As the whistling eventually subsided, the strenuous hissing of strong-arm wrestling filled the kitchen. Their elbows slid on the smooth wood-grain Formica. The table leaf began to shake and their hisses became the undignified UHUGHHHs of tennis aces. The leaf collapsed and they ended up on the floor. Not stopping amid the crashing of crockery, they then began a bout of kitchen-floor wrestling.

Mum, returning with a full teapot, guided it through the air above them, spilling a few drops. 'Hell's bells! Why don't you look what you doing.'

Dad had Ray in a headlock and, grinding his fist into his crown like a pestle, was giving him what he called the Knuckle Torture.

'Ger-im off,' gasped Ray, clearly in real pain. 'EEE'S A MADMAN.'

Dad's teeth were clenched and he was completely absorbed, a little crazed even. His grey hair brushed back at the front had gained some lift in the struggle and, with his heavy sideburns, this gave him the aspect of an ageing Ted, brawling with a young rocker in the town centre.

'Ger off! Ger off me, menk! Ger off,' screamed Ray.

Mum turned and, rolling her eyes to the ceiling in a glance that took in the clock, she fitted a cosy over the teapot and said, 'Soon be time for work, Bernice.'

My older sister could almost have been poolside. 'Soon,' she said, turning the page of her magazine.

In under an hour she was due behind the bar at the Turpin Motel, but she was still in her bathrobe. Her long blonde hair was up in a towelling turban. She'd do her make-up in the cab. In the wake of what was now the tenth Ripper attack, Mum insisted on her having cabs to and from work. Mum felt this caution implied no slur. The Ripper had started killing randomly now as opposed to previously confining it to red-light girls.

THE TURPIN MOTEL REMEMBERED

After the carriage clock on the telly had struck midnight, triggering an epidemic of various chimes all over the house and throughout the diocese, Mum rose from the sofa. 'Bernice still not back,' she mumbled, turning off the national anthem. The telly's diminishing static accompanied her retreat into the embrasure of the window.

At that time we lived in a pre-war council semi that lay in a dip between a natural rise and a railway bridge. At night, the geographic depression trapped and accentuated all sounds. Next door, the Partridges were hearing out the national anthem. Mr Partridge was in the NF and I imagined him observing it in a formal ritualistic way, perhaps involving his wife and kids. Out of the darkness, beyond the curtains, to the muffled strains of 'God Save the Queen' came the sound of quickening footsteps. Although that was a natural consequence of the slope, the accelerated tapping of heels evoked the Hitchcockian effect of being followed home.

'Is that Bernice?' I shouted to Mum.

'What?'

'I SAID – is that Bernice.'

'Pardon, can't hear you.' Mum appeared from behind the curtain.

'I said, is that Bernice,' although by now I could hear the footsteps going off into the distance.

'No,' said Mum, 'it's some silly girl with hardly anything on.'

In my mind's eye I accompanied this girl up to Battlegarth Bridge where the footsteps were fading. A train sped by drowning them out completely. I pictured the train – duddlee-duh, duddlee-duh, duddlee-duh-ing along, obscuring the girl with not much on. I saw passengers' heads leant up against speeding windows. Behind them, I caught glimpses of the girl through the flashing yellow and black of the carriages. The clipped sleepers rocked me into an uneasy kind of rhythm. I seemed to hear it long after the train was out of earshot.

'What?' I started as I heard my name.

'Billy, be a good lad, will yer, and go and meet yer sister from work. She's awfully late.'

Bernice, I knew, walked home to save the taxi fare Mum gave her. I wouldn't have minded if she hadn't the money. I don't mean in any way to be pejorative about my sister, or about prostitutes either, and in saying she looked like a prostitute, I only mean she resembled a stylised Hollywood ideal of one. Long blonde hair, high heels and all that stuff. Imagining her thus, I thought I'd better cut along. Outside, there was an imperceptible drizzle just visible in the halos of street lamps. Turning up my collar I hunched over, squaring off a shiver creeping up my back. I passed a news-vendor's shack. Under the harlequin paper trap, in marker pen, it said, THE RIPPER IS A COWARD.

At the top of the rise I stopped and lit a cigarette. A lone female approached. Seeing me loiter she crossed the road, heels clicking the kerb. She used a vague Green Cross Code to disguise a nervous glance back. The road was quiet but she gathered her coat about herself and broke into as much of a run as her skirt and heels would allow.

I saw myself as I must have appeared to her, a shadowy male figure lighting a cigarette, with perhaps a slightly sinister tilt to the head, half-hidden behind cupped hands. I tossed away the match and watched her pass the replica of Dick Turpin's gallows, on the very spot where Turpin had been hanged for horse rustling. The rest of the drag was dominated by the hanging theme: an off-licence called Dick's Offy, the Black Bess pub, Turpin Taxis, the Stand and Deliver take-away.

A little further down the road was my destination, the Turpin Motel itself. It looked strange and out of place, more the sort of spot you might come across on some lost American highway, checked into by travellers from *The Twilight Zone*. The impression it gave was that the owner, having stayed somewhere similar out in the States, had thought, Hang about, this'll go down well back home. It hadn't, B & B at the Black Bess being much more the thing. In fact, since the motel had opened some seven or eight years ago, it seemed to have been forever changing hands.

The current owner was a Canadian widow, Girlie McLeven, and it was she who'd made it over in the Turpin theme. She'd clearly once been glamorous and appeared every night with a fur draped over her shoulders, even though in warmish weather it made her sweat. Determinedly, she would mark her place at the bar with twenty menthols, a bunch of keys and a lighter, then proceed to get slowly soaked on perfumed gins until she passed out, leaving her perspiration hanging, slightly redolent of mother's ruin. To her left was a door, above it a green-lit EXIT sign. Every night she had to be helped through that door. She was at least, I thought, surrounded by reminders of her once glamorous life: a swimming pool, Martini umbrellas, a gravel path, *Tom Jones Live in Vegas* on a loop. Though generally empty and running at a loss, the Turpin Motel boasted all these attractions.

As I conjured up the Turpin Motel in my head, I wasn't really paying attention to what was happening on the street. Translucent fixtures and fittings were drifting across my mind, and it was through a pair of crossed duelling pistols mounted above the serving hatch that I saw, some fifty paces or so up the road, a figure making small adjustments to his dress. I slowed a bit and, blinking away the residual traces of Girlie McLeven's sequinned, backless dress, paused and lit a Sir Nige.

The red glow of the Turpin interior faded to the sodium pink of the street light under which, through the illuminated drizzle, Ziggy Hero appeared like the Exorcist. I timed my 'Hi there' so as not to catch him unawares, but it did, and as he jumped I realised that under the brim of his hat, he could only really see his feet and the patch of path in front of him. He seemed to be privately enjoying the way his trousers moved as he walked.

'Hi – sorry – didn't mean to, er, make you . . .' I pointed at myself. 'We met, the, er, other night – at Purd's . . .'

'The other night . . . thas right, man. Far out!'

I was lost for how best to respond so I just shivered and said something about the night air being chilly. He nodded and looked off into the distance, reminding me in a way of old Doc Slater. He stood for a moment like this, and then his expression changed. Screwing up his eyes, he said, 'Do you by any chance know a *bald* cat with a *thin* moustache?'

I turned to where he was looking, up the path of the Turpin Motel. From reception, the night manager, a slight, immaculately groomed man known as the Balding One, had seen us and, with one hand cupped against the glass was waving 'COO-EEEE,' fluttered fingers working an invisible glove puppet.

'Oh yeah. My sister works here, I'm just picking her up.'

Ziggy produced a bottle of Beefeater from inside his great-coat. He took a quick glug and then held it up to me. I took a hit then handed it back. As he screwed on the cap, he seemed about to say something, but frowning at his watch as though he had a pressing engagement said, 'Ah, gotta go.'

'Oh – OK – See ya then.'

'G'night.'

I watched as he walked away and then, after a few strides, he turned around but carried on walking backwards. He registered no surprise in seeing I was still staring after him and lifted some words back towards me.

'Sorry?' I cupped my ear.

'Are – you – coming – to – my – concert – man?'

'Oh – er – yeah, er, sure.' I didn't know about it but said, 'Yeah, sure.'

I turned away up the long gravel path to reception, towards the Balding One and my sister. The tiny stones crunching beneath my shoes sounded like money, like the intro to 'Love Is The Drug' by Roxy Music, but then as I got nearer I thought how it sounded more like old cat litter really. Suddenly the gravel was being kicked up behind me. I spun round and was surprised to see Ziggy running up the path, one hand holding on to his hat, the other controlling the flapping of his coat. Realising I'd seen him, he slowed and tried to regain his casual step.

'Bu-Billy,' he panted upon reaching me. 'Su-sorry man,' he wiped his brow, 'c-car's broken down, j'av any jump leads by any chance?'

'*Jump* leads! Well, no, I haven't, sorry, can't help you there.'

'Ah, uhm.'

He turned the question to the Balding One in reception who was regarding us curiously. I shook my head on his behalf and, indicating the empty car park, said, 'All the staff use taxis, in fact.' I pointed at the revolving amber light up the road. 'Why not try 'em, they're sure to have some.'

'Hmmm.' He considered this, crassly fingering sleep blackened by mascara from the corner of his eyes.

'I'll go with you, if you like,' I said. 'There's a driver over there I sortov know. He used to go out with our lass.'

I'M A SPACE INVADER

Looking in through the dirty window of Turpin Taxis, I said, 'Uhm, nope. Don't see him.' There were just two drivers in there, neither of whom I knew or particularly liked the look of. Nevertheless, Ziggy went in and, standing tall in the doorway, enquired about the jump lead situation. Sir Nige smoke swirled thickly beneath the faltering strip lights. One driver was sitting on a burst sofa reading the paper. The other was playing the Space Invaders machine. Neither gave the slightest impression of having even heard him. The Space Invaders carried on its nuh-nuh-nuh-nuh, building a tension in the air. Ziggy pressed his lips together and said, 'Please, don't be suspicious.'

A lone spacecraft peeled away from the squadron. The man at the controls writhed about in its hail of fire before slapping the machine with his palm. 'EEE-YES! Gotcha, you air-lee-un bas-tud.' The man on the sofa stirred, turned over the page of his paper and without looking up at Ziggy said, 'Puff.'

I accompanied Ziggy back to his D-reg Toyota. I couldn't make out its colour in the deluvian gloom of the library car park. Was it beige? I couldn't tell. What was for sure was that inside, under the wan interior light, was Vampirella, the girl I'd seen at Purdcake's the other night. Hazel, the tall beautiful one. She didn't look so tall sitting all alone in the broken-down car, but she was still beautiful. As we approached, she made some feminine fast checks and dropped something into her handbag. Then she began smoking like she was unaware of us, just out there on the traffic island. She gazed from the quarter-light as if watching some yacht perhaps, leaving St Tropez harbour.

Ziggy was talking rapidly, saying something to me in a low voice that I couldn't catch. He broke off apparently finding it all too hilarious to go on with. 'Ahh, it's jus . . .' He removed his hat and shaded his eyes, shaking silently. 'Ahh, it's too crazy.'

'What is?' I said. He even stopped and groped the air in front of him as though a wall should be there for him to lean on. 'What is it?'

'Ahh, by jingo.' He began vaguely slapping his pockets. 'Don't have a *bean* on me.' He was shaking his head at the incredulousness of it all. Running a hand through his hair, he put his hat back on, then from under the brim shot me a quick glance to catch my mood. Apparently encouraged, he broached in a slightly strained voice, still very Mr Newton, 'I don't s'pose you could lend me three or four quid, could you, man?'

I couldn't really, but I said, 'Yeah, sure.' I dived into my pockets. 'Comin up.'

With a few pound notes in my mouth we came to rest in front of the car where I continued to rummage for the remainder of the dough. Handing it all over I called out 'Hi there' to Dracula's bride. She gave me a smile, vaguely aware, I supposed, that I was helping out here, but obviously still a little wary of my much discussed madness.

'Oh, sorry, man,' Ziggy said, waving a hand as though scattering seed, 'This is Hazel.' He could have meant the car, the library, the dog shit on the path.

'Billy,' I shouted, pointing to myself. She nodded in spite of herself but then went about emptying her face of all expression. Ziggy seemed sort of anxious for her not to see the transaction but it was too late, she already had. He thanked me anyway.

I waved at Hazel. 'See ya.'

Her yacht was very far away now, out of sight, and her eyes began to shift around aimlessly across the library wall. She gave a sudden shudder as though birds had alighted from her frosty black limbs and then gave me a pleasant, if not a little automatic wave. 'Oh yeah, see ya.'

BACK AT THE MOTEL

'Coo-eeeee, Bernice! Your brother's here.'

I hung about in reception flicking through a few out-of-date style mags till Bernice was ready. Sifting the pages, Hazel's face dissolved, leaving me staring at a full-page ad. Gilby's Gin – the unwinder. I loved that. The unwinder. Up at the bar, with her head on the bar, Girlie McLeven was unwinding the years, her fly-trap fingers loosely guarding a half-drunk gin. A beer towel for a pillow. On her upturned cheek a diamanté earring lay shimmying against her liverish complexion.

All around, as if to compensate for the unsightliness of the slumped figure, Bernice was tidying up, straightening beer mats a half-inch or so and touching things into place just the way our mum would.

2HB HAIRDO

She looked good, Bernice, in her wench's theme uniform and often when I arrived, I'd find some travelling sales type at the bar doing his utmost to chat her up. They always reminded me of those soft 2B drawings you'd see in barber's shop windows, these types, and they'd be recalling a joke or funny story that had happened to them or one of their mates. Bernice, without looking up from her tidying, would nod and smile, and at the punchline, while maybe banging a beaker of coloured cocktail forks into order, would give just a slight, 'Ha ha.' And to be polite, 'Really! How hysterical.' And then you'd see these embarrassing-like grins stranded in their seedy faces. I fucking loved it when she did that.

I was surprised then to find her listening attentively to what I took at first to be the drunken slurring of another fat salesman. As I approached, he lit a Sir Nige, then loosening his tie he used the fat end of it to dab at some sweat on his brow. Like Girlie McLeven only two bar stools away, he was also on Gilby's. It was way past closing time and Bernice had draped a beer towel over the pumps on which she was now leaning.

'Cheers, luv,' he was saying. 'An wun vu yurselv.'

'Oh ta,' said Bernice, seeming not to mind that he was ogling her tits. She caught me a look through the optics and brought over a tatty old *National Geographic* and a lager and lime and set them down emphatically in front of me on the bar. I shrugged and, sipping my drink, began to read an article about the midnight sun. I found it pretty interesting, particularly the bit about all the suicide, so I tore it out.

'Who's that skinny rake I saw you talking to out there?' Bernice asked as we left the motel.

'Oh, I dunno really, his name's Ziggy, he lives in my old room. Who's that fat bloke you were talking to at the bar?'

'A detective. Something to do with Ripper case.'

'I think he fancies you,' I said.

'More 'n likely,' she said yawning, too tired at the end of her shift for false modesty. She linked arms with me. 'He comes in and gets pissed and starts talking about how they haven't got a flamin clue. I don't think he's supposed to say anything, about the case, you know, but I'm dead nosy so I just let him prattle on. What was he tellin me this evening? Oh yeah, apparently they're using *clairvoyants* now. Ah mean! But does he look the type to even read his horoscope?'

Bernice was a horoscope addict. Personally, I didn't want to know what was in store and told her so as she rifled in her bag for *Cosmo*, saying, 'Here – I read yours, Kid, it's quite interest . . . Where is it now?'

'Don't worry, Bern, I'm not too fussed.' If it was good I never believed it; if it was bad it would scare me to death.

'Oh ere we go – Pisces.' She read as we walked. '"There is a pleasing fluidity to the Piscean life, not only in the way that different parts of it overlap and –" whas that – "inter, inter," oh yeah, "intermingle . . . but also in the way you slip from one episode to the next without a visible break, however, certain transitions must necessarily be abrupt, with separation and severance the essence of the matter, you can duck the . . .'"

'All right,' I said, holding up my hand, 'it's fuckin terrifyin.'

MA YUMMY

I glanced at my watch, quarter to seven, fine, I'd be at Grimshaws's bang on eight to meet Ziggy. Apparently he wanted to ask me a favour, that's what Alex had said on the phone. I was kind of intrigued.

It was snowing when I came across the Coneheads; they were all splashing about in George Hudson's memorial fountain. One of them was up on George Hudson himself, pulling this Bruce Forsyth silhouette. He'd transferred a traffic cone from his own head to George Hudson's. Suddenly I was distracted by a shout from outside Jackson's Minimart. A Conehead was running out with an armful of nicked Fairy Liquid and an Indian shop assistant hanging on to his shirt tails tug-of-war style, shouting, 'Stop, THIEF!' With a deft twist of his upper body, the Conehead got away from the Indian and lashed out with his docker, catching the shopkeeper a blow to the stomach which sent him crashing back into a line of supermarket trolleys. The Conehead was biting the tops off the Fairy Liquid bottles like they were grenades. 'Ahuuuw, this stuff tests shite!' he wailed, spitting and pouring it into the fountain.

Bruce Forsyth had been watching the whole thing with an arm around George Hudson's stone shoulders. Inevitably he shouted, 'Din't he do well,' sullying the catchphrase of the great master, by whose standards, to my mind, all other game-show hosts fail miserably. The other Coneheads shouted applause although they were fast becoming lost beneath the detergent bubbles that were lathering up into an immense froth. Brucie Cone, in some celebratory way all his own, got his knob out and tried to piss on his mates. They in turn ducked under the foam and, reappearing elsewhere in the fountain, shouted, 'ARGHHHHH, tha wankha!' making furious tosser signs up at him.

'You fuckin fuckers,' roared Bruce. 'Cum ere.' He slashed the air with his piss, gyrating his hips like a girl keeping up a hoop. 'Yeh fuck-in fuck-ers.' The foam was now erupting over the rim of the fountain and creeping out into Exhibition Square, reminding me of some sci-fi scourge, eating everything in its path. It was too much to hope that it might devour the Conehead bastards. They re-emerged covered in suds like *It's a Knockout* contestants.

I crossed the square to Yummy's burger van. There was a long queue at the hatch and only old Ma Yummy serving. I was freezing and fancied a hot drink, something to take down the tab of Sunrise I had with me.

I was about to conduct an experiment with myself. I wanted to see if the acid would bring back any of my disorientation fits, the visual trails as Doc Slater had called them. Not because I was missing them, far from it, but now I was cured, sort of, I was curious to know what had caused them. I figured by tomorrow I'd know. If it was LSD or marijuana – I saw Doc Slater mouthing at me through a haze of smoke – I'd be experiencing those light trace effects by the morning. And if I started to have an adverse reaction, I had a precious Tunnel with me, the little pill guaranteed to subdue the most out-of-hand hallucinations. I felt its comforting shape in my pocket.

I turned into my coat to light a Sir Nige and when I looked up this Conehead bastard was rounding the side of the van. Fresh out of the fountain and soaked through. He was gasping and squeegeeing water off his face with his huge waterlogged hands when he suddenly stopped and, without warning, turned round to face this kid who he'd just pushed in front of. 'You fuckin say summat, pal?'

The kid hadn't said a thing. What he'd done, though, was drawn in his breath and then let it out slowly like he was saying, Fine, yeah, just *push* in why don't you?

'Hey, am talkin to you, TOSSER.'

This kid, a student by the look of him, began blinking and making strange regurgitating movements as though bringing up a stammer. A girl in the queue came to his rescue, tapping Coney on the back. 'Ere, arn't you fuckin freezin like that?'

'You what?' He looked round.

'Ah say, arn't you a bit cold?'

Seeing how this girl was fit, he put his shoulders back, like he was just out taking the night air.

'Ahw – nah, not at all. 'S mattur a fact, it's ovur warm for me this.' He grabbed the neck of his T-shirt and, pulling it to one side, he moved his head and neck around like he was agitated by the closeness of the day.

'You mus be mad, you,' said the girl, though she was clearly very impressed. He was steaming like a racehorse now and I was getting mesmerised by the way snowflakes, alighting on his body, were melting into the sealskin-like wetness of his black T-shirt. The impressed girl touched him on his chest.

'Yur soaked tut skin,' she exclaimed. He nodded, clearly very chuffed.

Ma Yummy said, 'Canna elp you, luv?'

As Conehead put in his order for fifty million burgers, I huddled in all my layers of warm clothing. I was wearing a T-shirt, a shirt, a suit jacket and an RAF greatcoat and gloves and I was still freezing. By the time Coney's order arrived, he was well in with the fit girl. He handed her a hotdog and they walked off together deep in some sort of conversation, which was good news for the student kid, who'd gone into a terrible trance. He was just staring at the front wheel arch of the van, wincing occasionally like he was holding in a wee.

'Yeah, canna elp you, luv?' Ma Yummy asked him, when it was eventually his turn. He glanced up and seeing the coast was clear breathed an audible sigh of relief.

'Canna elp you, luv?'

'Hu hoh . . .' He made saliva come back into his mouth, and on a second try he managed, 'Ahem, a hotdog, please.'

While his hotdog was frying Ma squinted at me in recollection. 'Teeeeea?' she said, 'just a splash a milk and . . . *no sugar?*'

'Thas right,' I said.

'You bin away, luv?'

'Yeah.' I hadn't considered myself such a regular. The thought depressed me.

While waiting for his hotdog, the student was getting braver. Irritatingly, he began tapping 50p on the metal serving hatch. When I looked over he was staring straight at me as though waiting for me to say something like, I think you handled that very well, pal, very mature of you not to get mad.

'Some people,' he said, tutting to the sky. 'Actually, he's lucky actually, because I'm a pacifist, you know, but I can pack quite a punch when I have to.' I couldn't place his accent exactly but there was no trace of irony in it. He wasn't from around here.

'Hmm,' I mimicked him. 'Well, he's certainly been a lucky chappie tonight then.'

The student nodded eagerly, not seeing I was taking the piss. I felt a tad sorry for him then. He wanted to pal up, asked if I knew where was good to go, but I blanked him. I had my acid to take and my meeting with Ziggy, so I paid for my tea and walked off. I imagined him at his lonely digs writing a lonely letter to his mother in Surrey or somewhere – 'Everything is fine here, people are very nice and I'm managing to make friends quite easily' – later waking slumped and cold over said letter, a Ma Yummy burger belch lingering in the intimate sadness of his crooked arm.

Over by Fairy Mountain, George Hudson stood at the summit of bubbles looking foolish in a traffic cone. The Coneheads themselves had all fled when they heard the pigs' sirens. Biting off my gloves, I searched my pockets for the tab of Sunrise. In doing so, I noticed how George Hudson's face seemed to be made up entirely of pigeon shit these days. Pigeon shit and green slime.

There's a local fable that's been on the go for donkey's that says, at the stroke of midnight, George Hudson moves his curiously cocked little finger. I've no idea how this legend was born. I dabbed the acid on my tongue and took a swallow of tea. Mum said that as a little girl she'd believed in the legend of the little finger, and one night had stood patiently watching and waiting as the last clock struck twelve. She was ironing when she recounted this to me.

'An what happened?' I'd asked, rapt.

'Nothing happened of course,' she'd said flatly. 'Part from I caught a good clattering for stoppin out su late.'

The pigs had arrived and were standing around outside Jackson's Minimart, looking bored as fuck. The Indian shop manager complained at them in a state of high vexation. The pigs looked over at me suspiciously.

'NO,' wailed the shop manager, 'NO NO,' and he began making irate traffic cone shapes with his hands above his head. From where I stood it looked as if he was praying.

A FREDDIE STARR

I had a sudden desire to get home and change into my white suit but it was difficult walking and drinking my tea at the same time. It kept slapping against my face as I tried to slurp it and it was scalding my lip. When I did finally reach home, somewhat drained, intent on reaching the sanctuary of my bedroom, the lounge door flared open and there was my dad.

'Freddie Starr's on,' he shouted. He wasn't just telling me this, he was accusing me of missing the beginning of it.

The Friday night Freddie Starr ritual had begun without me. Homebrew and crisps were laid out on the orange fold-out table in front of the fire.

'Your favourite programme,' he said, angling his chair in to watch me watching Freddie Starr. 'A say, laddie, yer favourite this.' I felt his knuckles rap my knee.

He knew something was up when I went the whole show without once cracking a smile. 'Are you all right, laddie?' he said. I nodded and, judging a lapse of time I thought to be natural, said 'Yes.'

When the ordeal was over I went to my room and changed into my white suit and a black polka-dot tie. My shirt needed cuff links and finding none I worked two ornamental keys from a chest of drawers into the eye holes.

BACK IN NO TIME

Purdcake's front room flickered orange from a roaring fire. I lay down facing the flames and was quickly lapped in by the glow. I saw faces in the flames, the way I had as a kid. Always so depressing the cold grate the next morning, all that grey and salmon-coloured ash.

Footsick came into the room and kissed me out of my reverie. Holding my face he kissed me hard on the mouth, disengaging with an exaggerated plunger sound.

'Ahhg, what th . . . oh, Footsick, 's you!' He slid his hand on to my inner thigh and began writhing his torso in front of me like a cobra, shifting his hand on to my crotch, 'Ged off, willya.' My heart rate had increased.

Footsick grinned like an iguana. 'Don't knock it till you tried it.'

'Yeah, listen,' I said. 'Listen, I wanna tell you something about that. Listen, Footsick, pack that in, willya.'

He stopped writhing and came and sat next to me on the edge of the sofa. I began talking and he nodded intently until I'd finished, then he got up. He was still nodding, and it seemed to me he was digesting what I'd just told him, persuaded and convinced by it. He turned to go and almost collided with Ziggy who'd just appeared in the room. I acknowledged him with a hand movement as Footsick disappeared. Ziggy stood around for a while caressing the brim of his hat then, when I looked up again, he'd also turned to go. I saw his shadow on the ceiling crease into two down the wall and slither away into the wedge of light visible above the open door. I heard murmuring down the hall and then Purdcake's face appeared above me. He was doing an impression of Anthony Blanche from *Brideshead Revisited*, though I didn't know it at the time. I thought he had hiccups.

'B-B-Billy, could you pu-possibly help me get the m-m-mattress down from the sh-sh-shove-me-up, dihr boy.'

I groaned as I got to my feet and went to lend a hand. The shove-me-up was claustrophobic and brightly lit in contrast to the convivial glow of the front room. The king-size was too wilful for us, flexing about stubbornly in the small passageway, getting wedged and caught up with bicycles and such. Ziggy's and I think Hazel's voices were on the other side of it, but I couldn't see them and I couldn't make out what they were saying.

I was visited by a sudden feeling that I'd been in the

passageway an inordinately long time; I hadn't asked where the mattress was going and I was wondering why it needed four pairs of hands to move it. The air here smelt fusty and the stale odour of the mattress was choking. As we wrestled with its swirling Slumberland design, all I wanted was to get back to the flames and the faces of the front room.

The mattress was eventually laid down on the floor of *my* old room where I recognised *my* old *single* mattress standing slumped against the wall, shamefully stained and sagging like a sorry refugee. When the king-size was finally manoeuvred into position, Hazel flopped on to it and, seeing how that must have looked a bit wanton, got up again and waited for Purdcake and me to leave. Ziggy just stood revolving his fedora in his hand.

'C'mon, Kid,' said Purdey, pulling gently at my sleeve. I heard the door close behind us.

TUNNEL

I seemed to wake partially and, bit by bit, on to my feet. I'd taken the Tunnel and was walking home, this much was clear. I looked down to discover my shoes, two unerring pale-blue flashes beneath me. I put my faith in them to get me home, they seemed to know the way. Knee-deep below, their Italian ancestors had tramped this route. According to notable psychic researchers, they had perished here at the hands of savage Picts during the collapse of Roman Britain.

Halfway up Strensall Hill, I was overtaken by an old creaking cyclist bringing up phlegm. I looked up in case he was about to goz at me, but saw he was already wiping his lapel where the phlegm had come back on him in the wind. The wind was freezing and I hurried as fast as I could but under the dulling effect of the Tunnel I felt like I was wading through black molasses. In the near distance I could just see the yellow light of the Sunrise All Night Chinese Take-away. When I reached it and went in I found I was the only customer. Even so, the woman behind the counter didn't look too pleased to see me. She took my order while shouting in a stream of angry Chinese to somebody I couldn't see in the kitchen. I wasn't even sure she'd heard me till she held out her hand for the money.

Back out in the chilly night air, the chips were steaming hot and needed a lot of blowing. I was enthusiastically doing this when I thought I heard a noise behind me on the street but, straining my ears a long while, all I could hear was the tinnitus ringing of burglar alarms far away in the shopping precinct. Apart from that there was nothing, save that annoying twitter ornithologists call the dawn chorus. It seemed to be coming from the life-size silhouettes of the frontiersmen Hudson and Etty. I started walking again, when a hand gripped my shoulder, and forcefully turned me round. There were two of them, and their faces loomed up distorted with hate. I heard my voice full of panic saying, 'Sos, pal, sos.' I didn't feel the first punch but it knocked me down. To a degree, my chips broke my fall, my face landing flat in their warmth. Perhaps I felt pain but I don't remember, I was numbed by the Tunnel. I dimly remember being rolled on to my back and looking up through half-closed eyes and registering the dark forms of the city's frontiersmen looming above me. Somehow they had descended from their plinths with their birdshit complexions and pointed Coneheads. One of them, Hudson or Etty, unzipped his flies and created shallow yellow puddles in the folds of my clothing. The other lifted a heavy boot and stamped it down hard on my nose.

THE MILKING OF HUMAN KINDNESS

Spying the Great Crested Grebe lying limp by the roadside, a milkman picked me up and drove me to casualty in his float. He took me right up to the automatic glass doors, his milk crates going jangle jangle over these speed bumps they've got in the hospital grounds now. When I thanked him for stopping, he told me not to mention it and, tapping a milk bottle, said something philosophical about, 'This stuff' – clink clink – 'being in short supply when it came from the milking shed of human kindness.'

In the hospital's glass doors, my bloodied reflection had sheered in half. As I stepped through my refracted self into the warm blast of air from somewhere above, I sensed the admonishment to vanity in the clipped swish of the glass doors closing behind me. I pictured Baz Barrel pointing the nibbled stem of his sunglasses at me, saying, 'You've godda good face, man – good structure.'

SOME THOUGHTS ON RETIREMENT

'I see yu've been duffed over,' said my dad, some two days later. I don't think he would have mentioned it at all if it hadn't been for a feature on the regional news that the ex-capital was the most violent place in England, person per square mile. Dad began on a theory about this while combing his hair in the mirror. I assumed a look of interest but it was all just so much more Vienna to me and I let my tongue begin work on some shred of marmalade that had been stuck in my back teeth all day. I don't remember the exact order of his words, only the gist of it. He explained how Blossom Street, the main approach to the city, was, in Roman times, lined with the mutilated bodies of criminals and traitors, their heads displayed on long spikes between the trees. The heavy scent of blossom contended with but couldn't prevail over the stench of rotting flesh, and the gutters would be awash with traitors' blood. Here my father paused to sprinkle a Silvikrin hair preparation the colour of mint sauce on his scalp. The Romans exhibited the remains as a deterrent to those approaching the capital with no good in their minds. He stopped combing again and looked round at me, tapping at his temple with his heavy forefinger. Riff-raff, think on.

Mum, vigorously ironing, sounded some disparaging note. 'DHOWUUUUH, get out, where you getting all this *rubbish* from, George?'

More than anything, Dad couldn't take interruption of this sort. 'Negative, negative, negative,' he responded aggressively, 'always negative,' which was pretty good coming from someone who really *was* negative. For instance – and it was this that I was mulling over a little later that day as I went to sign on – Dad believed that when you retired your employer should *shoot* you through the head with a *bullet*, because that's what they were really saying to you. 'You're done for now – no further use, Mr Glover – ready for the scrap heap.'

Such were the terms in which he presented his idea. This theory in particular I remember hearing many times over. I was about eight or nine when he'd first communicated it to me. He was smoking a roll-up, and standing in front of this same mirror combing his hair, when he broke away, bringing his hard-bitten countenance to within spitting distance of my young face. 'Done for – no further use,' he said, shaping his hand into a pistol and putting it up to his temple. 'Ready for the scrap heap.' With a click of his tongue he removed the safety catch, cocked back his thumb and blew a loud gunshot sound through his lips. Smoke curled away from the roll-up while the musculature of his mouth resonated with the sound of saliva rumbling like distant thunder in his throat. 'Then when they bury you,' he continued, letting his gun arm fall to his side and swing slightly, as though cradling something heavy to the grave, 'the worms eat you.' His arm became limp, expressing some eternal nothingness.

This was the contradictory nature of his thinking then. Straightforward on the one hand, and yet capable of advancing the fantastical notion that the ex-capital's violent past could somehow insinuate itself upon the present.

But to return fully to that Monday evening when I was probing my rear molars. The marmalade wouldn't budge. My dad was really smarting from my mother's interruption of his theory. With his forefinger still up by his temple, he shouted, 'Where my getting it from, Audrey?' Alluding to her dismissive remark he began to drill violently at his head with his finger. 'It's all up ere, Audrey – up 'ere, d'you see?' He drilled at the point where he proposed his employer's bullet should enter. 'UP HERE.'

Like I say, I was about eight or nine when he first communicated his thoughts on retirement to me. In terms of me holding down a job, I think it really held me back.

GHOST RIDERS

The next day, on my way to sign on, I was obliged to walk down Blossom Hill, so-called because of its many cherry trees. Local myth has it that they were planted there to cover up the stench of rotting flesh, for it was *here* that the decapitated heads of thieves and traitors and murderers would be displayed in Roman times. I thought of all those hessian-clad AD types approaching the city gates looking for work. I saw fathers' hands going to sons' shoulders as the little boys glimpsed between the cherry blossom the severed heads on their bloody spikes. I swallowed hard, clutching my UB40.

There were those who laid claim to seeing this type of thing for real, swore blind they had, swore for a living you might say. These fellows, for they were all men, were known as Ghost Riders. They advertised their tours of the haunted quarters on sandwich boards placed at windy corners. Around these, tourists would gather and wait for them to appear which, at dusk, they would, in full regalia. In our city they became a kind of cult. Perhaps it was this that had attracted Ziggy Hero to become one, or perhaps he thought the wearing of Gothic togs wasn't really work for him and only required a few small adjustments to his lifestyle: some timekeeping; a few damp afternoons in old bookshops, seeking out obscure references to the paranormal; a little practice getting up and down from a pony and trap in a top hat and cloak; and some experiments with the eerie light effects of carriage lamps.

Like I say, the Ghost Riders were a cult of sorts, and we learnt their names from the *Evening Echo*, though the stories weren't always the type to cut out and keep. We remember the case of Lasher, a Ghost Rider regularly too pissed to do the talk coherently. He drank at the Traveller's Rest and often fell to snoring in his cloak, his top hat shading his eyes while his nag pawed the tarmac outside. It was here, after some hushed negotiation, that Ziggy and he became partners. If he, Lasher, could hold it together to drive the trap, Ziggy would do the rest. He had a top hat and cloak somewhere knocking about and adopted the name Inglewood for this work.

Lasher, 'the red-faced beast' to quote the *Echo*, was so-called because he attacked his wife one night with the whip from the pony trap. Not quite to death, but it had ended up in public down on the cobblestones at the end of Grape Lane – her semi-naked and screaming, he with his cloak flailing wildly around him, oaths ringing in his wake. He was dragged away by the pigs. She sobbed into the cobblestones unable to look at the gathering crowd or touch, without flinching, the tiny droplets of blood beading up along the welt of the lash. The courts found him guilty of GBH and the tourist board revoked his licence.

After that, Ziggy kept him on as an accomplice. All Ghost Riders have accomplices, and these are usually the real desperadoes of the piece. I'd seen them in the dole office – Tuesday signers like me – ready to be Roman soldiers, half-hanged highwaymen, faceless monks and friars – a shifting medley of every ghost to ever haunt the town. They knew all the short cuts between the haunted spots, and could often be seen haring breathless down snickelways, cramming togas into duffel bags or hurriedly fluffing out highwayman's cuffs from Oxfam frock coats. But it's a tawdry affair, all those Turpin mock hangings, and ex-Ghost Riders past and their accomplices were a common sight at the DHSS.

THE RINGMASTER'S POSITION

When ex-Ghost Rider Ziggy Low – his surname had changed to coincide with a new favourite Bowie period – walked into the DHSS, the fedora was characteristically tilted forward. Not that the manner in which it was worn was the sole way of identifying him from others. More the fact that it was worn at all in the city of beer and sweets. His greatcoat was soaked and slung about his shoulders and the usual clutch of Queen Anne's schoolgirls was in tow. Shrinking back behind the jobs board, I watched as the swinging door wafted smoke across the room.

Ziggy's entrance caused a lull, the kind directors of westerns are so fond of, only the smoke left curling until slowly the talk starts up again. The talk here was about the cunt in the hat. Hard mocking voices. I shook my head sadly, recalling the other week when I'd accompanied Ziggy into the smoky minicab office after his car had broken down. 'Puff.' The door swinging shut seemed to announce the same opinion. Phouff.

Ziggy stepped forward with his P45. He didn't carry it off, as I was about to say, with his usual panache, but he remained as far as possible in character. Sitting down opposite an efficient-looking Indian woman wearing a sari and pince-nez, he handed her his UB40 and placed his elbows on the table, making a steeple of his hands, on the point of which he rested his chin, a new affectation but one I recognised from the cover of 'John, I'm Only Dancing'.

'Ahh!' I heard him say as she took his claim. Checking it at arm's length over her pince-nez, she pushed it back to him, along with a clear plastic pen, gnarled at one end, flooded at the other. Throwing a backward glance at the truants and the row of unemployed waiting in grey flexi-back chairs, his attention returned to the dotted line where he was not about to do his usual signature. Lifting his wrist, he paused for a moment as though signing a four-album deal with Island Records, then, with an exaggerated flurry, signed Arthur Bannockburn. He pushed the form back like a roulette wager. Beneath the brim of the fedora, his lips, just visible, puckered at one side like the knot in a balloon.

From another counter a sudden fracas erupted. A young West Indian kid, whom I recognised as the one who did the robotic mime act in St Samson Square, was getting some grief about his claim and lifted an anguished plea to the ceiling.

'Sweet Jeesus – when are we gonna get some RELIEEEEF?'

There was a short silence and then a smattering of applause broke out. The West Indian kid hung his head. Ziggy looked over, like all the Tuesday signers, only his response was different. I watched him eyeing the scene, transferring the balloon knot to the other side of his mouth then back again.

The Indian woman coughed and said, 'Mr Bannockburn – thank you, Mr Bannockburn.' She was holding out his P45.

Ziggy winced. 'Uhh, sorry,' and turned back to face the Indian lady. Leaning forward conspiratorially and tilting up the brim of his hat, he cleared his throat and said, 'Uhmm . . . it's Low actually, Ziggy Low.'

The woman regarded him for a moment over the top of her pince-nez, then, after an even silence in which Ziggy heroically met her stare, she said, 'Thank you, Mr Low.'

'It's OK.' He scrutinised her name badge as he rose to go. 'Mrs Patel, I'm only signing on.' There was a loud buzz as the automated queuing system flipped on to the next number.

Ziggy gave Mrs Patel a half bow, but the corresponding click of the heels was lost in the gravelly cough of the next signer who was already looming behind him. He was a big bastard, blinking incessantly. Too large for one chair, he'd been sprawled over two. His sheepskin was torn and trailing from his left hand was a boxer's-style bandage. Between his right thumb and forefinger he was agitating the USS *Enterprise* badge-shaped ticket.

On turning to leave, Ziggy narrowly avoided bumping into his vast chest. The Indian woman swivelled to her colleague and raised her eyes. Taking his seat the big bastard man turned his bulk round to stare at Ziggy, making a mental note to twat him if he ever saw him again.

JEWELS

I turned my attention to the jobs noticeboard. I really didn't want a job for the next forty-odd years – day in, day out – at the end of it a long-service watch inscribed on the back. I didn't want to return home one day after years of slog, chuck a catalogue on the kitchen table and say, 'It's all rubbish, Audrey.'

Employees at my dad's place, with twenty-five years loyal service behind them, were presented with a catalogue of stuff such as hi-fis, lawnmowers, watches. It was like with Green Shield Stamps, the best things were the watches, and even though you needed fifty million stamps for a half-decent one, suddenly that didn't seem like much in comparison to the twenty-five years my dad had put in to get the same thing. 'Tissot's nice,' my mum had said, passing the catalogue around the tea table. We had all agreed the Tissot with the day and date display was the best thing in there.

The numbers clicked over slowly. Now serving 61. I looked at the number in my hand, 63, the year I was born. Someone was calling it out, 'Sixty-three.' I'd tell them I was looking for a job that didn't necessitate retirement – something you could do right up to the end. 'Sixty-four, then.'

'Wait up, wait up, I'm sixty-three.' I got up waving my ticket in the air.

THE TRILANGER SCARE

The claims officer began yawning, showing me his fillings, 'Huh hoooww-scuse me, scuse me.' He rubbed his face. 'Yes – right – now then, about your search for work.'

I leant back and glazed over. I noted the Swiss watch on his wrist and absently followed the second hand round for half a minute or so before losing myself in the view of the sky in the slit window high in the wall. While he droned on, I started thinking of Dick Turpin swinging on his rope, and all the Dick Turpin impersonators swinging on their ropes, and Girlie McLeven slumped over the bar, slowly unwinding the years. I thought of my uncle William collapsed against the old wheelhouse of the Scottish trawler *Sweet Estelle* and of Dad and his retirement theory. Saw his boss shaking his hand and taking from a box of Black Magic a sumptuous-looking duelling pistol. Heard a click as my thumb cocked back, the sound of a gunshot cracked at the back of my throat, and I became aware of my nails digging into the flesh at my temple. My fingers were up there making the shape of a gun.

Adrian (I caught his name on his lapel) looked up. 'Sorry,' he said tersely.

'Sorry – got a headache,' I said, rubbing my gun fingers over my brow.

'Oh dear,' he said, his mouth twitching into an irritable smile. 'Nothing serious, I hope.'

'Oh, as a matter of fact,' I replied, watching his smile vanish, 'it is ahh, something I've suffered from since I was a kid. Sort of,' I searched for the word, '. . . hereditary, you might say.'

He let out a long measured sigh. 'Huuuuuuuuuuuuuuh, dear me. Sometimes I understand why we have wars.'

I glanced at his watch. All in all, it had taken a mere forty seconds or so to go through my schooling, qualifications, past jobs, interests and hobbies.

He was talking again now. 'I see you've had experience of Trilanger.'

'Trilanger? Uh, yes.'

I had had experience of Trilanger. It was where the sugar beet was melted with the cocoa powder to make the molten chocolate. I grew up with the smell of it drifting in from the factories across the estates and as a child the word Trilanger was bandied about like an oath. As I grew older still, it would keep whistling past my ear as though I'd ascended into its flight path. Teachers, parents, uncles would fire it in my direction. After a particularly poor report it would be, 'Well, looks like Trilanger for you, lad.'

During my final year at Hopwood Secondary, a scheme was introduced to give fifth formers a taste of work. Imaginatively the scheme was called Work Experience. I remember Toggsy, the games master who doubled as the careers advisory officer, blowing his whistle, 'OK, OK – listen up. On the sheets I've given you are a choice of jobs you can do on Work Experience

. . . you've got three choices – tick the three that you'd most . . . in order of pref . . . number one for the . . .'

Afterwards, Si, Ovo and Kitty Petch asked, with a fair degree of excitement I noted, 'What ju choose, Kid?'

'Choose?' I said. 'What from?' I showed them with what contempt I held the whole scheme, stirring the air with my finger and stabbing randomly at the page. 'I dunno, Assistant fuckin Greenkeeper at Pike Hills Golf Course, I think, or summat like that.' I shrugged. 'I don't care anyhow, it's just slave labour, int it.' Si and Ovo looked at me as though I hadn't taken the work experience too seriously. 'So,' I said, 'what did you lot tick?'

Kitty said, 'I'm doin British Home Stores.'

'What j'u mean yu're doin British Home Stores? Thas not a job, is it, thas a shop. What you doin *at* British Home Stores?'

She looked at me resentfully.

'It's better thun owt you chose,' she said, all up in arms.

'Oh yeah,' I said all cheery like, 'yu reckon? Well, we'll see.'

Pride comes before a fall as they say. Even in the arbitrary way I'd ticked the form, not in a million years, conjuring up as it did the image of topless blokes stoking furnaces down in the boiler room of some old steam packet, did I imagine myself heading to Trilanger. The morning of our results was incredibly hot as I recall, and the whole of the fifth form were walking around in shirt-sleeves, heads bent reading their Work Experience itineraries, some whooping with delight, others fanning themselves with the torn-open envelopes.

'What j'u get?' asked Kitty.

I was staring out across the playing fields, off past the rugby posts. 'Trilanger,' I said with a lump in my throat. I couldn't lie. 'But,' I added quickly, as she sprayed me with derisive saliva, 'I think there's bin some mistake.'

I sought out Toggsy. He was in his office buffing up some old rugger boots.

'Glover?'

'Sir.'

'What is it, lad?'

'About this Trilanger, sir.'

'No,' he said, running some spittle over the toe, 'no – no mistake.'

I was quite young when I entered that dark Victorian building. Despite the furnaces, it was darker still in the department known as Trilanger. You entered into that underworld through two normal-ish looking doors. From the top step the view was quite overwhelming and the bloke who was showing me round knew it. He gave me a moment to take it in, then shouted above the massive machinery noise, 'C'mon then, let's av you.'

In the labyrinth of gangways below, Neanderthals like worker ants were pushing things around on trolleys. As I descended the metal walkway they grew less abstract and I saw a face – all gnarled with snapped-off, stubby teeth. Jets of steam would suddenly ptssssss across my path, startling me. My guide left me at a row of open furnaces and, one by one, all the stokers stopped, leant on their shovels and leered at me. The most senior said, ''S jus like shovelling shite, young un.' He had many fillings. I traced the stares of those flighty grinning stokers up through a tangle of pipes and metal to one of the huge cauldrons of molten chocolate. Balancing on the edge was a Neanderthal, his overalls down around his knees.

MORE THOUGHTS ON RETIREMENT

Uncle Ray was a foreman at the chocolate factory and Mum said he would look out for me. He didn't, but I wasn't fussed. I'd met this bloke there I really loved, Chris. He was a mountainous man with a few wisps of white hair left on his dappled head and he had keen blue eyes behind wire-framed spectacles. He, like me, was a stoker, only he was leaving at the end of the month. Early retirement he told me one lunch hour. He spoke about it cautiously, leaning close over his plate of cabbage, his spectacles all steamed up. When he took them off to clean them on his sleeve, his eyes shifted about nervously as though maybe he was a fool to believe in it.

Chris was married but had no kids. I didn't ask why. During the war he'd played piano in a dance band. For reasons he didn't go in to, the Chris Barrow Seven had missed their big chance. He loaded his fork with pale cabbage, paused a moment, and then explained that, anyroad, the thing for him was to carry on playing. As he took a mouthful of cabbage, I felt suddenly sorry for him and for something to say said, 'Ah, yeah, you know, I'd love to be able to just sit down and play the pian . . .'

'I could teach you,' he broke in.

'Isn't it too late to begin?'

'Nahh,' he ran his fingers up and down the worn Formica, 'hits heasy to syncopate hif you've got han ear.' He tapped his fork and cupped a musician's hand to his ear, but as he listened for perfect pitch, he only seemed to hear the canteen din redouble in intensity. Gravy dribbled down his fork on to the vestigial web of skin between first finger and thumb – the area where snuff is traditionally taken.

After Chris retired, lunch hour became a solitary affair. Sometimes I'd spy old Uncle Ray laughing and joking on the other side of the hall. I'd always be ready to acknowledge him but if he saw me, he'd look blindly past and, taking hold of his tray, stride off purposefully in the other direction. Fuck him, then. Instead I'd sit alone and think of Chris, imagining him on his old Norton Dominator motorbike, with his wife in the sidecar wearing a headscarf. Apart from jazz, what Chris liked was to find a sequestered spot on the North Yorks moors for a bit of a picnic and to check out the wildlife. Rare birds, endangered butterflies, wild flowers, that sort of thing.

On his last day there, as I'd been saying my goodbyes to Chris, Uncle Ray had come up to him in his capacity as foreman to wish him well and insincerely shake his hand.

'So what you gunna do wi all yer time now then, Chris?' said Uncle Ray.

Organising his thoughts, Chris raised himself to his full six foot five and, as though he could already glimpse these things, started slowly. 'I want,' he began, 'to see a *Clouded* Yellow[1] and hopefully a Golden Oriole[2] and . . .' (As he talked Uncle Ray looked mystified, then kind of resentful. He tried to enlist me with a glance, something to the effect of, always knew this bloke were tapped. I looked away, just as he did in the dinner queue.) '. . . and a Lady Slipper.'[3] Chris lowered his eyes to meet Uncle Ray's again who, turning out his lips and with a slight shake of his head, said, 'Ah dunno what yer on about, mate.'

ERRAND BOYS ON ACID

Saturday morning, Bernice came into my room and I knew by the way she said my name she wanted something. 'Billeee.' She ran a fingernail up and down the door, sort of moving her shoulders about in a coy way. She'd just dumped Graham, last week's Mr Wonderful, and she couldn't face him. 'Would j'u go round there for me and pick up a box of me things?'

It was a sunny day, I wasn't up to much, so I agreed. On my way I bumped into old Ziggy again.

'The sun machine,' he said, 'is coming down and . . .' like a child with a toy aeroplane, his hand made a slow silhouetted

---

[1] Clouded Yellow: A rare butterfly, in general a roof dweller, occasionally descends into sunny glades.

[2] Golden Oriole: Migratory visitor to northern Britain in very few numbers.

[3] Lady Slipper: Once widespread in the limestone hills of northern England, this flower has now been reduced by collectors to the point of extinction.

descent out of the winking sun, '. . . we're gonna have a party.' He opened his hand to reveal . . . nothing. 'Yeah, yeah, yeah,' he said conclusively, as though this was all and more than you could ever ask for.

By association with his words, and as I stared into his empty palm, as though to fill it, I recalled the sunrise I still had in my top pocket. I thought of producing them, but as my two fingers scissored about in my jean jacket pocket, I remembered my promise to Denise.

I told Zig I had to run an errand and good-naturedly he shrugged. So it was, the pair of us sauntered over the rise with no particular cares. He had his crummy portable tape recorder with him and we listened to 'Memory Of A Free Festival' all the way.

Graham was friendly enough in his jeans and checked shirt. He'd been sanding floors and we'd had to bang like fuck over the noise of the machine to be heard. He came to the door with a dust mask hung loose round his neck. He handed me the box of Bernice's stuff, blowing at a light covering of sawdust that had settled on it saying, 'Phoo, sorry bout that.' Then, as we were leaving, he said, 'Oh here, I asked your sister to buy me this for my birthday.'

He was brandishing a copy of *On the Road* by Jack Kerouac but wouldn't you know it, it turned out he'd been given two, one by his mother. He laughed and, laying the book on top of the box next to the hairdryer, said, 'I think by the looks of you, you might get on with it. It was by a beatnik in the fifties, wrote most of it on toilet paper.'

Graham tried to be casual about being dumped, saying it was mutual. I nodded. 'Well, great,' he said, and began to fiddle with his dust mask as he walked us down the path. You had to despise people like Graham and I hated to think of him fucking my sister. I really did.

Ziggy and I didn't go home immediately. We sat by the side

of the road and I alone dropped the acid. Ziggy declining in the manner of someone who declines to speak whilst trying to catch something off the radio. I took out Bernice's hairdryer from the box and, blowing dust off, it pretended it was a gun and shot out all of Graham's tyres on his TR7. Ziggy picked out a make-up compact and applied some blusher to his cheekbones. Then, using the mirror, he dazzled a passer-by. Zig, I realised, didn't really take drugs yet his behaviour was always strangely in keeping with the abstract. I disentangled a suspender belt from a copy of *Cosmopolitan* and flicked to an article about better sex called 'Non-verbal Cues'. I was sitting uncomfortably on *On the Road* so I took it out of my back pocket and read the first page of that as well. When I looked up again, Zig was still angling the compact at the passer-by. She was away down the street now.

THE CUTTING EDGE OF MEN'S MAKE-UP

'Billy,' called my mum up the stairs, 'telephone.'

She was cupping her hand over the mouthpiece and making a face. 'It's that queer-sounding sort of chap – Purdcake.' In the moment between me holding out a hand for the receiver and her giving it to me, she surveyed me as if through the eyes of a long-suffering landlady, me very much the . . .

'Queer?' I said, taking the receiver.

'I don't mean what you mean.' She drew herself up indignantly and moved over to the window ledge where she produced a hanky from her sleeve and began polishing the sail of a small brass yacht.

'Hello, Purdcake.'

'B-B-Billy, w-w-word has it, my dihr boy, you can su-su-su-suck yourself off.'

I caught Mum's eye and made a big flapping elephant's ear

with my hand. She moved away, muttering, 'Well, I'm not listening.'

'I did that *once*, Alex,' I said. 'I don't make a habit of it.' I'd made the mistake of telling this story to Footsick the other evening after he'd tried to seduce me. I was actually trying to explain to him how I knew I wasn't gay. One night, I'd managed – by supporting my neck with a caterpillar draught excluder that Bernice had made at school, and bringing my legs over my head in a yoga-type movement – to get my knob in my mouth. It was a strange experiment that obliged me to consider the sensation of what it felt like to have a cock in my mouth. I'd never considered, while wanking, how a cock felt in my hand. I began to think about the pleasure the giver of oral sex gets beyond the enjoyment derived from pleasing the recipient, in this case myself. Me giving myself a blow job was sort of confusing. I kind of saw the thing through, though, and after I came – came in my mouth *and* swallowed – I was left with that question, 'Well, how was it for you?' I was able to answer truthfully enough that, novelty value aside, it actually wasn't really that good.

'You what?' I said. Purdey was talking.

'It's Ziggy. Are you listening to me or what? He wants to ask you a favour. He wanted to ask you the other night but you were too out of it. He's doing this gig and he wants some designs doing for T-shirts and posters and things. I told him you were good at that stuff.'

'Uh, you did, did you?'

'Yes.'

'Uhmm. What is it he wants exactly?'

'I don't know. I think he's got some kind of an idea. You should meet up with him tonight maybe.'

'OK, bout eight?'

'Eight's all right.'

LAY THE REAL THING ON ME

With a day to kill I thought about calling on old Baz Barrel. I found his card and gave him a ring.

His place was in the attic of this old Tudor house. The kitchen and bathroom were all one and doubled as a dark room and his bed was separated off in a corner behind a clothes rail. All around the walls he'd got his photos up and framed. When he saw my face he said, 'Oh no, dude, whor appened?' I made light of it but he said, 'Oh, man, them Conehead bastuds are too much.'

'I could certainly live without 'em,' I said.

He screwed up his eyes and began considering me, moving his hand back and forth in front of my face. 'Hmmmmm, might be able to do somethin this side, Dude.' He slapped his cheek and, lighting a joint, ducked under the roof beams towards me indicating his photographs. 'Whad uh you think?' Dropping his voice very low, as though involving me in a special moment, he whispered huskily, 'They're fucking beautiful, aren't they, dude?'

I didn't really know what to say. They were cheap stylised fantasies, Roxy Music album sleeves taken on a frame or two into porn. His models, not that they were models, were local girls he'd met in clubs and pubs. He didn't pay them but like he said, 'It won't cost you owt, just gim a ring.' I wondered where the cool people were that he'd suggested would be stopping by.

'Fuck,' he said suddenly. He'd cut his hand pushing aside the clothes rail to reveal more photos of girls. One photo had a pair of red knickers draped over the right-hand corner of its frame like a saggy rosette. He stopped sucking the vestigial web of skin between forefinger and thumb and began talking me through them, shaking his hand in the air now as though he'd burnt it.

'This girl's like – whu hoooo! Red-hot, man.' I looked at the girl. She was sitting on a toilet. 'We've done some great things with her,' he said. He seemed to imply a whole team was behind him. The girl was naked except for white roller skates and round her neck pom-poms – tied, untied, hanging forward, held saucily over her tits.

'They're just studies really,' he said, pushing the clothes rail back. 'I'm more into these.' He pointed up to another set of photos hung higher up. 'These are like ma most recent.'

This time the girl was cinched into a Morticia Addams-style dress, balancing on a railway line and turned three-quarters to look at the camera, slowly unzipping. 'That's Hazel, isn't it?'

'Yeah,' he said, surprised that I seemed to know her, 'yuv made her aquaintance-ship, dude?'

'Yeah – well, no – not really. She goes out with Ziggy, doesn't she?'

He considered this the same way he'd considered my face. 'Uhmmmmmm, I don't know if you'd actually call it going out, dude. You know Ziggy, do you?'

'Yeah, well, no, not really, I've met him a few times.'

Baz smoked through cupped hands like an owl impersonator. His expression softened and he rocked back on his heels and closed his eyes. Smoke poured out of him.

Just at that moment the biker from the Traveller's, Fizzy Paul, turned up. He looked as though he was in a bit of trouble.

COOL PEOPLE STOPPING BY

Baz scowled. 'Ah, fucking bezny,' he muttered under his breath. 'Scuse a sec.' His expression hardened into a worried frown. There was a brief pow-wow in the doorway. I gathered he didn't have what Baz wanted but gave him a brown paper bag instead. Baz looked in it, then up with a silent What's this then? Paul shrugged and sniffed and came all the way into the room. Apropos of nothing he began talking about *Apocalypse Now* and tried to explain this bit where the helicopters rise above this ridge in the sunset – he kept glancing about him as though he half expected one of them to loom up suddenly outside the Tudor attic windows. He was in a real lather. He could hardly get the words out and his hands shook as he lit a Sir Nige. Baz came back into the room and sat down saying, 'I know which bit you mean, dude, you mean the bit where the helicopters are playing Wagner and . . . hang on a tick, av got the record somewhere,' and went to flick through his stack of LPs. Paul had all this speed on him, which he started doing without offering us any, saying, 'Nah, nah . . . you don't want any u this . . . it's . . . rubbish.' He sniffed and attempted an American accent, 'It's like nay parm int morning.' Then the doorbell rang and he got really paranoid and went and hid in the wardrobe, getting me to shut him in, and muttering, 'I'm not here, right.' Once before he'd got in and twice after I'd shut the door he shouted, 'Cunt bastard greenfly.' I asked a few people about this later but nobody knew what it meant, they all told me he was mad anyway and that he'd been in Brayburn san for a bit.

It turned out to be Ziggy at the door, on his way home from town. On seeing me he put out his hand and as we shook he said, 'I've thought about you a couple of times.'

He'd managed to get some rare book on Bowie. Taking off his fedora he sat straight down on the sofa and started reading it, read this particular bit out loud that said Bowie's left pupil was unusually dilated from where he'd been punched in the eye at school. He paused then read it again, this time more to himself than for our benefit. Baz went to the toilet and when he came back into the room the draught from the toilet door set some wind chimes gently jangling. Ziggy was still stuck on this sentence about how Bowie had got hit in the eye, only now he was mouthing the words to himself, sort of turning them over in his head, and I noticed him tapping at the cheekbone under his own left eye. Then, retracting his forefinger into his fist he began placing slow-motion punches there, sort of braving and steeling himself against their increasing weight and speed. After a bit of this, though, he stopped and looked down at his fist with apparent disappointment, then he turned to me and Baz and said, 'Could either of you guys punch me in the eye, d'you think?' Neither of us really felt like it. But just then Fizzy Paul sort of fell out of the wardrobe – I'd almost forgotten about him. He was totally wired on all the speed he'd done and really into punching Ziggy, though he made a great effort to conceal his excitement, suggesting instead he was merely being obliging. 'Sos like,' he said, 'but ah couldn't help overhearin you and . . . well.' He flexed his muscles and prodded his bicep. 'Am definitely yer man, like.'

Ziggy pointed to his eye and egged him on. 'C'MON, MAN, LAY THE REAL THING ON ME,' and so saying he jumped up and hit his head on one of the low Tudor beams. 'Ohouw, man.' He staggered back unsteadily, holding his head, 'Whoaa, moon age daydream.' Before he could regain his balance, Paul waded in and smacked him one, only he missed his eye and hit his nose which started bleeding really badly. Ziggy went down clutching his face. He had to go and lie on Baz's bed and turned all of what was left of a pink bog roll dark red. Baz went and got some ice. Paul came and stood at the foot of the bed looking really pleased, though he kept saying, 'Sos, pal, sos.' In all the rumpus, the wind chimes had begun to jangle again above the last track on *Apocalypse Now*. 'The End . . .'

PEAS

A few days later I saw Ziggy on the bus. He looked pretty terrible and was on his way to County Hospital. I was on the way there myself to have my stitches out from the Conehead incident. It seemed Ziggy had still been going round getting people to hit him in the eye but not many punches had been on target. Nothing had happened to the size of his pupil but he had been getting a lot of headaches and experiencing blurred vision.

I was seen to quite quickly and had to wait for ages in reception for Ziggy. It was kind of depressing and I was about to go when Ziggy came out wearing a perforated eyepatch in a prosthetic flesh colour. The medicos told him that if he wore it a few hours a day it should help him focus.

Outside the County grounds he said, 'I thought about you once or twice . . . I wanted to ask you something.' He started feeling in all his pockets. I thought for a moment he was going to ask me if he could borrow another fiver, but then he produced a crumpled piece of paper and was attempting to fold it out against the wind and the rain, smoothing it down against his thigh. It was a paper bag that he'd scribbled on. Looking up through the drizzle, he said, 'Alex told me you were a good artist.'

I made a modest octave with my right hand. He carried on smoothing out the drawing on his thigh until the rain began to smear the ink. He looked up and winced.

'J'u fancy a drink?' he asked

'Got no money.'

'That's OK. We won't need any – c'mon, t'aint necessary.'

'Where we going?'

'Don't be suspicious,' he said, 'it's not far.'

We trudged along in silence till we entered the red-light district – such as it was – one narrow street that ran down to the river. In the relative shelter of the tall warehouses he handed me the paper bag refolded. 'It's just a rough sketch,' he said. 'I want you to think beyond this.'

For a moment I couldn't work out where and how I'd entered his scheme of things to the extent that I could be called upon to think beyond this, or think beyond anything for that matter. But a glance at him showed me that I surely had. 'What is it?' I asked.

'It's how I want the poster to look.' It was also symptomatic of him that he assumed I knew what poster it was he was talking about, but then again, I did.

'It needs some looking at. Alex said you could do it.' He bestowed a hopeful glance on me.

I folded it into my pocket. 'Yeah, OK, I'll take a look at it.'

Only one prostitute was braving the weather and she was huddled so far under a large umbrella you could hardly see her. The river was rising and rushing along, the colour of cold coffee. We came to a line of barges and stopped at one converted into a type of nightspot. 'This is where I'll be playing,' he said. A closed sign was hanging from a rope across the gangplank. Ziggy strode over it shouting 'Anyone abouuurd?'

Somewhere down below someone stopped playing the saxophone and answered, 'Down here.' A metal spiral staircase went down into the hold which was sparsely furnished with round wooden tables and stools and, at the far end in the prow, there was a rudimentary stage area. The saxophonist we'd heard was standing up to greet us. His gleaming sax lent his smile a certain pizzazz.

'Hey, Ziggy.' He was an old beatnik guy with a beard and Lennon specs. While they shook hands, he touched his finger tentatively just below his own eye. Ziggy waved the question aside and, turning to me, said, 'This is Joby Schmidt, it's his place. Joby, this is Kid Glover, an artist.'

'Not really,' I began, but I could see that Ziggy was pleased with the way this sounded – 'an artist.'

Going behind the bar, Joby said, 'Sounds more like a boxer.' He brought up some beer bottles and started opening them. 'Vell, j'u vanna beer, Kid?'

'Great.'

'Ziggy?'

'Just a water please.'

'Vasser,' he seemed to mumble disapprovingly. There was some trace of accent I couldn't place – possibly German. 'Hee-ar you go,' said Joby. He peered at the stitch-marks left under my eye. 'Hmm – you look a bit like a boxer too.' He glanced at Ziggy then at me. 'Ha, you guys only got von good pair of eyes between you, ya.' He found it funny as hell and while he laughed Ziggy and I exchanged glances. Just an imperceptible glint, a moment, that was all, a silent You and me, man, against the world, or at least that's what I fancied.

'Joby's teaching me to play,' said Ziggy at length.

Joby stopped laughing abruptly. 'Huh, nothing to teach, he's a goddamn natural.' He unhooked his sax and offered it to Zig in the same aggressive way he'd offered me the beer. 'Here, man, go on – play.'

Ziggy declined at first, but then acquiesced. He tried to get the strap over his head but found it wouldn't go past the brim of his hat. In attempting to get it back off he somehow managed to get it all caught up. While he untangled himself I looked out of a porthole at the river rushing by. A family of swans was sailing past, backwards. I was still looking at the river as Ziggy began to play, *sotto*, and I didn't actually realise for a few seconds that he had in fact begun.

Without being corny and attaching too much importance to that eye contact of earlier, it was, you might say, if you were that type of romantic guy, like he was playing to the tempo of the current and the beautiful swans that were sailing by so white and unperturbed. I wasn't even expecting him to be any good but he was, he was really good. It was all Bowie of course – a kind of medley of stuff flowing in and out of each other, all very accomplished. Joby perched on a table and began rolling a joint. With his tongue to the paper he looked at me over his glasses as if to say, Well whadid ah tell you. I nodded. Joby's sense of style depressed me. It was crass irony: Hawaiian shirt in winter, odd socks (one luminous green, one pink and decorated with crotchets and quavers). One thing though, he didn't muck about rolling a spliff. He had the dexterity of years of practice. He offered it to me and I took a long drag and turned away to watch the river again.

I recognised a melody now, 'Young Americans'. I knew some of the words but mostly mouthed what seemed to fit. *Sit on your hands on the buses of divers, blushing at all the apple stealers.* (Ziggy would later correct me on this, 'Not apple stealers, man, Afro sheeners.') I took another drag of the spliff and turned to pass it back to Joby. To my surprise he was reaching up to kiss a hippie goth woman who'd just appeared in a wet fur coat. She'd come in on tiptoe, I guess so's not to disturb Ziggy's playing. She had two small boys in school uniform with her, Joby's I assumed. He ruffled their hair and then, like they knew the drill, they drifted aft. Their mother smiled over at me and turned to take a blowback from Joby, shutting her eyes and swaying to the music. Ziggy had closed his eyes too, and when he finished playing he was surprised to see the new arrivals. We filled the hull with a smattering of applause, all except the kids who were quietly peeling apart beer mats while waiting for their tea.

Joby's woman, Amanda, asked us to stay and divvied up some fish and chips she'd gotten on the way back from picking up the kids, saying: 'No no, it's fine. Don't be silly, look! Here, I don't want all these.' As she ladled out mushy peas, Ziggy held his hand over the steaming plate and, in that rather hesitant and apologetic style of speech characteristic of Mr Newton, said, 'Uhmmm, thas sufficient peas for me, Amanda.' He looked round the table approvingly. 'A man should spend time with his family.' At which Joby burst out laughing and clapped him heartily on the shoulder.

'Ah, you vill be ze death . . . ze death.'

LIFE WILL BE THE CRIME OF THE FUTURE
(P.S. SORRY FOR BREATHING)

Later, I hooked up with Purdcake and we smoked a joint and took a short cut home through the old brick quarry by the railway sidings. We were both completely stoned and for a laugh we thought we'd climb on the roof of the old goods depot. Drizzle had left the lead slates slippy as hell and they were impossible to walk across, we had to kind of crawl and even then I lost my footing and began a heart-stopping tumble towards the guttering. At one point I had to prostrate myself against the tiles and claw myself to a halt like a cat. My fingernails filled with wet mossy gunge and began to bleed a bit. I broke out into hysterical laughter, the sort of laughter brought on by fear, and Purdey, who wasn't enjoying himself one bit, shushed me hissing, 'You wanna get us caught or what? They've got night fugin watchmen here.'

I imagined the security guards playing poker dice some twenty or so feet below us. I think Purdey was half expecting them to come running out with dogs and flashlights. His progress on all fours was slow and then, when he tried standing, he looked shaky, like an apprentice surfer. 'Jus shutin fuk it, will you, I mean jus *shut it.*' His voice sounded vexed and was broken by a cowardly tremor. 'I hate heights,' he hissed, softly now.

His remark seemed to affect my own balance and I began to think something terrible was about to happen. A signal arm dropped close by our heads and the overhead wires hummed with electricity. Then there was a loud creak, like ice cracking on a pond. I spun round and caught a glimpse of the cold fear that had spread over Purdey's face as he looked down. There was the terrible sound of glass fracturing and giving way and in the confusion I lost my balance momentarily and slipped. All this happened in just a fraction of a second. When I regained my feet, Purdcake was being eaten by an ancient skylight that had been camouflaged to the same grimy viridian as the whole roof, and now he had disappeared up to his chest in its great glass jaws. It had held him just long enough for that awful look of horror to register on his face. Then he was crashing through, almost a splash, shards of glass glittering around him. A flash memory of a midnight stroll on Scarborough sands, an unsuspecting Brother Ray falling into a rock pool. The long train roared by and yellow light from the carriage windows flickered across the roof illuminating Purdey's cadaverous complexion.

'HAANG ON!' I shouted above the express. Scrabbling over, I grabbed at him, got hold of his leather jacket. My hands were sweaty and his jacket began slipping from my grasp. He strained as though trying to give birth to the next few seconds of his life. I clawed, leather joining the blood and moss under my fingernails. Somehow I managed to haul him out, but not before a stubborn shard of glass sliced open his trousers like a crisp packet. He let out a horrible wail as we fell back in each other's arms. Quickly he disentangled himself and began clutching his inside leg where blood was already pumping out. It spread in dark-crimson blotches across the cream silk of his knickerbockers. He started to bray at that point, like a child's impression of a Japanese machine gunner. 'Aga aga fuck! Aga aga fuck!' Over and over. 'Aga aga fuck!'

'Shur up,' I snapped. 'Shur up, willya.' Now I was getting paranoid about the guards below. Any second now, I thought, there'll be alarm bells ringing and guard dogs going grrrrwh and all that type of thing. I couldn't understand why there weren't already. Crucial poker throw perhaps, causing guards to ignore shower of glass and dangling baroque-a-billy feet. I heard nothing though, it was all quiet, only the night was listening and Purd's moans felt far off, in a different dimension. All I could think about was how unnaturally green the moss growing round the skylight looked. But that might have been the pot.

Purd had limped up to a large chimney stack and with his back to its solid brickwork was struggling out of his knickerbockers. Gingerly, baring his teeth, he revealed a nasty-looking cut running down his inner thigh. 'Fuckin look a' this,' he screeched, becoming really hysterical. 'Ohmygod, ohmygod, look where it is! Look where it fuckin well is! Jesus, could a' had ma bollies off.'

'Hold on, hold on, yur-ahrite, yur-ahrite.' I ripped off my T-shirt and started swabbing the blood as best I could. There was a lot of it but it wasn't as bad as it looked. All the time I was swabbing he just lay there as if he was dying in some army field hospital with a musket ball through his leg and groaning, 'Oh, God, could a' had ma bollies off.'

'You're lucky,' I said. 'It's just a surface wound. Look.'

'I can't,' he said. He was sort of shielding his eyes with the back of his hand like he was in a swoon or something.

'Fuckin LOOK!' I told him. He lit a Sir Nige and dramatically throwing away the match sat up. 'See?' I said.

He was surprised, then disappointed. 'I nearly fuckin die and that's all I've gotta show.' He cast bitterly towards the skylight.

We smoked till the bleeding stopped and every now and then he dabbed at the cut then tasted his blood – like icing. 'Oh, God!' He sucked his finger. 'Why do these things always happen to me – tell me?' Calmer now, he was back to doing his Anthony Blanche impression, abandoned in the fall. 'Can you imagine, dihr boy, a thing like this ha-ha-happening to friend Z-Z-Ziggy?' I could actually but I said not. 'No, that's right. But tell me though, don't you think dear Ziggy is just a touch toooo cool. I mean, I spent all day yesterday with him over this design and he didn't say two original words, or if he did I can't remember what they were and when dear Ziggy does say something . . .' He began on some speech he had down cold from the latest episode of *Brideshead*, Anthony talking to Charles Ryder over some discreet candlelit dinner, 'When I do hear him talk,' continued Purdcake, raising his voice above a passing goods train that seemed to go on for ever, 'I'm reminded of that in some ways NU-NU-NAUSEATING PICTURE OF BU-BU-BUBBLES!'

I wasn't into bitching about Ziggy so I looked away. I was struck again by how green the moss was and how many moths there were flying about, then I realised why it looked so luminous. There was an electric light coming from the shattered skylight. I crawled back over to it and looked in. A dusty fluorescent tube was hanging from chains in the ceiling – it didn't light much. I pitched in a penny, hearing it ricochet off metal-sounding objects, clang ping ting. I couldn't see what was causing it but after a bit my eyes made out the floor. It suddenly looked a long drop. There was obviously no nightwatchman on guard, the warehouse was disused and in a bad state.

The drainpipe we'd climbed up had been rusted to a reddish rub like flake tobacco and there was no way I was going to trust it or any of the guttering to support me going down. I became concerned. I gave the fluorescent light a shove making it buck about on its chains, illuminating snatches of the depot to left and right, and I spied the metal stacking shelves just beneath us which my penny must have ricocheted off. The shelving suddenly suggested itself as rungs on a ladder. Purdcake was still bitching bout Ziggy. I called over to him. 'Hey, av you thought how we're gonna get down from ere?'

'What?' he said, though he'd heard perfectly well, because his face was suddenly aghast.

'Here, come here a sec, willya.' As he approached in his underpants, sliding down gingerly on his arse, his trauma began to return. 'Oh, ohmygod, ohhhh God, please God, I'll be good I'll be goo . . .'

'Look!' I shoved the fluorescent again. 'See there!' I pointed in. 'Some shelves we can climb down.'

'Oh no. No no no no no. No fuckin way.'

'That's it, Alex, there is no other way. Look, it's just like climbing down a ladder. You lower yerself down and then just step on . . .'

'Oh, God! You first,' he said, gazing at his gash.

TEN THOUSAND WATTS OF POWER

'Su breeze, Alex,' I shouted up to him from below. His face peering down at me looked extra sick lit by the fluorescent. He made a huge song and dance, even crossing himself I think, or maybe he was swatting at moths. Something suddenly smothered me, smelling meaty – it was his bloody knicker-bockers that he'd thrown down.

As I waited for him, I looked around in the dark and made out a load of cardboard boxes sitting on the shelves. Obviously the depot *was* still being used. Directly in front of me just a few feet above, I could just make out the printed words:

> Phillips 100 x 40 watt – Blue
> Phillips 100 x 40 watt – Orange

So when Purdcake finally got down and said, 'What you doing, where's my trousers?' I said, 'Hey, Purdcake, help me with these boxes, willya. I've had an idea. Let's nick some of these light bulbs!'

FAMOUS FOR FIFTEEN COUNTS OF BURGLARY

The *Echo* devoted a whole paragraph to the break-in at the Malburn Lane Goods Depot. I was shocked at how wilful they assumed the damage was, but pretty relieved to learn the police were treating it as the work of the notorious cat-man, a local operator whose break-ins were characterised by their daring aerobatics. In perpetually evading capture he was a latter-day Raffles, a kind of Milk Tray man meets Hannibal Hayes.

I was just mulling this over when Mum said, 'George, are you *ever* gonna get a light put in that damn coal shed?' I nearly choked on my tea.

Along with a lock on the outside toilet door, a dynamo on Bernice's bicycle, and a hundred other odd jobs Mum nagged Dad over, there was nothing unusual in her bringing this up except that, unbeknownst to her, less than fifteen or so feet away from where we were having tea, there were two hundred-odd lights concealed among the rafters of the same, oft-referred to damn coal shed.

'I'll av a drop more tea if there is any, Dad,' I said, holding out my cup. It rattled in its saucer like laughter.

'I'll do it tonight, Audrey.'

I relaxed back into my chair. He said this every night.

However, in the event, I couldn't have been more mistaken. The two crates of stolen bulbs were discovered that very same night by off-duty police officer Bill Pullman.

PICKERING TO WHITBY LIGHT GAUGE RAILWAY ENTHUSIASTS

About Pullman. He was a fat bloke Dad had met at a steam gala. They were both members of the Pickering to Whitby Light Gauge Railway Trust. My dad was an occasional volunteer signal-man, Pullman was a driver. To my surprise, him and another bloke, Ron Henderson from the bowls, turned up after tea to help my dad lay some concrete in the back garden. When I came down into the hall, Ron was struggling in through the front door with some kind of cine film projector, swearing at its weight.

'Bloody hell, George, this bastard weighs a ton, wer canna stick it?'

Dad, who never swears and doesn't normally tolerate swearing in the house, held open the sitting-room door. 'Ho ho, yes. Righto, Ron – just put it down there I think.'

The idea was that before laying the concrete they were going to show some super-eight films which Ron, a keen amateur cameraman, had shot on the Pickering to Whitby line.

Ron and Pullman both smelt of beer and I guessed they'd had a few before towing up, knowing as they probably did that Dad was more or less teetotal and, apart from some home-brew in the bathroom that's probably still fermenting in there, never had anything in to offer guests.

Mum made some tea and brought it in on a tray with a saucer of Peek Frean iced gems which she offered round. Dad went over to the curtains saying, 'Ah you right there, Ron?'

Testing a spool this way and that, Ron nodded, tongue out in concentration, and as Dad drew the curtains, sending the room into darkness, Bernice opened the door and stood framed in the light from the passage.

'What's going on?' she said. 'I've come to watch *Top of the Pops*.'

As Ron set the projector going, Dad crossed the dusty conical beam of light and for a second his scowl was caught in a series of scratched and flickering numbers counting down his overalls:

8

7

6

5

'Close the door,' he said irritably. 'Just come in and sit down a moment, willya, and take an interest for a change – this won't take long.'

Bernice was due at work later and was half dressed in her wench's outfit with a dressing gown of lightweight fabric over the top. She came in and perched on the arm of the sofa, crossed her legs and tried twice to pull the material of the gown over the smooth denier of her tights, but the material was too silky and each time she let go of it, it just slid away again. Ron watched her do this, looking her up and down approvingly and licking his lips. He was one of those blokes who couldn't keep his leg still for a moment. Nodding up at Bernice, he said, 'As she ever bin on the Pickering run, George?' As he said this he began to lightly drum his fingers on his jumping limb.

'Uhmm, no, Ron,' said my dad, clearing his throat. 'She hasn't.'

'Don't know what yu're missing.' He turned back to look up at her. His leg, working at an invisible sewing machine, was running up some fantasy about Bernice and him on the Pickering to Whitby light gauge railway line. As Ron winked up at her I thought how perhaps his amateur camera work wasn't confined wholly to railway footage. His beered-up leer came back level with her breasts, oscillating from upper thigh to cleavage and back. Bernice, being perched on the arm, looked down at him with amused contempt and somewhat encouraged him by making a big thing of crossing her legs. Dad coughed nervously and Pullman came to the rescue shouting, 'Here we go,' as the amateurish credits ended and a sudden speeded-up rush of passengers' and fellow enthusiasts' heads appeared, waving into the lens of the old Bolex.

'Huuuh.' A hoot of derision from Ron, trying now to impress Bernice by humiliating Pullman. 'J'u recognise that fat whelk?' There was a sudden cut to the train nameplate, LINDA, lost in smoke. 'Uhoow, he's gone.' Ron's lens pulled back to show the whole of little Linda puffing out clouds of the stuff. He pointed at a train driver's uniform that was occasionally visible, hunkered over the cab.

'Huoooow, it's that fat bastard agen.'

'Hu ho,' went my dad.

Running down the platform like a Beirut reporter, Ron jumped on to the observation car at the very last moment, and off chuffed Linda, out on to the Yorkshire moors. Ron was now filming from out of the back of the guard's van and whenever Linda appeared round a sharp curve in the track he'd say, 'There she is, by heck – little beauty, hey,' and so saying he'd shoot a furtive glance at Bernice who'd lost interest now and was looking down at her nails, pushing her cuticles back in an offhand manner.

I excused myself and went upstairs. I tried on a few threads, spun a few sounds and threw some shapes in front of the mirror. When I came downstairs again the film show was over and they were preparing to lay the concrete.

I was halfway out of the door and away up the street when I was vaguely aware of being troubled by something. In the kitchen, from the corner of my eye, I'd seen Dad hand Pullman a flash lamp, and I deciphered now just exactly what it was – his mouth all crammed with iced gems – he'd said: 'You'll find everything yure looking for in the coal shed, Bill.'

END OF ROOM SERVICE

It was past midnight when I got home, drunk and swaying under the wisteria and dreaming of bed. Through the front door I could see the light from the sitting room seeping into the hall, silhouetting all its familiar clutter. I fumbled for my key in the latch, imagining how this drunken scratching at the lock would be making the old man bristle with contempt.

Quietly shutting the door behind me and tiptoeing across the hall, he made me jump by calling to me from the sitting room. I stopped and trod back a step, looking in. He'd returned his attention to the slapstick of collapsing the projection screen and

I assumed his seething mood was down to the struggle he always had with that particular piece of equipment.

"Lo zer, Dad.' I saw his frame stiffen as he heard the slur in my voice. 'Whoz up then?' I took a step inside the room. He answered with his back to me, bent over and fiddling with great vexation at a metal catch.

I didn't get what he said exactly because he seemed to be grinding his teeth. Something like, 'Oh, yu've done it now.' In his intonation I could hear the two hours of brooding silence behind those words. Now, when he stood up in front of me, abandoning the ruse of collapsing the projector, I felt my stomach shrink to the size of a troubled pebble.

'What is it?' I heard myself saying.

'WHAT IS IT?' He lashed out, cuffing me.

'Ahh.'

'WHAT IS IT?' He cuffed me again and I staggered back into the hall where I felt myself jar against the understairs cupboard. 'I'LL GIV YOU WHAT IS IT.'

'Ahhg! What you doin? What you . . . Stop, willya.'

He pointed into the kitchen at two familiar boxes now slightly covered in coal dust. 'WHAT ARE THEY?'

'Uhh.' I blinked at the boxes thinking, Oh fuck, but my wits were dulled by drink. 'Just some light bulbs, Dad.'

'You think they're just light bulbs!'

'Truly!'

'TRULY! He lashed out again. 'TRULY! AHLL GIVE YOU TRULY!'

I slid down the wall under the blows, crossing my arms above my head to protect myself. Felt a bang spread across my face as a serge-blue knee, smelling of oil, cracked and flattened the gristle of my nose. I let out a nasal 'Arghhhhh'. The world darkened before my eyes, pain followed the shock, spreading out to meet Mum hurrying downstairs in a rapid gown and slippers.

'GEORGE, GEORGE!'

And from somewhere behind her Stacey came crying, 'Mameeee.'

BACK OUT THROUGH THE UNDERGROUND CAVES

The next morning I waited until I heard Dad disentangle his bike from the yard before venturing downstairs. Mum was at the stove vigorously frying bacon. She was tight-lipped for a while, bar the occasional damn and blast as fat spat at her from the pan. Then, without looking up, she said, as though we'd been talking all along, 'Once a nark, awiz a nark. Pleece are never off duty, Billy, you shud know that.' She pulled the face of a nosy copper and, using the bacon slice like it was a flashlight, pretended to shine it around the inside of the coal shed. 'Routine that,' she said, returning her attention to the bacon.

It wasn't such a big heist in itself, but there were fifteen unsolved cases of burglary in the vicinity. The narks were treating this as one of them.

'What, you mean Pullman thinks I'm the cat-man?'

'Dhouuuw be daft.' She pointed the bacon slice at me. 'But listen, Billy, he's on the spot, isn he.'

I shrugged. She turned back to the stove.

'Just this once Pullman's going to turn a blind eye. Just this once, mind. You shud be thankful yu're not getting done. First thing now, tunight, wi jolly well want them light bulbs off the premises. Ju hear me?' I nodded, she sighed. 'What on *earth* possessed you?'

I poured some tea and put my cup down carefully on a coaster that had a faded design on it. As a kid I'd always thought it was a hula girl's naked back but now, for the very first time since I don't know how long, I saw that what I'd thought was a naked back was in fact the space between an elephant's legs. I was amazed by the discovery. As I stared it seemed impossible to see it as anything *but* an elephant's legs. It was maddening in a way and I felt an odd sense of loss for the girl of my mealtimes.

Mum set down a fried platter in front of me. '– And that's what am tellin you,' she said flatly.

'What?' I said, alert to her again.

'Well, what av jus said, Billy.'

'What j'u mean?'

'Well, haven't you been listnin?'

I looked up at her. 'Uhmm . . . yeah,' I mumbled, unsure. My glance fell back to the coaster.

'So that's what we think then. You could probably go stay at one of your friends for a while though, couldn't you?'

'Ah,' I said, nodding. 'OK.' I guess I'd seen it coming since the Freddie Starr show. 'Sure.'

But as I ate my breakfast, my mind was still taken up with the space between those elephant legs.

PART II

THE SELF-CATERING YEARS

The Wigwam was actually just a normal Georgian house – well, normalish. Inside, all the dividing walls that weren't load-bearing had been knocked down in some long-forgotten DIY drive and replaced with sheets and blankets which had gradually assumed the dirty air of permanence. To come in and out of any of those rooms you were thereafter obliged to part the blankets and duck slightly, the way you see Red Indians doing in films.

Ovo and Si were the core residents, but there were others like Deeb who'd come and go, stay a week, a fortnight, a month, two. It was an end-of-terrace house except there was no longer a terrace – all the other houses leading up to it had been demolished by developers several years earlier. The Wigwam remained because former occupant Gilbert Rathbone had refused to be turfed out. In huge white letters on the gable end he'd painted:

Gilbert Rathbone
HERE NOW
No. (you couldn't read this word) THREE WEEKS

This halted the developers and for a time the wasteland where the old terrace used to slope away became a gypsy site. Those houses still standing on the other side facing the Wigwam were slowly getting vandalised. Then one day – I'd like to think it was a sunny day – Tangster Rise, all that remained of it, was given conservation status.

Long before this, when I was eight or nine, the Rise had been one of the places Brother Ray and I used to go when he worked for pest patrol. They paid twenty-five pence per rat's tail and provided a plastic bag to put them in. Brother Ray shot them, picking them up was my job. It was seasonal really – when the becks flooded, the rats would come out of their holes; grisly work for an impressionable boy like me and it would sometimes put me off my tea. But it was good pocket money and the terrace being overrun with them it was always easy to fill a bag.

A few years after the rat-catching, I started a paper round that took in the Rise. It was OK in summer but in winter the dark nights and the drizzle and my fear of things that moved in the shadows would set me on edge. I had this chronic three-speed bike that I remember was permanently stuck in third. Another thing – it had something wedged under the mudguard that trailed in the spokes, making it tick intimately through the darkness. Generally, I liked that, but when the ticking became louder and slower, it meant that I was approaching the crest of the hill, derelict and demolished but for that one house – Gilbert Rathbone's.

Although later I came to profit from his lonely stand, in my paper round days the solitary sulphurous glow emanating from behind the blanket at his window did nothing to heighten my spirits. Twisting the rubber grip on the handle bar, I'd make motorbike noises with my lips and speed away as fast as I could peddle. At the bottom of the hill I'd turn in my saddle and catch a look back at his house, standing all alone in the twilight. I could just make out those words on the gable end: GILBERT RATHBONE, HERE NOW, No. (?) THREE WEEKS. I always puzzled over that missing word. It was obliterated by a blackened residue from where a kid's fire had burnt too close to the wall.

Apparently the developers had tried everything to get him out – money, bribes, promises, threats, more money, the heavy brigade – but he'd seen them all off. His neighbours, the Jacksons, had taken the money and gone to Spain. Everyone else had moved into the new high-rises over the way until finally he'd been the only one left. He just didn't want to move. While waiting for his change in shops he'd say, Maybe Spain would have been all right when he was younger, but now he wanted to stay put. He said it was right and proper that an old man should be allowed to stay in his own house where his memories were, that he'd face what was coming when it came. And he did. When he bared his arse to the bulldozers, top brass were summoned. He threw bits of the Jacksons' house at them and at the *Echo* photographer who'd somehow got hold of the story. Demolition work had to cease, leaving the Jacksons' taste in wallpaper cruelly exposed. Here and there a shelf, a calendar, a poster of a forgotten pop star – incredibly, these things remained. The men with hard hats stood around and watched. 'Old bastud,' they muttered hoarsely in the chilly November air, staring off into space. He of all people, though, the old bastud.

When he'd been young, when he could have gone to Spain, he'd put folk in mind of Marlon Brando. He'd been the professional misser of the last tram, a friend to milkmen. They'd have done anything to count him among them. Now they told their children not to play near him. Gangs of older kids occasionally shied stones at his windows, mostly all broken anyway. Of course he'd let things go during the stand and it had got harder. No one to turn to, not much in the way of money coming in, no meals on wheels or home help or anything like that. Lack of sympathy failed to disturb him, though; he remained defiantly the old bastard on the Rise.

Was it normal, though, not to see an old man for three weeks in a row? To hear his dog howl the place down night after night? I don't know. The new residents – Barratts dream house types in pastel trousers – had been too busy banging and sanding to notice. One of them had complained of an unbearable smell;

seemed to be coming from the end house on the other side of the road. A small crowd gathered at the gate as the ambulance arrived. Wearing oven gloves and masks, they brought him out, not in the wooden box he vowed they'd need, but a zip-up bag covered with a blanket, his body making the shape of a war landscape for kids' toy soldiers. 'Poor bastud,' people now said. Strange how hostility turns to regret when it's too late.

There were no beatnik impressions written on toilet paper – only this arse end obituary that the *Echo*'ll never print: 'Just how do you identify a stinking old corpse as the tattooed young man who'd put folk in mind of Marlon Brando, a friend to milkmen, and say, "Yes, that's him."'

TELL US ABOUT WHERE YOU LIVE (CONTINUE ON AN EXTRA SHEET OF PAPER IF NECESSARY)

On a damp and soundless afternoon, under an off-white sky, I knocked at the Wigwam to ask if I could stay a while. The house had been sold before it could even come on the market, to a second-generation Italian immigrant, Gianlucca Ovodicci, who let his son Daniel and Daniel's friends live there rent-free in exchange for doing work on the place. A sleepy Ovo answered, yawning in his vest and pants. 'Huh huuuooooohuw,' he stretched. 'Yu've woke me up, yu bastard.' He trailed back inside, disappearing behind a sheet. I followed him in and found him in the kitchen lighting the stove for tea. While he filled the kettle I told him my situation. 'Hmmm,' he said, blowing on the gas ring to try and get the flames to catch all the way round. His fanning the blue tongues with his hand seemed to take for ever. I had the feeling he was doing this to buy time while he came up with a good reason why I couldn't stay.

'A watched kettle never boils,' I prompted nervously. Eventually he settled the kettle on the hob where it began to rock. Scraping back a chair, he sat down and, looking at me over yesterday's breakfast pots said, 'Yeah, OK.'

Yeah, OK. Relief spread through me like a river in flood. I'd been scarcely aware of sitting down but now I relaxed back into the rickety wooden chair like it was really comfy and searched my pockets for a Sir Nige.

'You can av attic room,' said Ovo. 'Needs clearing out, mind, but you can probably share Si's room till you sort it. Thuz a spare bed in there, or kip ont sofa down ere. S'up tu you.'

'Great,' I said, 'that's great, really great, man.'

He broke in, uncomfortable with my gratitude. 'Yeah, you know about deal wit rent, durt yuh.'

'Uhmm?'

'Basically, you can either pay rent, *or* you can do work ont spot.' He gestured around him, pulling a face as though he were squinting after some train he'd just missed. 'Thus lots tu do like and ad sooner you did that really. Work's come to a bit uv uh standstill lately but ah wanna get it goin agen. If yu cud mek a start up there,' he pointed to the ceiling, 'it ud be good cos it's still rammed full of the old grogger's gear and I wanna ged it out – it stinks. Maybe you can bag it up and tek it to Oxfam or summat – one uv them spots you get yur suits.'

'Oh sure,' I said. 'Listen, thanks again and sos for waking you.'

He took a dog-end spliff from an ashtray and bending down made several attempts to light it off the stove. ''S . . . OK, s'just . . . I'm – on – nights – this week – fuuuuch.' He withdrew his face sharply from the stove and, inhaling deeply, ran saliva over a singed eyebrow with a crooked little finger. 'Normally,' he coughed out in a huge cloud of smoke, 'norma . . .' he broke off to bring up phlegm, cradled the oyster on his tongue over to the sink where he spat it out, flushing it away with a blast of cold.

'Yeah, normally,' he raised his voice over the noise of the water hammer in the pipes, 'if SOME FUCKER WEKS you up and yur on shifts, they get punished by aving to do more housework.' Looking around it was hard to believe that Ovo was quite so house-proud. 'Ah wanna get it really nice,' he said when the hammering finally subsided. 'We're livin like fuckin students.' He shook his head and looked down. ''S that all yur stuff?' He pointed to my grip.

'No, I just dint – you know – in case . . . I've got some more to pick up from home, cupla boxes.'

He glanced at his watch. 'I'll gi you a lift ovur if you want, av got time before ma shift.'

MAN IN WOOL

Next day, when everyone had gone to work and I was alone there, I brewed up tea, piping hot, and with biscuits on a tray climbed the steep stairs to the attic to start the tidying. Halfway up those creaky old stairs, taking care with my tray, I heard a noise ahead of me. There for a moment was a horrible apparition of Gilbert Rathbone, hanging from the spindle, squirming in front of me, HERE NOW. Kicking at the air, I missed my footing. Everything slid on the tray – a listing liner feeling – and hot tea slopped out, scalding my hand. 'Jeesus fuck!' I waved my hand in the air. 'Jeesus.' A little bit freaked, I edged around the empty space where I thought I'd seen the writhing figure and, at the top of the stair, I paused and looked out of the dirty landing window. I was up in the eaves where his legend began. Outside a packed ledge of sleek but scrawny violet and viridian crops took fright at something below, a cat maybe. I stepped back as a frantic grey wing beat several times against the dirty pane before flying off. I spilt more tea. 'Bastud pigeons.'

The attic door, painted an odd shade of green, was closed. Supporting the tray on my knee I pushed it open, blinking several times to adjust my eyes to the crepuscular gloom inside. The room was piled high, full of stuff that looked as if it was waiting to be sorted for a jumble sale. There was an over-powering smell of damp, like from a quayside. I felt up and down the flaking wallpaper for the light switch, but when I flicked it the bulb blew, making me jump and spill the last of the tea. I was on edge.

A single skylight covered with a film of dirt lit the room, but it wasn't enough to work by. I realised, as I went downstairs to get a new bulb, that this would be the first time I'd have occasion to use a stolen one. That thought at least cheered me up. The previous evening, Ovo, good to his word, had taken me home in his old Viva van to pick up the rest of my stuff. Mum had looked out an old leather case for me without a handle and said there was no mad rush to bring it back. The bottom was lined with a yellowed *Evening Echo*. It smelt a little fusty, so I took it out and sprinkled some drops of Snookered aftershave in the bottom then began filling it. The fusty smell mingling with the cheap aftershave seemed somehow to strongly evoke the place I was going to.

Packing wasn't as easy as I'd imagined. I'd made three piles of stuff.

Keep   Don't know   Get rid

I found myself cradling a bunch of stuff – a snowstorm, my diary – so I put them in the Keep pile. The aftershave with a red snooker ball for a top – Get rid. A David Essex LP began in the Get rid pile but somehow, like a pea under the three cups of a street hustler, weaved its way in and out of Don't know, Keep and Get rid so many times that I found myself staring at it in something akin to a trance when Stacey came into my room in her nightie. She was rubbing her eyes and frowning. 'What choo dooin?' she asked in a puzzled voice, as though I was a strange character from her dream.

'Sorry, Stacey, did I wake you up?'

She came and sat on the bed looking blankly around her.

'Stacey?' She nodded. 'Would you like my record player?' She nodded eagerly, her chin going all the way to her collar bone. 'Would you like this record?' She shook her head. 'No? C'mon, it's a good one, I jus haven't got room for it.' She wasn't sure. 'Listen,' I said. 'Shall we? It's really good, you'll like it, I'm sure?'

The old radiogram had a very bassy sound and a deep crackle that resonated through the lyrics. 'We gonna make you – a star star ahah – a staaaaaaaaaaaaaaaaaaaar.' She mouthed along, reading the lyrics off the song sheet, swinging her legs.

I loved Stacey, her innocence and all that. I hoped she wouldn't turn out like Bernice. I hoped maybe her tits wouldn't grow so big. Sometimes it seemed the whole of a girl's future round here could be shaped according to her breast size. I picked up the newspaper that had lined the case. 'Pervert tells police: Stay cool!' I began to read, even though, like the words to this song, I practically knew it off by heart. ' "A pervert threw a bottle at a policeman last night, magistrates were told today. Daniel Ovodicci, aged 17, was caught stealing women's underwear from the washing line of a house in the Battlegarth area. On being arrested, he told police, 'OK you cops, stay cool OK.' Ovodicci was also charged with . . ." '

How that cutting came to be in the case I don't know. I suppose Mum must have kept it because it was someone she knew who'd made the news. It wasn't one for the mantelpiece though – Youth Saves Girls From Drowning type thing.

I put the paper in the Get rid pile.

THE AGONIES THAT ARE EXIST IN THE
ECSTASIES THERE COULD HAVE BEEN

When everything was packed, I went to say goodbye, giving a
little cough as I entered the lounge. It was as smoky as old Doc
Slater's surgery. Stacey had come down and was sitting on the
sofa. Mum was abstractedly ironing. They were both watching
an old black and white film, *Brief Encounter*. It was just about to
end, you could tell by the music. Mum, with her steam and her
cigarette smoke, had turned the lounge into a hazy extension of
the famous station waiting-room scene. Trevor Howard and
Celia Johnson were sitting in silence, looking into two untouched
teas. There was nothing to say. Their entwined fingers were
doing it all anyhow. At the next table a lot of tittle-tattle could be
heard – 'So I turned round to him and said '"Ooooh fancy."'

Mum, with an effort, wrenched herself away from the telly and
turned to look at me. 'Turn that down a minute, Stacey!' she said,
and when Stacey turned the volume down, *Brief Encounter* could
be heard coming muted through the adjoining wall. Stacey tried
to turn the volume down some more until she realised it was
coming from the Partridge family's telly next door. This seemed
to somehow taint the tender farewell scene. The actors' voices,
the station tannoy announcing departures, tainted my goodbye
too. Mum's face, still able to follow what was being said, brought
to mind an eavesdropper with a glass to a wall of air.

'Oh, you're off then. Have you got everything?'

'Yeah.'

'You won't forget the – you-know-whats.'

'No.'

'Mind you don't,' she said. 'You don't want to annoy yur
father any more, do you.'

I didn't answer.

'No,' she said. Then breezily, 'Right, well – you're off then.'

'Yeah.'

Just then the tannoy came through the semi wall. 'Train now approaching platform eleven is the three thirty-eight to London Vic–' The announcement was cut to canned laughter – the NF had turned over to a sitcom. Trevor Howard's lips now moved out of sync like dubbing on a cheapo porn flick. I waved in the steam and smoke, 'I'm off then.' Stacey looked round blankly. Mum murmured a detached, 'Bye then, luv.' It could have been Ma Yummy speaking.

Outside I was handing the bulbs up to Ovo when I spied my dad at the top of the Rise. He had dismounted his bike and was standing on one pedal, free-wheeling down the slope.

'Ah yu're off then, lad?' he said, applying squeaky brakes.

'Yeah.'

He bent to remove his bicycle clips and agitated them like lobster claws. 'Righto,' he said, nodding. He seemed to want to say something, some fatherly advice perhaps. With his thumb he slowly and absently rang the croaking bell on his bike then, as though the sound had woken him from a dream, he reached decisively into his back pocket for his wallet.

'Billy, ah say!'

'Yeah.' I turned to face him but he looked away. Perhaps he didn't want to look at the dark circles under my eyes.

'Look, I'm sorr –'

'Sorry.' We both began speaking at once.

Dad turned back to face me. 'Ah, least said soonest mended.'

'Yeah.'

'Well, uhmm.' He looked into his wallet. His fingers pincered out a fiver then he changed his mind and pulled out a ten. 'Here.' He thrust it into my hand.

'Thanks, Dad.' I pressed my lips into a smile.

We didn't go in for hugging but he did slap me on the back. 'You'll want to be with your friends anyway,' he said, looking at Daniel. 'When I was your age . . . couldn't wait to leave home . . .' He began to wheel his bike up the drive. 'We'll see you at

Christmas no doubt,' he called back.

Ovo jumped down. 'That the lot?'

'Yeah.' I clapped dust from my hands. 'Least we won't have to buy a bulb for a while,' I said. 'That's as long as you don't mind the colours.'

'Not as long as they're Yorkshire's popular price[1] I don't.'

From out of nowhere Stacey suddenly appeared and nearly knocked me over.

'Oooooof, Stacey!'

She clung on to my leg.

'Heeey,' I said. I wanted to stroke her hair but my hands were all sooty from the coal shed.

'Ah'll get int van,' said Ovo, making himself scarce, never comfy with emotional stuff.

'OK, I'll be wi yu in a minit.' I crouched down level with her face. 'Don't cry.'

'Not crying,' she said, crying.

'I know you're not.' I smiled. 'C'mon, it's not like I'm going to Mars.'

I led her back up the crazy paving, assuring her I'd take her to see Santa like I'd promised. No, I hadn't forgotten. Under the ivy in which a family of robins always nested, I held her face and kissed her head. When she looked up at me her cheeks were streaked with black, sooty fingermarks.

DEAD MAN IN WOOL

The blue light didn't do much to cheer up the attic, in fact it kind of made it worse. I worked quickly, bagging up the old-person smell of death (as you might say, if you were that type of morbid

---

[1] Free

guy) into bin liners. In a wall closet I found a few Sunday bests, shoes and an overcoat plus a stack of ancient porn tied up in string. One of the suits was a blue woollen Dunn & Co., pinstripe, slim fit. I tried it on. It didn't fit like a glove as I was about to say, but it looked reasonable. Gilbert Rathbone must have been about the same build as me – tall and thin, lean rather than lanky I like to think. The stuff in the closet hadn't been as affected by the damp as the stuff lying about on the floor. I sniffed it. It smelt OK. I checked myself out in the mottled mirror. It looked good – gangstery.

I kept the suit on and took a couple of large bin bags into town with me on the bus. At the MIND shop, the two old crows behind the till thanked me, diffidently at first but then regarding me with increasing suspicion when I asked them if they'd had a copy of the 'Ancient Mariner' in. They were searching their memories but not for the book, they were trying to place me. I just managed to stop myself from saying Ciao.

I was glad to get rid of the bin bags, though. On the bus people had kept glancing over as if I'd committed a murder and was getting rid of the evidence. Even after I'd ditched George's effects, his smell seemed to linger on around me, rising to my nostrils in the rain. George and I were becoming intimate: I was wearing his clothes, I'd leafed through his porn. A line I'd read on the letters page came back into my head, something to the effect of: A man in coming years will look more wistfully at the wrinkles in his penis than those upon his face. I don't know why this had stuck with me so, but it had, and as the bus pulled away I was aware that I was staring at the old man's crotch sitting opposite. I was aware of it because he'd crossed his legs and was glowering at me.

The morning's activities had left me with a morbid feeling that I couldn't shake. Perhaps it was the suit. In the pocket I'd found a pre-decimal penny and my fingernails gathered a lot of loose tobacco from an old pack of Players Weights.

I decided to blow some money I didn't have on a decent lunch at Plunkets. Plunkets was a brightly painted place with old creaking timbers. One bit of wall hadn't been decorated since the sixties because it had been flamboyantly signed one night by all the Rolling Stones including Brian Jones. The waitresses were cute, mostly university students topping up their grants.

As I entered, bringing in a gust of cold, a tall flustered blonde looked round and, with a wide sweep of her arm that showed a patch of sweat, indicated I could sit anywhere I could find. They were busy, so I took a seat up in the gallery area. A fan heater at my feet was noisily achieving nothing. I bent forward, warmed my hands in front of it, and that's how I was when a waitress's midriff appeared next to me in my peripheral vision. My eyes travelled up to her breasts, which were rising and pushing against her T-shirt as she sniffed the air around me. It was Hazel. When she recognised me she stopped sniffing and said, 'Oh, hiya, it's you! Din't recognise you.'

'Oh, hi,' I said, surprised. I straightened up and removed my bobble hat. 'So this is where you work, is it?'

She nodded, looking round and clicking a pen in her teeth. 'Yeah, for ma sins.'

She took the pen out of her mouth and flicked her hair back. I'd read in one of Bernice's magazines that if a woman fancies you she unconsciously plays with her hair, touching it into place and coyly teasing strands of it across her upper lip and stuff. Encouraged, I made some small talk during which she continually turned her head around, eventually telling me in a low voice that her boss didn't like it when she talked too long.

'Ahh, right you are,' I said, plunging into the menu. 'Righto.' As I perused it, I began wondering why it was that she was sniffing the air around me, and then I thought that it must be the old suit that had got wet in the rain and was emitting a powerful smell of moths. I'd heard that Salvador Dali had once covered himself in rotting fish essence in order to be sure of making a definite impression on a woman he fancied. She was physically sick in his presence, but later she married him. Perhaps I didn't stink bad enough.

All the main-course meals were numbered but I'd sort of lost my appetite. Randomly I ran my finger down them. 'Oh, here,' I said, tapping the menu, 'I'll have a twenty-three.' I hadn't a clue what it was but I remember Paul telling me it was Aleister Crowley's favourite number, a magic number.

'Twen – teee – threeee,' jotted down Hazel. 'Great. Anything to drink?'

'Yeah, a beer, please.'

'Cool.'

When Hazel promptly returned to tell me there were no twenty-threes left, she found me sniffing all over my suit, up and down the arm like a dog, from the armpit to the cuff – sniff, sniff, sniff. While doing nothing for the temperature of the room, the fan heater was clearly wafting the odour of Gilbert Rathbone all over the restaurant. I pretended to be listening to my watch. Shaking it, I frowned and then brought it up to my ear again. 'What's that you say?' I feigned abstraction. 'No twenty-three? Uhmm, Oh kaaaaay. I tell you what, that was the only thing I fancied really.' I lit a Sir Nige nonchalantly and started to get up. 'That was really why I came in,' I said, 'for a twenty-three.' I offered her a shrug.

(Later, when I went round to Fizzy Paul's place, he told me that the magic number was actually five, which was the sum of two plus three, representing the five points of the pentagram.)

8.20 SLEEPER TO KING'S CROSS

Deeb stood up swaying and did a couple of neck exercises. 'Uuuughoow nora . . . fancy another, uh s'pose you're skint, uh,' was the gist of what he said, but the alcohol had worsened his natural speech impediment and he talked now as though trying to pluck a hair from his tongue. I offered him money but he wouldn't take any, in fact the rest of the night he frittered away his pay packet in front of me with all the zeal of a pools winner. He was trying to prove something, I don't know what exactly. That he had more money than me? Well, that was never in doubt. When two blondes approached us for a spare ciggy I pointed to Deeb and said, 'Ask Viv Nicholson.'

He nodded, offering his Sir Niges magnanimously, as if to say, Yeah, next to you, Glover pal, I am a fucking Viv Nicholson.

'You got a light?' one of them asked. Her candyfloss hair was up in a semi-beehive. Pinkish at the roots graduating to peroxide white, like trifle. It was brittle with hairspray and held the light.

With a series of dextrous movements I produced a petrol flame. They blew out smoke in unison and looked around in a dreamy way, apparently appreciating the pub decor. Wisps of song lyrics from the juke-box rose and fell on their lips dissolving into la-la-las where they didn't know the words and of course Deeb jumped up to get them drinks. With money in his teeth his speech impediment was strangely disguised.

The blondes made a big thing of asking for Pernod and blacks with ice and lemon. 'And in a tall glass,' they called after him, their hands doing sign language up and down to show what they meant. He paused for a moment as though he thought they were calling him a tosser. Seating themselves they took an age organising their limbs in front of me as though I were a Swiss finishing school mistress.

'Heeeeere you go,' said Deeb, returning with a tray piled high with crisps and drinks. 'Two Pernod and blacks, wernt it, ladies.' While he lifted their drinks towards them, he whispered 'King's Cross' to me behind the cover of his arm. Then, to them, 'Hey up, manners! I'm Deeve, and dis is Kid.'

125

'Deeeve?' They said in unison.

'Thhh-teeve,' said Deeb, trying not to get wound up.

'Oh, Steeeve. Well, hiya, Steve! I'm Paula and this is –'

'Ritz,' cut in her mate, in a way that belied Beryl or something. Not that there's anything wrong with the name Beryl.

Paula was the one with the candyfloss hair. Ritz's was just bleached blonde. Reaching up she pulled at a strand of my hair and said, 'What's yur name, j'u say – Kid?'

'Kid, yeah,' I said, feeling odd talking to her as she fingered my hair, her mouth slightly open. 'Kid Glover,' I said, 'or Billy, if you prefer. Kid's just a nickname.'

I was about to say I preferred Billy these days when Ritz said, 'Oooh, Kid I think. Meks you sound like a boxer.'

Deeb unleashed spumes of ale. 'Boxer!' He wiped his lips. 'Cunt fight his way out ov wet paper bag, this lad.'

Ritz ignored him, dabbing at the tiny globules of spittle on her face. Turning to me, she said, 'Du you dye yur hair, Kid?'

Deeb gave out another wild hoot like he thought she'd said this to try and embarrass me. Ritz made a big thing of ignoring him and I said, 'Yeah – Polly blonde,' and, leaning back, 'from Boots.'

We smiled at each other and Deeb shook his head sulkily.

'What the fuck y'on about, Glover?'

'Hair dye,' I said, without taking my eyes off Ritz.

Ritz laughed.

'Fuckin hell.' Deeb shook his head. 'Touched,' he offered to Paula, who smiled, more to be acknowledged than in agreement.

'*Grum*py,' said Ritz, and giggled bubbles into her Pernod.

I was getting to like Ritz. Paula was a thicker-set version with not much to say as though all her energy was in her hair like a Marvel character, Torch or someone. Her lips were unusually thin but she'd argued a Cupid's bow way up over a slight moustache – somehow it made her look stuffed. Her eyes though were kind and slow, like those of a patient horse. Getting up, she mumbled something to Ritz about accompanying her to the juke-box. Bending over the Wurlitzer glow I could see that the fake tan on her legs lay in uneven stripes. Under her green fishnets it reminded me of the way onions come in their grocery sacks.

Deeb was looking her up and down, stroking his moustache like some matinée cad. 'You av her, right?' he said.

'Whatever you say, Steve,' I said, trying for sarcasm, but he didn't detect it. He nodded and started to mumble the names of English towns, sloshing his ale from cheek to cheek like a good vintage.

'Grantham – Peterborough – Stevenage.'

'What you on about?' I asked.

'It's railway talk,' he said. ''S how sum uv the blokes talk about doin it at t' railway.' He explained how sexual progress was gauged in terms of distance travelled on British Rail's Edinburgh to London King's Cross line, journeys invariably begun with the purchase of a platform ticket. 'Like when they came up for a S'Nige. When ah gave em one that meant I'd bought me a platform ticket, then after I got drinks in – I'd booked me seat. J'u see?'

'So hang on,' I said, trying to grasp the gist of it. 'You mean like – say Selby's . . . ?'

'A wayside halt.' He shook his head. 'Nowt to get excited about, just snogging or feeling up ont outside uv clothing. Doncaster, though, that's mebbe like one hand down their blouses, titting up, you know. Peterborough is like when yu've just got em down to their knickuz . . .'

I looked over at Ritz and Paula. Ritz was shaking her head, dismissing certain tracks Paula was suggesting or, I suddenly thought, perhaps they weren't discussing music at all.

'Grantham like . . .' Deeb was saying, in the swing of it now, 'you've got their fucking knickuz off. Approaching Stevenage is like up but not in.'

'So what's that then?' I interrupted, imagining him being hauled off by some angry parent or having some other unforeseen derailment. He grinned a silent You know it, Glover pal, and said, 'Yeah, yeah.' He had, you might say, if you were getting into the spirit of his metaphor, a head of steam up now. 'Yeah, yeah! Up but not in right,' his head bobbled about as though crossing points. 'But King's Cross, right – King's Cross is like,' here he threw his head back to the ceiling and wailed out, 'UP TO THE BUFFERS. All the waaaaaaaaaaaaaaaay.'

'Hmm, good one,' I said, watching Ritz and Paula returning from the juke-box.

Ritz looked at Deeb with unconcealed suspicion and addressed me almost accusingly. 'We think wiv seen you before! You know that Ziggy Low, don't you?'

'Uh, yeah,' I said, a little taken aback, 'as matter of fact I do.'

'Seeee,' she hissed at Paula, then turned back to me. 'Are you going to his gig ont barge, then?'

'Uh, yeah, I will be going, yeah,' I said, conscious of Deeb's train timetable rustling noisily in his throat.

'Can a cum wi' yu?' blurted out Ritz.

I couldn't say no, it would have put a downer on the evening, so I said very formally, 'Yes, of course you can,' knowing I'd never call the number she was already smudging on to the back of a beer mat with lip-liner. I put it in my inside pocket.

Ritz said, 'Heey-er!' and gave me a kiss on the cheek. I glimpsed Selby. Their first choice came on the juke-box – Blondie, 'I Am Always Touched By Your Presence Dear.' They knew the words and sang along, even beginning to dance a little. The Forge, though, just isn't the sort of pub you do this in. Me and Dicko had been here on the occasion of Valerian turning up in his mother's jumpsuit.

ME, I DISCONNECT FROM YOU

Valerian was a choccy basher and worked at the same factory as my dad, but if you asked him what he did he said he made sweets for the children of the planet. His real name was Alan and he'd been through a bit of a Bowie phase himself. Nothing to compare with Ziggy, mind. Ziggy was a performer, an interpreter, and Alan was just a lookalike, a clone, I suppose. You'd see him at the Roxy standing around wherever there was some dry ice puffing out. Sometimes, if they played Numan, he'd do his robotic dancing. I can see him now, struggling against the general exodus to the bar, all alone on the dance floor, his movements becoming extra jerky as macho types threw money at him. He'd duck and ride the loose pennies, staying cool, never getting mad, like ice like Numan. The men were Prat men and there were many such examples on the planet.

Alan had undoubtedly been a real Bowie fan though, in his time, and told me once that he was going to Bridlington Pier to have the front cover of the *Aladdin Sane* album tattooed across his whole back.

'That'll take a while,' I said.

'I know. Thas why am off fu t' week.'

All week then I imagined him stripped to the waist under the tattoo gun at the end of blowy Bridlington Pier, the *Aladdin Sane* face buzzing into being on his back. I thought of him sitting astride a chair, his elbows resting on the back of it, like some method actor. I saw the blue and red lightning striking slowly down his spine.

When I next spied him cycling up the Rise, he had on a Wrangler jacket. On the back, in place of the tattoo, he'd had the thing embroidered instead. He faced a lot of derision for that. For Alan, though, it was a sensible decision, because not long after that he changed his name to Valerian and became a Tubeway Army fan. He started dressing like Numan and was the first Numoid in the ex-capital.

Valerian lived at home with his mum, herself a good-looking Barbara Stanwyck clone, and it was a Friday night then – dressed in one of his mother's black glazed cotton sugary jump-suits with epaulettes and a cavalry slash zip – that he crossed the worn-out coconut Welcome mat of the the Olde Forge Inn and caused a bit of a stir. He had the look down cold, he'd even slung a shiny red plastic belt Cossack-style across his chest and round his waist. Hanging from his hip was a little matching pouch in which he kept his lipstick and what-have-you.

There was something of the lone stranger entering the cowboy saloon about his entrance into the Forge that night. An epidemic of silence and head-turning accompanied him as he walked slowly to the bar. He didn't falter though, he kept on walking, his silent spurs going chink chink chink as he swayed through the parting crowd of real men drinking real ale. The sugary coating on his jumpsuit sparkled worryingly as he reached the troubled light from the optics.

'Coke, please,' he said to the barman. Coke please – now that was downright silly and the Prat men were definitely offended. He was mucking about with some heavy stuff here. There was total silence. Dave the landlord – a big bastard who kept a baseball bat behind the bar in case of trouble – just stared and made no move to serve him. The real men supping real ale closed in. One of them came up close and started whispering in his ear how he was going to alter his facial design 'n' all. Valerian stood impassively for a while and adopted a transporter podium stance, his right hand grasping his left forearm just above his digital watch. He didn't get mad, or lose cool, he just turned to this bloke and said, 'Me – I disconnect from you – we are glass – I die, you die.' All Numan lyrics of course, repeated like a mantra, and I imagined old Gazza coming up with them one night, getting tough with himself in the mirror. For one glorious moment he had them. One glorious moment – a second, maybe two. Then the violence erupted. He was kicked to the floor, and on his hands and knees he began to crawl towards the door, the way he'd just come, back through these same bodies who'd parted for him and now scrummed over to kick and tip beer on his sugary-coated back. At the worn-out coconut Welcome mat he scrabbled to his feet and pegged it off down Grape Lane.

Dave threw the baseball bat (as I say, kept in case of trouble) to some animal who was bursting out of a three-button T-shirt. A shout went up and five blokes ran after him in a pack. They caught up with him at the end of Grape Lane. One of the prossies gave him away huddled behind a bin and watched impassively as they worked him over. Two weeks off work's worth. With torchlit Wagnerian pageantry, the men lit lighters and carried their leader aloft, back up the lane to the Olde Forge Inn where drinks were waiting on the house.

UP TO THE BUFFERS

It was in this same tolerant atmosphere that Paula and Ritz were going through their Blondie routine. Soon enough the cavemen were beginning to stir. One or two emerged from the shadows and shouted things I didn't catch.

We left sharpish and Deeb hailed a cab.

'Dringwood Av . . .' hiccuped Paula to the cabbie, 'Avenue, scuse me.' She said it like she took taxis all the time. 'Number fi–five, oh, thas right, just ere's fi–fine.' When we got to their house there was a pause, then Deeb paid and tipped the driver and we all got out. Ritz linked arms with me as she picked her way across the grass verge in her heels. I knew they were going to invite us in from the way they'd nudged each other in the cab with their knees.

Ritz was still singing Blondie and it was really painful listening to her do the guitar bits in between the verses. Suddenly she broke off. 'Well, Paula, wha'd y'think? (hiccup) Shall we invite these waifs and strays in for a drink?'

Paula was standing like a stork, handbag up on one knee. Rummaging, she mumbled, 'If I ever find the soddin key.'

I was picturing the scene behind the frosted wheatsheafs on the door. Through the pane came a dim orange glow that perhaps was an electric fire. A train rumbled by and while the wagons clipped the loose sleepers Ritz's face tilted up to me. I bent forward and kissed her on the lips and from the corner of my eye saw Paula fit the key in the latch. The Welcome to Selby sign just flashed past as we stumbled inside, knocking over, in our drunkenness, a stack of phone directories that got kicked down the hall. In the front room, fast approaching Doncaster, we seemed to have left Deeb and Paula far behind on some branch line waiting-room sofa.

On the hearth rug I saw my outstretched hands caressing Ritz's tits through her bra. Something of the zombie about my mesmerised squeezing was communicated back to me by her eyes. Her blouse quickly became gypsyishly draped around her shoulders. We manoeuvred into a lying-down position, her on top, tongue out, the very picture of concentration as she unfastened my trousers. It took strong tugs from side to side to get them down. I arched my back and lifted my arse to make it easier. My cock slapped out against my stomach and she made a grab for it as though it was going someplace, like in *Alien* when the baby alien bursts out the bloke's stomach and hares off. I have to say I'd have preferred a more teasing approach, her painted nails carving around my groin a while but, anyway, there we were, and the hot thud of expectation was welling up in me all the same.

While Ritz seemed to be going through some learner-style gear change, rubbing the smooth material of her red knickers against me, I suddenly became aware of the two-bar electric fire which was beginning to scorch my exposed thigh. I tried to ignore it even though it was getting hotter and hotter, but after a while it became so unbearable I had to roll Ritz over on to her back so that now I was on top. Instantly, my flesh was relieved by a draught from under the passage door. This didn't last long, however, for the fire soon began to roast my other flank. My cock was also getting hot and Ritz's thigh above her stockings was turning a gammon pink. I was fairly cooking in the lubricant saliva she'd spat into her palm and was working up and down my shaft. I wanted to tell her to turn the fire off but I didn't want to hear myself trying to say, sexily, D'you think you can turn off one of the bars on the fire for me please, sugar, they didn't seem the right words for the moment. Also, the fire provided the only light in that little sitting room and I didn't fancy the cold ticking darkness that would follow. I had a sudden mental image of Ritz trailing saliva up and down my shaft then blowing on it to cool it down. In mulling over how best to communicate all this, the pages of one of my sister's women's magazines fluttered open in my head, turned it seemed by the same draught from the passage that was cooling my thigh. The pages fluttered a bit more then stayed open at that article about better sex called 'Non-verbal Cues'. I tentatively put some of these non-verbal cues into operation and was amazed to discover that Ritz responded as if it was telepathy. I found I could sort of control her movements with a held-in breath or by the merest tilt of my chin. Slowly, Ritz uncupped her breasts from her bra, then let her hair, slightly crimped, fall in a corrugated heap on my chest. She arched her back and brushed her breasts against the head of my cock, bringing each nipple quickly erect, catching her breath as she did so. I got quite turned on as she did this and my cock throbbed at the extent of its erection. I lifted my head to watch her face coming into proximity with my cock, but she was lost in all that hair. I felt her breath on me and then her tongue, and then the inside of her mouth soothing my boiling veins.

Deeb, over on the sofa, obviously hadn't read the article about non-verbal cues in *Cosmopolitan* and I felt Ritz stiffen all over as he growled at Paula.

'Get down there.'

I'd been trying to forget all about Deeb, blank him out, but I could make him out plenty now, legs all akimbo on the sofa. Paula, who'd started off nestling up next to him, had been bundled down into position on the floor. Deeb was pushing down on her head. 'Go on! Get down there.'

Outside a goods train rumbled past shaking the foundations of the house. I thought I could detect some non-verbal resistance in Paula's naked back. She was big, Paula, like a swimmer is big, but no match for Deeb. As the train trundled out of earshot, Paula's struggle seemed to go with it. I couldn't see Deeb's actual face but I could tell from the shape of his red moustache curled round his critical gape that he was watching her sucking him off. Woe betide her if she caught him with her teeth.

Not liking to hear her gag so, I began to groan, fake at first, but then real sensations took over and I started going, 'Ohhhhh yeah! Orrrr God yeah!' and stuff like that. Stuff I'd hate to hear played back to me on a tape recorder. After the rough clasp of Ritz's hand, her mouth was soft and cavernous, not too teethy either. I felt my way into her rhythm. My thighs of course were burning to hell, but by now I couldn't have cared less if I'd seen them begin to smoulder on the verge of combustion. I was breathing through my teeth, 'Ohh God,' and, 'Ohh yeah,' when I remembered there'd been a distinctly unpleasant odour when I'd come into the house. I'd first got a whiff of it when we'd opened the front door, down along the passage it had got stronger still and once in the room it had become just short of overbearing. Even in all the sexual excitement I'd had to sip at the air so as not to become nauseated. But now it was suddenly undetectable. I only smelt the *mélange* of Ritz's perfume, her cunt smell (sweat, slightly singed by the tightly coiled filaments of the fire) and the stale after-pub waft of Pernod and fags. 'OH GOD, AHUOW YEAH!' Using my elbows to support me, I raised myself up, straining the muscles across my stomach. I was about to come, there was no holding back. Her hair was so much heavy rock, banging up and down at groin level. With my forearm, I swept up a bundle of it, hoping to catch a sight of myself climaxing in her mouth, but those crimped locks kept falling back over her face. I glimpsed her forehead, saw how her foundation was rubbed patchy with sweat, her skin pink and shiny beneath. I squeezed my eyes tight shut, making fiery electric spheres of orange jostle on my retinas, and ejaculated. The 'OHHH God yeah!' noises amplified in my ears as I threw back my head and jerked my hips. Ritz's hair stopped pulling in my hand as she slowed up to swallow. She seemed to be concentrating very hard. In a few seconds I was dimly aware I'd feel guilty about her doing that swallowing thing.

As though she'd intuited these non-verbal thoughts of mine she looked up with an expression I couldn't fathom. My cock was still bulging in one of her cheeks and perhaps it was this that made the nature of her look hard to grasp. It felt unnatural now to be propped up on one elbow, watching my stomach contract and ripple like a belly dancer. I became aware of the skin on my elbow taking on the imprint of the rug and Ritz's hair began to itch my palm. I watched her swallow and as she did so her eyes flicked up at me again. I flopped back while she milked me dry.

The unknown odour had meanwhile returned, and my leg! My leg felt like a blacksmith's face. I was ready as all hell to jump up and call it a day, buckle and zip my way down the passage and out through the frosted sheaves of wheat into the cool night. But old Ritz kept up a kind of insistent momentum at my groin. And my poor testicles! They'd been cooked in their possum skin by the fire and I could feel the little purple thread veins pulsing as she made them bulge with her rough hand. The last sparrow's tear of my ejaculation was awash in her saliva, but still she kept on. I was really flaccid inside her mouth and kind of embarrassed and not a little helpless. She clearly hadn't been as satisfied by the non-verbal exchange as I had and was trying by sucking and intermittently wanking me to get me hard again.

I did actually manage to get hard again. A shined chunk of steel at the end of her stiletto was sticking into my calf leaving an impression like an Allen key. Mechanically, I got into position between her legs and pulled the damp crotch of her knickers to one side exposing her cunt. I'd sort of forgotten about her cunt and I experienced a new surge of excitement as my knuckles lightly brushed her moistened lips. Having already come, I knew there'd be no fear of another premature ejaculation. Fucking her, though, I was very detached. I could smell that powerful odour again, what was it like? Ammonia and cauliflower, cat litter unchanged since the romans? I couldn't work it out. I tried to blunt my olfactory senses by focusing on a half-eaten pack of Polo Mints above the fireplace.

Ritz closed her eyes as I fucked on in a steady rhythm. Increasing the pace, she began to writhe from side to side, reminding me of my little sister Stacey making a comfy hole for her head in Scarborough sands.

STICK ME ARDER YU WANKER

Ritz suddenly yelled, 'AH DURT NEED YOUR LOVE.'

I turned my face away. What the hell did she mean she didn't need my love! Wasn't that taking a lot for granted? It was all I could do to retain my erection, but in accordance with her *very* verbal wishes, I set about sticking her as hard as I possibly could. Our pubic bones banged away and I began to fear internal bruising. It worked for her though and she made a very big thing of having an orgasm.

Afterwards, as I got off her and slumped back against an easy chair, Ritz lay her head on my chest and together we gazed into the glow of the fire. As Ritz brought her breathing under control, the intermittent saliva-type noises of Deeb, *still* being sucked off, filled the darkness.

'Poor Paula,' giggled Ritz.

'Hmmm,' I nodded, and stroked her hair.

Perched on the hearth was an ornamental blue tit. A line of epoxy resin had beaded up around a break in its beak. It had a queer look in its eye like it could see the bad mend and was peeved about it. My eye wandered from one ornament to another and I noticed that many of them had been mended in the same ham-fisted way.

Ritz began whispering to me like we were in church. She'd transformed into a little kitten.

'You what?' I said. For some reason I was whispering too.

I wasn't really listening to her, I was concentrating on the blue tit with the break in its beak. I heard mention of Ziggy Hero and his concert, though, and how she thought she might come with me – 'Can ah cum? Ah wanna cum,' over and over again. I wanted to tell her that after that 'Stick me arder' business I wouldn't even consider it. I wanted out now.

Deeb's climax was a bind to sit through. When it was eventually over and all the grunting had subsided, I heard Paula climb back up on the sofa and snuggle up next to him. The sofa springs creaked as she leant up to whisper something in his ear. Deeb seemed to stiffen and there was an odd silence into which Paula whispered, 'Oh, Steve, ju luv me now?'

I think – though I wasn't sure – she was probably joking. Either way there was no justification for what came next. Deeb sent her flying and she landed all in a heap between Ritz and me on the rug that had imprinted itself into my elbow. As she struggled to get back up in a tangle of undress, Deeb got off the sofa and with a facial expression I'd be obliged to call fearsome, snarled, 'WHAT? After what *YOU'VE* jus dun!'

She was struck dumb. She'd landed badly on her coccyx and her brown horse's eyes brimmed in the firelight, full of confusion and pain. She began rather automatically to pull her bra strap up, touching off a response.

'Yoooooooou BASTUD!' she screamed, struggling to her feet. She used the mantelpiece to help herself up and grabbed an ornamental windmill that she shied at Deeb's head. 'Twatty bastud!' We flinched as it smashed against the wall, exploding in blue and white smithereens, just missing Deeb, who ducked with stunt-double precision. A Delft clog landed near me.

Deeb was shocked. Paula was spitting insults at him, advancing at bayonet speed. I scrambled to my feet in an effort to calm the situation, tripping and hopping and pulling up my trousers. Paula was right up in front of Deeb now, spitting in his eyes, and I knew he wasn't going to take that for long. I made a lunge for her, wrapping my arms right the way around her to try and pull her away. Her back felt clammy pressed against my bare chest. She struggled to get free, still spitting. 'Wanker, yu're a bastud, yu're a wanker.' He seemed to come out of his daze and grabbed her face, making her lips pucker up like someone doing a goldfish impression.

'Fuckin shur it, SLAG! One more fuckin peep . . .'

'Wanker, yur a twat, yur a wahhhhh . . .'

Deeb let her have it, an economical movement of the head as he did up his fly. The back of Paula's skull struck my nose in a domino effect and I reeled away, staggering blindly into the middle of the room. Oh, God. I felt the familiar drip drip drip of the old vino in my cupped hand. 'Fuck!' I opened my eyes, Paula was right next to me, she was bending forward too, her hands up to her face as though she was recovering from a terrific sneeze. When she straightened up though and took her hands away there was a thick smear of blood – gory, like special-effect blood – all around her mouth and teeth and gums. Her voice was hoarse and came to me above a harsh ringing that had begun in my ears. I think from what she was saying she'd had Deeb's type before. 'Thas right, hit a girl! 'S all yu're fugin gud fu – prick laka fuckin worm anyway. Hit me – go on! Go on then, worm! COME ON . . .'

'SHUDUP!' bellowed Deeb.

'Why, yu're *not* scared? Come on, *wormar*!'

He pointed a finger shaking with rage. 'JUS SHUDUP *RIGHT*!'

'Steve,' I yelled. 'Fuck's sake, man! What you fuckin doin?' He didn't hear me. 'STEEVE!' I stumbled towards him pulling up my trousers.

'Come on,' cried Paula, sticking her face right up in front of Deeb's. 'Do it!'

He knew he was being goaded, that he shouldn't let her control him like this, but he kicked out anyway.

'AHHG God, no!' Paula screamed and creased over. Her hands shot between her legs and I saw she was cupping her crotch, retching as though about to vomit on the carpet. I felt my own hands suddenly nursing my own crotch and winced while I listened to Paula's terrible moans and then I felt myself being pummelled from behind. Ritz was battering on me like a door. 'Fuckin bastud, fuckin bastud.'

'What?' I wailed. 'Wa'nt me!' I shot a furious look at Deeb, who glared back.

Ritz went to try and comfort Paula who was crying. 'Come on, Pauls,' she was whispering, 'come on, babe.' With an arm round her broad swimmer's back she was guiding her doubled-up form out to the kitchen.

I bent down level with Paula's face. 'Are you OK?' I asked, my voice sounding stupid. Paula stiffened and, trying to summon up the strength to tell me where to go, managed only a sort of liquefied grunt and some spits of blood. The look she gave me said it all anyway.

'I'm sorry,' I stammered, 'I'm really sorry.' When I'd thrown my arms around Paula she must have thought I was restraining her to give Deeb a free nut. Ritz punched me again with her hard little fist. 'Fuck off, you! Arnt you dun enuf? Ger out.' She tried pushing me away. 'Ger out or I'll call t' pleece.'

'All right, we're goin,' I said, backing off. 'We're goin. Jus wanted to know if you were all right – ah you sure . . .'

'FUCK *OFF*! AH YOU THICK *OR WHA*!'

I took a deep breath and wiped her phlegm from my face. This was such a fucking bad scene. I couldn't work out how it had happened exactly, except that it was all basically Deeb's fault. I fucking hated him for this. He was standing by the door like a primate caught in the confusion of actually standing up for the very first time. His upper body was hunkered over with the weight of his huge arms. I yelled at him to come and shoved him with both hands out into the hall.

In the street he glared at me. 'What?' he asked, holding out his hands as though if I gave him a wry smile now, we could laugh about it in the morning.

'I don't believe you,' I said, shaking my head.

CHRISTMAS TOKENS

On Christmas Eve I took Stacey to see Santa but he made her cry.

The nearest grotto was in an old railway wagon in the sidings by the market. There was just a piece of tinsel nailed above the sliding doors. Santa was a big shifty-eyed bastard. He looked like he'd done away with the real Santa and was using his grubby outfit as a disguise. I don't quite know why but I was reminded of something Pete once told me about John Huston, how Huston's idea of an action-packed film was 'a mind in turmoil'. This Santa would have excited the hell out of old John Huston.

In the afternoon I went to the Theatre bar and found Ziggy in his usual spot. I asked him what he was doing for Christmas – turned out he wasn't doing anything. His aunt was away to her sister's in Doncaster so he was spending it on his own back in Halifax. 'Come to our place then,' I said, and at first he said no but when I insisted he nodded and said 'OK, man.' I called Mum to ask if it was OK. She wasn't wild about it but, it being Christmas, she said all right. In the background, I could hear my dad, who'd caught the gist of the conversation, shouting aggressively, 'We don't *want* anyone, tell him we don't want anyone!'

I suppose it all went off OK, apart from the quiz of course.

When Ziggy had arrived in the morning he was his usual self – very polite to my family and all that, asking where he should put his coat. Of course he'd kept his fedora on through dinner. Later on, we went to this quiz which had been organised by Dad's cronies from the Pickering to Whitby Light Gauge Railway Trust. Fortunately Pullman wasn't there. The bloke whose house it was at was called Dave Farnsworth and apparently he hated Pullman. Farnsworth was a parrot dealer. The week before Christmas though – which he reckons on as his busiest time – all his parrots (and judging by the amount of empty cages there'd been lots of them) had died of a rare parrot virus. It was quite depressing sitting there with all those empty cages in his front room, and the tinsel through the bars was an odd touch, I thought. Every now and then you'd find a tiny bit of grey plumage down the side of the settee or sometimes see a feather floating slowly through the air like there'd been a pillow fight.

The quiz was taken very seriously and it had been pretty

much even-steven all the way, so much so that the result hung on the final question. The answer to that question was really obvious – wig or toupee. There was no conferring allowed and it was all up to Ziggy. Everyone on our team was looking at him willing him to come out with it. The thing was, the woman sitting dead opposite him was so obviously *wearing* one that Ziggy couldn't bring himself to say it – for fear, I suppose, of causing embarrassment. But while he was umming and ahhing it was more painful for the woman because it was like she could hear everybody silently shouting, 'Wig, it's *fuckin WIG!*' over and over in their heads. Eventually, Ziggy, who was sort of stroking a fragment of feather on his chin, gave a shrug and said, 'Ahh, by jingo, mind's a blank.' Farnsworth, who because of his birds was having a crap Christmas anyway, shouted, 'IT'S BLOODY WIG, YOU BASTUD.' He was really pissed off about losing and started making a lot of snide personal comments about Ziggy wearing make-up and dyeing his hair. Ziggy sat there silently just sort of twirling this feather.

ENTER THE GEORGE AND DRAGON

On Boxing Day we went round to Auntie Sheila's. She'd bought me a W. H. Smith's book token and said, 'Yur mum told me you wanted "The Rime of the Ancient Mariner" or something. Anyway, I wasn't sure so I thought if I get you this you can go and get what you want, can't you.'

In the evening, we went to a disco at the George and Dragon. The DJ, some smooth bastard with a Bryan Ferry hairstyle, was giving all the girls the eye. For some reason – probably because Si was dancing with Clare Crocker, the best-looking girl there – this DJ bastard was making sarcastic comments over his microphone about Si's dancing and his hair and his clothes. Si shouted something back but it was lost in the music. He started dancing again but really stiffly and self-consciously so that eventually Clare gave Si a little smile, shrugged, and just sort of drifted back over to where her mates were sitting. Si stood there for a few moments while everyone carried on dancing around him, and I could see he was taking the sting of humiliation particularly badly. Simon had decided some time ago – I don't know when exactly, maybe when we were at school – that 1) he had to be cool, and 2) he wasn't going to take any shit from anyone. He was really het up with this DJ and feeling uncool and he didn't know what to do about it. Eventually, he made a movement as though he was being helped into his jacket, and shouldered his way off the dance floor. I stood up from our table and craned my neck over the swaying heads just in time to see him disappearing out of the back door to the car park.

The DJ came over his bingo microphone: 'Must ha bin something ah said?' He shrugged, holding out his hands in mock innocence, making the girls giggle again. We nearly got into a fight with some kids at the next table when one of them turned round to us and said, 'Your mate's chickin shit, int ee?' It was weird really because despite his fancy clothes the last thing Si was was chicken shit. I never heard tell of him backing down from anything. The reverse in fact – at school his nickname had been Si-co, somewhat predictable, I know, but nevertheless.

While we waited for him to come back, last orders was rung at the bar, the DJ put on a slow number and, to add insult to injury, got down to dance with Clare himself. They did this slow smoochy waltz round the floor right past our table. Deeb picked up his pint as though he was examining it like a good wine then casually in a loud voice said, 'Slag.' In the same casual way, he took a long draft of his beer. Clare had her back to us and I saw her stiffen, but the DJ just pulled her closer to him and, sliding one hand down on to her arse, winked at Deeb – quite a cool response really.

I got up to go for a piss and said I'd have a look for Si while I was at it. It was pitch black outside, but as I took a couple of steps in the gravel, a trip light came on and illuminated the whole of the car park and some of the oblong beer garden too. It had been snowing again and everything was white. The picnic table where we'd sat in summer was covered with a fresh powdery snow in which little birds had hopped, leaving their tiny tracks. 'Si – hey, SIMON! It's meeee, Kid!' I shouted. I saw something move down by one of the children's swings, but when I stared into the darkness it was mutant eyes belonging to some woodland creature that flashed back at me. A fox or a badger. Before I turned to go back in, I reflected on what a beautiful and silent night it was in the beer garden compared with the noisy tension of the crap disco inside. I walked over to one of the picnic tables and scooped up a handful of snow, rubbing it in my face. I was quite loath to go back inside really so I hung about and smoked a couple Sir Niges and thought about that animal with its mutant eyes and old Keith fucking Michell at number one with 'Captain Beaky and Ratty Rat and Somebody Toad'. I imagined the animal I had just seen getting back to his burrow where his family had been anxiously awaiting his safe return. I saw them all huddled in front of a roaring fire, winter berries and strange drinks made from holly roots on the table. The thought pleased me. It was Christmas after all.

EXIT THE GEORGE AND DRAGON

The last dance was over and the house lights were on. Bar staff were clearing away and apart from some drunk people who'd lost a bag or something, we were the last ones there. I picked up Si's jacket that was still hanging on the back of his chair. 'Come on now, gents, pu-lease,' called the barman, upending a stool on a table. The DJ was over at the till getting his money from the landlord. He smirked at us and ran a hand through his thick lustrous hair. 'Fuckin go ome, you,' shouted Deeb, to which the DJ stuck his chin out at him like he was shaving and, crooking his little finger, scratched his chest. Deeb went wild and we had to pull him back and the landlord said, 'Right, you lot – OUT. And consider yerselves barred.'

The bouncers showed us the door. Outside it had begun to snow again. It was fucking freezing and there were no cabs so we went up the side of the George to shelter – just far enough along to keep an eye on the road in case of a cab. I put Si's jacket on to keep warm and, feeling in the pockets, I said, 'He's got his keys and money and everything in ere.' I pulled out a pack of hopeful toggys. 'Even a pack of three for Clare. Where the fuck j'u reckon he's gone?' As I said it the trip light at the back of the pub came on and we saw a silhouetted figure carrying something heavy over to a transit van parked in the corner. It was the DJ, come out to start loading up his gear. He was whistling the refrain of the last dance – 'morning, afternoon and night' – 'Body Talk' by Imagination.

'Away,' said Deeb, 'let's go fuckin nobble t'cunt.'

Ovo said, 'Ignore im, cart you, it's Christmas.'

Deeb began to strip off his new Fiorucci cardigan and was giving it me to hold when the timer on the trip switch plinked out and the car park was plunged once more into darkness. There was a startled cry and the metallic whine of the transit's back door being forcefully slammed. We all looked over. There, pressing for all he was worth on the back door, as though giving the transit a push start, was the unmistakable figure of Si Knight. He'd sandwiched the DJ against the back of the van, so all we could see of him were his snazzy shoes scuffing at the gravel in panic. Si let the pressure off the door and the DJ buckled and wilted to the ground, clutching his calf. Si pulled him back up and deftly gave him the head. The DJ began to howl but Si smothered his mouth with his hand, dragging him round the back of the van.

'Away,' said Deeb, his face lit up. 'It's Si, he's fuckin doin im,' and he was off. We followed at a run across the gravel.

It transpired that Si, after he'd disappeared out the back, had been circuiting the car park seething and muttering in the snow, brutal fantasies running through his head when all at once he'd come alongside the transit with Ace Mobile Disco painted on the side. Looking around for a weapon to do some damage with, his eyes alighted on a decorator's old wire brush sticking out of a snow-filled bucket, and suddenly Si had an idea that seemed to make him almost sick with anticipation. He weighed the brush in his hand and made a few practice swipes, breathing out 'Oh yu-ess' in the cold night air, and that's how he was when the DJ, having reached the transit with his box of records, was gently sliding them into the back. Si got him in a headlock and, when we arrived on the scene, was viciously striking at his head and combing his well-tended hair with those steel bristles, pulling out great clumps with a horrible tearing sound. Blood was flowing freely down the DJ's face that was contorted beyond all recognition.

Seeing us, Si growled, 'Giz a fuckin 'and, willya.' Daniel kept looking away like he was going to be sick. Even Deeb had recoiled a little to see the DJ's instant case of alopecia, fleshy areas of ripped scalp where moments before there'd been lustrous black hair.

'Ger his other arm,' ordered Si. Deeb bent down and got the DJ to his feet but he couldn't stand and his legs gave way. Si helped Deeb scoop him up and together, all three looking perversely like comrades, they took him, an arm each, over to the transit's wing mirror.

'Look,' growled Si. He angled the wing mirror in a bit and slapped the DJ's face. 'LOOK! Can you see, you sen? MR FUCKIN COOL. NO BIRD WILL EVER FANCY *THAT*.

EVER AGAIN.' The DJ sounded like he was swallowing his tongue. He'd vomited and silent paroxysms were running through him as though he were epileptic or something. His sobbing was on a higher frequency than we could hear, a sobbing audible to bats, and perhaps the woodland animal I'd seen earlier with the red mutant eyes. Ovo turned away, pulling a face like someone had a laggy band trained on it. Si had removed a clump of the DJ's long black hair from the wire brush and was holding it under the DJ's nose like a Fu Manchu moustache. Deeb fleeced his DJ clothing till he found his DJ wages and slipped the notes into his own pocket. Si let go and the DJ fell to the snow, curling into a foetal position. His hands and arms were shaking like a Parkinson's sufferer as he brought them up over his head, but his head was too painful for him to touch. He was in unbelievable agony. Si bent down to whisper to him. 'The name's Knight, remember t'name when you look int mirrur.'

And so ended the festive period. When eventually we got home, Si went straight to bed. Both Daniel and I were horrified by what we'd witnessed and even Deeb had stayed more or less silent on the long walk back. The Wigwam's sparse decorations, the streamers and the fake snow in the corners of all the windows, couldn't cheer us.

'Roll on New Year,' said Ovo gloomily. 'Now we got a war to look forward to.'

'What?' I said.

Reaching up, he tugged at the streamers which slowly fell about him. Holding out his arms he was momentarily turned into the Christmas tree we never had.

'That DJ,' he said, 'I reckon I know him from Elland Road. I think he's one of Dave Scar's mates. If am right he's not gunna jus sit back and tek summat like that.'

NEW YEAR

Second January 1981. There was a news flash on the telly that they'd caught the Yorkshire Ripper. Two coppers in Sheffield arrested him for having stolen number plates. After all that and he gets caught for stealing number plates. There was a prostitute in the car with him and the boot was full of hammers and everything. She must have felt like the luckiest woman in the world.

Up and down the road people reacted as if it was like we'd won the war or something. I felt relief for Bernice, working in that wine bar and coming home late every night. It hadn't been easy on Mum and Dad. I hadn't really realised what a big thing it was until it was over. There were reporters everywhere and women breaking down in tears. I watched all the footage half expecting to see Bernice being interviewed. After leaving home she'd lived just over the way from where one of the bodies was found. It was like Yorkshire had been holding its breath the last five years.

THE RED AND BLACK FEAST

The pre-war wiring at the Wigwam, exposed during the DIY drive, had been tampered with, and the bulbs were always blowing. It wasn't long before all the lights had been replaced with the blue and orange ones. They were low wattage, and their sombre radiance wasn't so much light as non-darkness. 'Weird's an overused word to my mind, but it was often the first word used by visitors to the Wigwam during those winter months.

One night in late January, having just drawn heavily on a spliff, Ovo said, 'You know, I can't open me lungs up enough to ger it all in.' He dug himself repeatedly on the chest where he guessed his lungs were. 'J'u know worra mean, like?' He was out of gear and drawing for all he was worth on a number of roaches.

'You're desperate, man.'

'Fuck off. Think of all those starving hippies in India who'd be fighting for this roach.'

He'd just rung Fizzy Paul. Paul was, in his own words, 'a twenny-four-hour person', always good for an eighth of black, day or night. Occasionally, he'd get more exotic stuff like these Nepalese temple balls that Ovo had been so mad for. Paul didn't really get the vibe that he wasn't liked, or if he did, he chose to ignore it. Sometimes he'd hang around for days. For some reason he'd taken a liking to me, and though I enjoyed his company, it could get wearing after a week. He was one of those blokes who had countless theories. He'd also seen too much *Clockwork Orange* and everything was malenky this old droogy and a bit of the old and all that call.

(I say he liked me, but I'm basing this on a fleeting incident one night just before Christmas. I'd been leaving a party at Purdcake's when Fizzy Paul had come after me into the hall. 'Hey, pssst, Billy, here a minit.' I'd thought he wanted to sell me some drugs but he'd said, 'We haven't talked yet you and me but,' he'd flicked his finger between our front lobes, 'I feel we're on the same wavelength, you and me, old droogy, we're on the same wavelength.')

'J'u know what ah mean, Billy?' Ovo was saying, looking like he was imploding.

'Sorry, what?'

'Ah say, j'u know what ah mean, ah carn't like opun me lungs up enuf to ger it all in.'

'Oh yeah.'

Ovo glanced at his watch. 'Where the fuck is he anyroad, the greebo bastard? I hope he int gunna tek ages to ger ere then fuckin hang round t' place for ever. Don't you think,' he added thoughtfully, therz summat a bit weird about him, Kid? . . . I mean . . .'

He'd barely said this when there was a knocking at the door so loud it made Ovo fairly jump out his skin. I cleared off upstairs. I wasn't in the mood to get out of it. The walls billowed behind me as Ovo opened the front door. I heard him greeting Fizzy like a long-lost brother.

'Paul mate! How are you? Come in, come in. You got the . . . yeah? Ah fantastic! You – are – amazin. Cup of the old chi?'

I winced as Ovo ingratiated himself with this bit of Nadsat and then, to my great irritation, they came up the stairs, Ovo saying, 'We're in here.' They pushed through the blankets and sat themselves down either side of me on the bed.

Paul set up his scales and while he hunkered over them, I tried to catch Ovo's eye, as if to say, What yu doing bringing him in ere, you cunt? But Ovo's eyes were fixed on the lumps of black which Paul was drawing from a plastic wallet, the type banks use for loose change. Eventually, after a lot of squinting and nodding, he sniffed and said, 'Tenner.' Ovo, who'd had the note in his hand for the last hour, held it out to him. Paul tucked it into his top pocket and said, 'Shall I do the honours?'

This is what really wound up Ovo. Paul was gonna smoke most of the dope he'd just flogged him. Soon, also, he could be expected to go over to the fridge, where, bending down on his haunches he'd hold the door ajar and nod in at its contents as though mentally preparing an omelette. But usually he'd come away gnawing on a hunk of cheese. Crumbling the resin into a trench of tobacco, he said, 'Pinhead's all you need a this stuff to get comp-*leet*-lee trashed, like *way* over the horizon, man.'

Ovo and I wondered why, then, he'd put in at least *ten times* that amount. 'You gorra whole fuckin pin-cushion's wuth in there, man,' Ovo grumbled.

Paul smiled and carried on crumbling. This weird antagonism created a bad vibe.

Plumping up one of my cushions for his head, Paul lit the joint and leant back. 'Speak no evil,' he said. My room quickly filled with thick hashish smoke. The joint was passed to me but it had the opposite effect of what was intended. I'm not good on this, I heard myself thinking, so resolutely that I wasn't sure I didn't actually mumble the words under my breath. I felt vulnerable and abnormally sensitive. I rested a hand on my increasing heart beat and closed my eyes trying hard to concentrate on becoming calm. The billowing walls seemed to be mimicking my uneasy breathing.

''S fucking weird in ere, innit,' said Paul.

'What?' I cracked open my eyes and gave Paul a sidelong look of cold displeasure.

'These sheets and weird fucking lights,' he continued, oblivious to my response and, using the joint, he indicated the room as a whole. 'Yeah, I always feel a bit disorientated when I come ere.'

'Hmm,' I said, thinking, Well no one's forcing you to stay, but instead I said, 'Yeah, teks a bit of gettin used to.'

From the other end of the bed Ovo got up and mumbled, 'Fuck – com-pleeet-lee outers.' Then, seemingly for Paul's bene-fit, 'Bed ways is best ways, old droogy,' and walked out through the wall like a somnambulist. I got up too and coughed as if to say, Right, let's all vacate, hey. But Paul just sprawled back on my bed in his dirty, smelly Originals. I'd seen him in these day in, day out for, well, for as long as I'd known him. In fact, the only time I'd seen him take them off was outside the Traveller's one lunchtime. He'd pitched them into a circle of biker types and said, 'Right, lads, piss on em!' Then after they'd all relieved their bladders, he'd got back into them – trousers and jacket – and stood there steaming like a racehorse and inhaling the piss smell as a fell walker might appreciate a field of spring rape.

'Hey,' he drawled, reaching for my reading light, 'j'u know about this, man?'

'What?'

'This!' He went over to the dressing table trailing the light flex behind him like he was Jim Morrison on stage or something. He sat down and stared into the mirror, holding the bulb under his chin like it was a cut-throat razor. 'It's what Aleister Crowley calls the red and black feast,' he said. 'Try it.'

'Who's Aleister Crowley?' I asked.

'*Who's* Aleister Crowley,' he said contemptuously. '*Who is* Aleister Crowley.'

I took his place in front of the mirror and held the blue light under my face. 'Jus let yur eyes kind ov glaze over, but keep staring in to them and don't blink – whatever you do, don't blink.'

There was a fair bit of warmth coming off the bulb but the reflection in the mirror was a very cold unsmiling thing with sunken eyes that produced in me an instant shiver. I was reminded of an Aztec relic flashed over by an explorer's torch and, as Paul suggested, I let my eyes glaze over and, as I did, my face began to separate into planes of light and shade. I became aware of looking older and older, and then, not so much old like an old man, but more like early man, primitive man, a mud man, a Golem. I was drawn into the mirror, further and further, and then my image began to shift and I became by degrees a horrified spectator of myself. My eyes got very dry from not blinking. The face in the mirror began to sneer, do things I knew I wasn't doing. Creepy. I had gooseflesh on my back. All that crap from my subconscious, massed like woodlice under an upturned stone. I saw a man, like a man you might have trusted for years, a neighbour or a jolly family butcher, only stripped of whatever civility he boasted of on his striped awning. I saw old Doc Slater and felt 'The Ancient Mariner' moving soundlessly across my lips. And then I seemed to see Paul dicing his finger between our frontal lobes and saying, 'You and me, man, we're on the same wavelength, old droogy.' I was aware of him following the flex to the wall where he pulled out the plug plunging us into darkness. Then I heard his hand slide up and down the wallpaper, looking for the light switch, and when the amber bulb plinked on above me I was pretty freaked.

After a while I said, 'Shit, that was we-ird,' and in this instance I could find no fault in my observation.

LOVE AND UNDERSTANDING – THE POST-RIPPER YEARS

When Ziggy appeared at the door of the Centurion café, he was still in his greasepaint from the Haunted Walk. Stomping his feet and brushing snow off his cloak, he hung up his top hat and cane, then, using a rolled-up copy of the *NME* as a telescope, he found us through the thick smoke and steam in our usual booth.

'Hey there, Baz, Billy.' He greeted us and nonchalantly clicked his fingers for a waitress who ignored him. She was pissed off because he'd been standing outside for ages, just on the verge of coming in, and with his back against the door he'd been having some kind of altercation with Charlie and Sandy, the drummer and bassist from his band. A couple of times he'd attempted to break away from them, cracking open the door with his bum and letting in sharp draughts of cold and snow that had chilled the girl on the till. Leaning his dark cloak flat against the door, the pane had become mirror-like, reflecting her angry swivel.

'Just had to break up the band,' said Ziggy, spreading the *NME* out over the condiments. He'd bought it for the Bowie exclusive and set straight down to reading it.

'You did phwhat, dude!' said Baz, spraying tea. 'But whad about the gig?'

'Yeah,' said Ziggy, frowning at something he was reading. It was the first interview Bowie had given for quite a while. He'd been away on a health kick and returned. 'Rested, relaxed and *tanned*!' Ziggy lifted the word up at us. 'Tanned!' he said again, with the same inflection Aunt Shee had used when she'd received news from Cyprus that Kitty had got married. (*'Married,'* she'd said, letting the full weight of that word settle on everyone before reading on.)

Beneath the frosted orange lantern that lit our booth, Ziggy began to stroke his cheek, glancing down at the white Pan-stick on his palps, every now and then rubbing them together as though trying to get rid of dead hair from a comb. Throughout the article the interviewer kept remarking on how much orange juice Bowie was drinking these days, and how many Gauloise he would smoke. 'Nununuhnuhnur,' said Ziggy. 'Only halfway through the morning and he's into his second packet of Gauloise.'

The angry waitress from the till came over and clumsily set down Ziggy's coffee.

'Thanks,' he said. 'Oh, and ah, scuse me!' She stopped and turned back to him with an impatient sigh. Ziggy made her wait until he'd finished delicately tipping the slops from the saucer back into his cup. 'And, ahh, can I have an OJ chaser? An orange juice and orange juice,' he added quickly, seeing her getting even angrier.

Baz and I had been silent all this time. Ziggy looked at us, taking a sip of his coffee, and said what I'd been waiting to hear, 'I like the poster, man. I was wondering . . . if . . . I mean – I was wondering if you guys were doing anything tonight?' He put down his coffee and, steadying a hand on a wall of air in front of my face, mimed the pasting of a poster with a large brush.

FLOWERS, NEW CLOTHES, AND A CAR TO TAKE YOU THERE

We arranged to pick up Ziggy outside the Theatre bar at ten.

As we swung into Etty Square, I spotted him leaning against a lamp-post. It was still snowing and the wind was trimming embers from his cigarette. Suddenly his hand went up to his hat but . . . too late – the wind had skimmed it away and was leading him a dance over to the fountains where he caught up with it, goose-stepping to trap it under foot. He brushed it down and returned to the lamp-post, glancing at his watch and pulling the collar of his trench coat up around his ears like a Cold War spy.

'Hey, Ziggy!' we yelled, but he didn't hear. 'HEY, ZIGGY – ZIGGEEE!' I got out of the car and started across the square, feeling like Dr fucking Zhivago in all the snow.

Zig was shouldering out the blizzard, trying to light another cigarette with the old one-handed trick. Match after match blew out. Eventually he got one to light and I saw the sustained flame in his cupped hands. He turned towards me, tossing the match away and stepping beyond the glow of lamplight. I noticed how, as he held out a hand for me to shake, his teeth were pure white and his skin had an orangey glow like a sort of Indian, like I once saw Peter Sellers play Birdy Numnum or whoever he was. He splayed his fingers as though drawing away a veil of mystery.

'Self-tan,' he explained.

'Self-tan, of course,' I said. 'Thas really good, man, but, er, look – you got a liddle on yer collar here.' I indicated an orange tidemark.

He was frowning down at his shirt when two girls approached. I'd noticed them standing smoking in the dark cloister-like walkway that ran along the side of the Theatre. I could see that they had been staring at Ziggy and me. They began to walk towards us in their long black leather coats, every few paces falling against each other trying to stifle fits of hysteria, and as they emerged one of them was pushed forward to speak. She almost banged into us and she looked back at her friend who hissed, 'Ask him, then.'

The designated spokeswoman turned back to us. 'Ere,' she said, addressing Ziggy who was taking drags on his cigarette. She clamped a gloved hand over her mouth to suppress her hysterics. 'Ere, have you got a Schhhh-meeeel car?'

It was one of those moments when Ziggy's affected Bowie voice repaired to its Yorkshire roots. 'You what!'

But the girls hadn't heard, they'd collapsed into fits of laughter, awakening dormant smokers' coughs, both of them choking and bent over, clutching at their throats.

'Away, Ziggy,' I said, beginning to steer him across the road.

'What did she say?' asked Ziggy, looking back over his shoulder. 'Have I got a Schhhh . . .' He drew out the sound the way she had, like a wave at the seaside.

'A Schmeeel car,' I said, 'I think.'

He looked at me for an explanation. 'Schmeeel car?'

'Sorry, dunno,' I said, which was true, I had no idea, although to quote my mum it sounded vulgar.

Baz all this time had been watching Ziggy in the rear-view mirror.

'Hey, Baz man – Schmeeel car mean anything to you?'

'You what?' said Baz, his eyes narrowing in the rear-view mirror.

Later, in the Black Horse, where we'd arranged to meet Hazel and her friend Jane, Ziggy went straight to the toilet. Hazel and Jane were at a copper-topped table patterned with tiny hammer blows.

'Where's Ziggy?' she asked.

'He's gone to the toilet.'

'Ah!'

'J'u wanna drink?'

When I returned with the drinks, Ziggy was sitting with them.

His shirt collar was wet but the stain hadn't budged.

When the bell for last orders rang and we all looked at the log fire. Nobody really wanted to make a start on the posters. Ziggy ran a finger round inside his damp collar. 'Shall we get goin?' he said.

In the car, Baz and I took some speed, smoked a joint, then dropped off Jane. Hazel thought she'd come along for the ride. She didn't know about Schmeeel cars either.

IN THE BACK OF A DREAM CAR 20 FT LONG

It was a bastard to begin with, the wind wrapped the posters round us one second then tore them free like kites the next. We worked in pairs and took it in turns to keep the motor running in case of cops.

It was during one of my stints behind the wheel that Hazel moved forward into the front seat and said, 'Billy, d'you have a light, darling?' It was the first civil thing she'd said to me all night. The tip of her fag felt like it was tickling my ear but when I turned sideways she was still about a million miles away at the other end of a long art deco cigarette holder.

'A light, sure.' I got out my Zippo and, in flipping up the lid, lost it like a bar of soap in the bath. It disappeared in between the hand-brake and the passenger seat. 'Hang on, hang on.' I began scrabbling around, getting caught up with the fucking hand-brake and became aware of my face level with Hazel's knees. My cheek was grazing her stockinged leg. 'Ah, got it.' I came up and blew at my hair. 'Phew, sorry about that.'

As I eventually lit her up, I couldn't help wondering if she thought I'd fumbled the lighter on purpose in an attempt to look up her skirt. I thought it best to bring this idea out into the open. 'You know . . . kids at school used to . . . try and see up the student teachers' skirts and . . .' The drumming of my fingernails on the dash evoked the clatter of pencils. To my surprise she laughed and said that didn't happen much at a girls' school, but it reminded her of a Mr Sourby whom they used to try and get flustered. I felt for him immediately and as I asked her quickly, just for something to say, what she was going to do when she left school, I was in fact imagining Mr Sourby running a finger round his hot collar.

'Me,' said Hazel, pointing at herself with her long black glove, 'I'm a prostitute, me.'

'You what?' I blurted, and she laughed again, this time throwing her head right back. She laid a satin hand on her neck, took another drag on the old diamanté-studded Sir Nige holder and with her composure back began to explain. It was something she'd overheard at school, something another girl had said. I don't know if she was trying to make me feel bad about asking that same type of question or whether she just didn't want to let me in on her modelling aspirations at that precise moment in time. I asked her if the girl was serious. 'Oh yes,' said Hazel, 'she was.' Apparently she worked out of Harrogate, which had the highest rate of teenage prostitution in England. Genteel Harrogate, all fine bone and antimacassars. This third former had met some guy who started to pick her up from school, sometimes in a lorry cab, sometimes in a flash red car. He always parked just out of sight of the headmistress's office, behind a hedge, down Simber Lane. Apparently, though, if you were playing hockey and you knew he was there, you'd glimpse flashes of the red paintwork through the privet. This was as much as she knew but the overheard remark had stuck and become a kind of catchphrase among her friends. We talked about Harrogate's seamier side for a while. Hazel reckoned it was the cocaine hive of the North.

'How d'you know these things,' I asked, 'or is that an indiscreet question?' She laughed again and we talked about cocaine and drugs. Hazel brought up Frankie Dibbs and his smack habit. I said that Frankie had been cultivating his drug problem just so's people would talk about him – which is why I certainly wasn't going to. Everyone was talking about drugs, droning on, 'Yeah, you know, the thing about smack, man, is it's like a river,' or, 'the thing about speed is . . .' I didn't care but the fact that me and Hazel were chatting away like this was something I didn't think possible. There was a pause as perhaps we both reflected on this, and then Hazel said, 'Billy, d'you remember when we first met?' I told her I did. She smiled and took another drag of her Sir Nige, choosing her words. 'I wanted to tell you something about that night.' Pausing, she glanced up the street to where Ziggy was busy pasting up his own image on a closed-down shopfront. While we'd been talking, Baz and him had worked a fair bit ahead of us. The CLOSING DOWN – FINAL REDUCTIONS – EVERYTHING MUST GO in swirls of Windolene was now obscured by Ziggy's smoking silhouette.

'I like the poster, by the way,' she said.

'Thanks,' I replied, 'but go on, will you. You were saying, the night we met.'

'Uhm, oh yeah.' She took another drag on the Sir Nige. 'Well, when you came into the room, well before you came in actually –'

'Yeah?'

She smiled and brushed away some fallen ash. 'Well, you'd called and . . .' but before she could explain she was interrupted by angry shouts ringing out in the night. Baz and Ziggy were returning in an undignified bucket run to the car, sploshing glue everywhere.

'Eh up, let's go,' panted Baz, 'some old grogger's calling t' pigs.' At a first-floor window, above a To Let sign, I noticed an angry fist in the billowing nets. I sped off down towards South Bank where we laid low, you might have said, if you were that type of dramatic guy.

Baz said, 'Well, thas me, I'm dead.' He asked to be dropped

off near his flat, doing an Ant Hill Mob impression that seemed to draw the last of his energy. 'Yous nuts can keep the car if you wanna carry on.' He began to yawn. 'Bring it back when yu've done.' He got out and then tapped on the windscreen. 'Don't wek me up bringing it back though. Jus put keys, you know, under t' bin.'

Ziggy and I continued fly-posting for another hour or so while Hazel huddled on the back seat. We worked in relative silence. Once, I caught his eye and we exchanged uncertain smiles. We were just about done when the car broke down. Ziggy free-wheeled into a bus stop, then tried to start it again, but it was dead. We had to push with Hazel at the wheel calling out nervously, 'Oh, God, help, I've never driven a car before, whadda I do? Whadda I do?' She steered all over the road. The gritters hadn't been round yet so the road was still covered in snow making it almost impossible to push. Ziggy slipped and banged his nose on the rear bumper. He stood up panting. 'Woah, woah, slow down.' He took off his hat and wiped the sweat from his brow, inadvertently smearing his fake tan. Coughing like a consumptive, he put his hat back in place and dialled the air. 'I'm gonna call Baz.'

Under the kiosk light, he removed the fedora again and scratched where the headband had rubbed. Then, lifting his eyepatch, he dabbed at the sweat that had gathered there like condensation in the lid of a teapot. With one hand on his hip, the other arm thrown languidly behind his head – I recognised the pose from *The Rise and Fall* – I heard him say, 'That's right, man, I think it could be the starter motor.'

'Uuhruhluuu luhlu!' I couldn't make out Baz's reply too good but he sounded pretty pissed off.

'Stone Bow, thas right, by the old Odeon, next to . . .'

'Whurululuuuluh.'

'Twenny minutes.'

'Yeululuduh fuhun uh nuhwuh wuur urruhhh.'

'To an *hour*! OK, OK, we'll be here. Hey – hello – you there – yeah, bring some cig . . .' but Baz had hung up, 'some cigarettes,' said Ziggy, replacing the receiver.

I was beginning to feel the cold again. 'Ziggy,' I said, cradling my arms about my chest, 'can you lend me yur hat and coat, man, am gonna get off?' I sneezed. 'I think I'm coming down with something, feel like shit. Lend us yer coat, willya?'

I'd got mafted while I worked and I'd left my coat on a wall by Foss Island garage. When we went back, it had gone – keys, money, the lot. Uncle Ray's treasured RAF greatcoat. I felt really sick.

'Ziggy, lend me your coat, man?' He went and looked in the window of Blue Lagoon Travel. It was late, after three, and I didn't feel like hanging around fiddling with Radio Luxembourg while he and Hazel curled up on the back seat. Just then Hazel emerged shivering from the car, her mascara beginning to pandarise. 'I want to go home,' she said. She didn't stamp her foot but it came out that way. Ziggy turned to me, his arms organising themselves into an appeal. He was really laying it on, Hey, man, did I mind and all that, Suffragette, Hazel really shouldn't walk home on her own.

'No, of course not,' I interrupted, 'only I'm going that way myself. I could walk Hazel home if you'll just lend me your coat.' I could see him thinking, the girlfriend could go yes, but not the coat. He gathered it closer around him. There was a silence and I noticed that Hazel seemed to want to pee. She took a step towards Ziggy and smiled back at me weakly. 'Baz'll only be twenty minutes,' she said.

'Yeah, to an hour,' I said. 'By then I could be dead.'

Hazel looked down and made an arc in the snow with her shoe. Ziggy looked the other way as though he was a little embarrassed for me.

'OK,' I said, resignedly, 'fucking go then, I'll stay and catch bastard pneumonia.'

They murmured thanks. Hazel stepped forward and kissed my cheek.

On the back seat I watched them disappear. There was still a faint warmth in the leather from where she'd sat, which might have caused a greater stirring in me had I not been so fagged out. I opened the book that Ziggy had left me to read, *The Great Gatsby*, but I found myself reading the lines two or three times over. '"No one ever rightly knew who Gatsby was. Some said he was the son of the Kaiser' . . . 'No one ever rightly knew who Gatsby was some son of the Kaiser."' I kept getting distracted by the scent of Hazel's cheap perfume that contended but couldn't fully prevail over the stale smell of cigarettes and breakdown. I kept hearing her say, 'I'm a prostitute, me,' and feeling the brush of her stockings on my cheekbone where she'd kissed me. Then I got to wondering again what it was that she was going to tell me before we'd been interrupted. I worked my hand under the belt of my now off-white Jaeger trousers and down into my pants. I managed to encourage a tired fantasy, but I had to keep one eye open for Baz and couldn't sustain anything.

SITUATION VACANT

I didn't see Ziggy for a few days after that. I'd caught a cold and was dosed up at the Wigwam on Beecham's Powders and afternoon films, cursing him, he hadn't even called. However, when Tuesday came around I saw him at the dole office. I ducked out of sight behind a noticeboard, watching him like everyone was. After signing he swept by to rejoin the Queen Anne's groupies by the door.

I returned my attention to Situations Vacant. The chef's job at the Bernie still needed filling. I thought of their advert, some fucking actor grinning and saying, 'Treat yerself to a Bernie. As much as you can eat.' Every time it came on, Ovo would swear and stick two's up at the telly and say, 'Treat yer *slag* to a Bernie.' There was no way I was going to go and work for Bernie Inns.

'You gorra spare ciggy, pal?'

'What? Oh, er, yeah.'

A big bastard was standing right next to me, almost seven fuckin feet. I offered him the pack. He took two.

'One fu later,' he said, sticking a Sir Nige behind his ear and looking down at me as if to say, You gorra problem wi that, pal?

'Cool,' I said.

'You wha?'

'Nowt.' I turned my attention back to the orange fabric noticeboard.

'Zat your mate in t' 'at?'

'Pardun?'

'That lad in the fuckin 'at. Am askin *yo* if he's your mate.'

'Oh, *that* lad,' I said. 'Uhm, well, yeah, yeah – I know him.'

'He looks a right pillock, dunee.'

I didn't say anything, instead feigned interest in the Bernie job. I began reading it half out loud, running my finger over the line, 'Nnu nuh nuhr, applicants must supply references and . . .'

'If ah see im am gunna twat him,' said the mountain man.

'Uh huh.'

'Yup. Ah'll 'av you 'n' all if you ger int' way. Thanks fu ciggy, knob end.'

I was aware of him giving me a parting stare, then walking away.

Outside Merchant's House, I glimpsed Ziggy and his entourage already halfway up Swinegate. Hazel was with him. I would have hailed him but I didn't want to appear like a fucking sycophant schoolgirl. I did want to see him though. So I hared round the block, slowing up as I approached the top of

Swinegate, hoping it'd look like I'd just casually bumped into him coming the other way. But when I got to the top of that street, there was no sign of him, so I began to wander back down it.

Swinegate was pedestrianised for tourists. Its shops, most of whose signs began with the words Ye Olde, had once been pet shops and chemists and one, a greengrocer's called Eric's, had been run by two old women, one of whom had a beard. At the top of the road outside Brown's Tea Rooms was a hippie pavement artist looking nervously at the sky and holding his palm up to check for rain. He was pulling back a soaked polythene sheet to reveal a chalky Madonna and Child. But there was no sign of Ziggy. I browsed among the shops a while, trying to picture parrots and hamsters, carrots and King Edwards among the snowstorms and keyrings.

Eventually, I came to rest outside the great Huxtables, out-fitters to the trade. Even without a sign saying as much, Huxtables was without doubt Ye Oldest shop in the street. I recognised my dad's boiler suit in the window, faded by the sun except under the arms where its dark-blue cotton resembled patches of sweat. I was dazzled suddenly by the sun coming out from behind a cloud, reflecting off the buckle of a brand-new bib and brace. Squinting, my eyes travelled along its out-stretched rays————————— and back————————.

This morning had differed from no other morning of late in that I'd contemplated the day ahead in the short time it took to roll and smoke a joint. This was followed by hours of staring into space. I was reminded of the previous evening round at Fizzy Paul's. I was there buying an eighth and Fizzy, while making attempts to light one up from the candle, had said, 'That . . . wunnuv . . . the . . . accumulative effects of smoking dope is . . . an appreciation of the minuscule.' He'd slumped back in his chair gazing closely at the now glowing bud. 'Hmmm,' I'd said, 'good one.'

As that particular memory fell away I was left staring once more at the workwear in Huxtables' window, thinking of those who were trying to stitch me up in a job I didn't want. Trilanger, the Bernie, Vehicle Body Repair – cheerless sweaty apprenticeships in bib and brace. Now then, about your search for work, Mr . . . Mr Glover. When you gunna get yerself a proper job, Billy. A proper job, a career, Kid. I could take it from the Benefit gang, even from Mum and Dad, but not from the Planet of the Mates. Although Si and Ovo had been friends since school, they were becoming strangers to me now. Just the other day, Ovo of all people had asked me virtually this same question. When I'd looked at him in disbelief, he'd growled, 'S'not smart, Kid. We're too fucking *big* to squeeze through turnstiles now.' I was taken down by that. Looking back, I think it was just his way of showing his frustration with me. They'd all been putting by for a foreign holiday, a fortnight in France, St somewhere or other. When I'd pulled out saying I couldn't afford it, Si had offered to put in for me. I'd declined, saying I'd never be able to pay them back. 'Stop ere then, Kid, and fuckin rot in yer fart sack.'

I'd been thinking about what he'd said to me about the turnstile. I had it in mind to go and curse him off a bit about that, just to clear the air, like, then hopefully have a decent chat with him about stuff, Larry life and all. When I'd found him, though, he was kipped out on the sofa snoring his head off. I cursed him anyway, nothing much, just, You fat bastud. It was him who'd always been too big to squeeze through turnstiles, and invariably I'd always ended up paying his way. I'd whispered it so's not to wake him. The walls whispered back.

The hall at the Wigwam had been particularly draughty of late. For extra insulation Deeb had hung a tarpaulin in the corridor, lifted from the railway. Across it, in large stencilled letters, it said, PROPERTY OF PULLMAN BODY REPAIR WORKSHOP. Some of the words were obscured by oil stains leaving just the word BODY swaying imperceptibly in the draughty passage where Gilbert Rathbone had hanged himself.

'It dunt do to dwell on it,' Ovo had said, but I couldn't help myself. It was the third spindle along on the landing, the loose one no one had bothered to repair. The one that rattled when you started upstairs.

I'd talked about it one night with Ziggy in the Ebor. 'It's as though,' I'd said, settling into the booth, 'sometimes I see him, like he's still hanging there. I know he's not, but sometimes I have to go like this to avoid him.' And here, to make my point, I'd limboed out of the booth like a show-off at blind man's buff.

'Although I wasn't there,' Ziggy had said, raising his cup to his lips, 'he said I was his friend.'

'Hmmm . . . yeah, good one.' I'd frowned and sipped my tea.

I suppose in some ways old Gilbert Rathbone was my friend, or at least he was the reason I eventually left the Wigwam; and that, from a man who'd gone struggling and in pain, was a gesture I could only look on as being saintly. Which went along with how I thought of him anyway, very much the martyr.

I remember that particular evening as a series of dwindling pleasures – beer, crisps, a Ski yoghurt, a repeat of *The Great Escape* – blunted by long periods of boredom that turned by degrees into a general sense of unease. The others were all on nights so I was alone in front of the TV. I could barely get any reception on One and *The Great Escape* was practically unwatchable. But there was nothing much else on. The volume, always sporadic, had just given in to a low buzz that matched the acrylic knit of the picture. I switched over for *The Generation Game* and turned down the volume, letting it all just wash over me, like a downer. Once or twice I'd toyed with myself mechanically but I remained limp. Something about the restless movement of the sheets in the draught made it hard to keep my eyes closed.

It was a noise that set me off. The Wigwam was an old house without walls, apt to make the odd noise, but this was different

– a short dragging followed by a sound like a . . . like a crisp packet being ripped open. In need of distraction I scrabbled about the ends of the settee for some of Deeb's pornography. I sifted through it, and settled on *Back Door*. Suddenly, I felt a faint but distinct rush of fear. Slamming myself back against the cushions, I was able to check it against the comforting humiliation of contestants on *The Generation Game*. I tried to concentrate on the pages of *Back Door* but the magazine began to feel clammy in my hand. I didn't respond to any of the couples having intercourse, nor any of the weird prose translated from the German: 'The cellar was barely furnished with a table and a bed but our heroes didn't notice, they were too busy having their pricks taken care of.' They were too busy having their pricks taken care of! I realised I'd read this last line about five times without taking it in. My eyes had even strayed over the German: '*Da Lynn im Grunde genommen auch nur Groschenhefte* . . .' The noise was out in the hall, closer now. My penis was lying limply on my pants. I tried to switch my attention to the medley of household goods going by on the conveyor belt: coffee-maker, fridge freezer, barbecue, cuddly toy. I flung the magazine at the sheets, it landed like a miss on a coconut shy, open but partially hidden by the returning hem of the dirty fabric that seemed to whisper its opinion of me. A sudden gust of wind rattled the letter box and volleyed rain against the window and a shiver goosed over my scalp. 'There's no one here but me!' I shouted out, but my voice was flat and did nothing to dispel the strange atmosphere. I decided I would go upstairs. Whatever it was that was keeping me frozen to the spot couldn't be worse than a warm bed would be pleasurable. Balancing Ovo's Centenary drugs tin and a glass of beer on the copy of *Back Door*, I turned the telly off. It shrank to a white dot, and it was by its accompanying glow I entered the passage.

At first, I didn't see him hanging there. There was a naked blue bulb up at the top of the house and an orange one bathing the passage. I slid through the sheet and turned off the hall light and it was then, trying to balance my beer, that I noticed an unfamiliar shadow in the passage. I approached the stair, my free hand groping through the blue gloom for the banister. A faint sound took up the space. I froze and listened. Then it was louder, no mistake. The spindle overhead, third along, creaked like a gibbet. I heard my name on the draught, 'Biiiiiileeeee.' I screamed, I think. I don't know. I was so fucking scared I ran backwards through the wall and the sheets tore free and wrapped themselves around me. I was swaddled like a mummy and fell to the floor. I tried to sit up, tear the sheet from my face so I could get over to the door and fucking get the fucking fuck out. And then, above the hammering in my chest, I heard it: slow creaking footsteps on the stairs.

As the lights went on, the sheets were pulled off. Si, Deeb and Ovo fell about killing themselves laughing. Deeb was bollocko except for a pork-pie hat, speeding to fuck. He grabbed the Ewbank and was tearing round the room.

'You fucking wankers!' I yelled.

'Whoooooow, look who's talking,' said Si.

'Hey, Kid – yu've gone white as a sheet.'

They all fell about at that.

They'd been planning this for weeks, knowing how freaked out I was about the old Gilbert thing. The dummy had been pieced together in the attic from old clothes and straw. It was no penny guy, though. Even in my trembling anger, as I stomped upstairs, I was struck by the attention to detail. The hair was real, swept up from the barber's floor. I gave the thing a voodoo kick in its knackers and it was only later, remembering Ovo uncharacteristically and insistently sweeping up after a kitchen haircut, that I realised the Polly blond locks were in fact my own.

It had been at Christmas, while spraying fake snow in the corners of all the windows, that we'd begun talking again about all of us doing something, about getting out.

Si's cousin Dave Elmer had long since departed. He sent us postcards from all over the world. We'd read them in silence and prop them behind the clock on the mantelpiece. Bit by bit the palm trees and beaches would work their way into some spliff action. Ever since then, doing something, *really* doing something, became known as 'Doing The Elmer'.

'Nearly did the fucking Elmer today,' said Ovo, the night after they'd spooked me. His voice was momentarily muffled as he came through the sheets, balancing his Centenary drugs tin and a cup of tea. Every week he'd say this, without fail.

'Oh yeah,' said Deeb, trying to separate the beer-soaked pages of *Back Door*. 'How come?'

'Yeah,' replied Ovo, gazing at what was left of Dave's postcard.

I didn't say anything. Deep down I knew that, along with that hanging certainty in the hall, no one at the Wigwam was ever going to do the 'FUCKING ELMA', I shouted out, reacting to and banishing my thoughts.

I was back standing in front of Huxtables' window and had caused some passers-bys to jump. I watched them gather in their kids and hurry along. I passed a hand over my face, Jesus, and looked at the overalls again. The sunbeam reflecting from the buckle on the bib and brace had gone. Ziggy Low, the hope for a brighter future. Even if he hadn't called me I was suddenly filled with a strange love for him. I brushed hair from my eyes, the sudden movement drawing my attention to my own reflection, there among dinner ladies and plumbers' mates, uncannily positioned beneath a chef's hat, the faceless old hessian mannequin playing perfect host to my features. This was the job the DHSS would have me do, ten times more frightening than Aleister Crowley's red and black feast. I saw myself sweating over a huge cauldron, growing old. The clouds in the blue sky moved thunderously across the dark glass to the sudden accompaniment of a fairground waltz. I caught the reflection of an organ grinder with a chattering monkey. He was doing that big elbowy thing, cranking his machine, stirring my imagination. I returned to examining myself as a chef again.

There's no telling how long I'd have been compelled to engage in this painful speculation, had I not been startled by Ziggy's ghostly reflection hoving into view on Huxtables' front window, followed by the usual troop of Queen Anne's schoolgirls in their green uniforms and short pleated skirts. Cut off at their knees by the tiles below the fenestration, the procession made its way over to the far wall. The fedora weaved in and out of the plumbers' mates, dinner ladies and chefs. I spun round on my heel. They'd reached the top of the street and were passing the chalky pavement artist.

'Hey, Ziggy!' I yelled. They were coming out of one of the teashops further down.

'Oh, hi, man,' he called laconically.

I started up the street towards him. We were both too cool to stop and chat but carried on the conversation in passing.

'How y' doin, man?'

'Cool, man, cool.'

Some of the Queen Anne's schoolgirls had lit cigarettes and, as usual, were making a big thing of smoking them. Hazel was among them, her hair plastered to her face by a shower of rain. She gave me a smile and I nodded at her. I nodded at the organ grinder too, and at his monkey, and I was still nodding when Ziggy said, 'You're coming to the gig, yeah?'

Had he betrayed a note of concern? I nodded. 'Yeah.' We drew level, then over my shoulder I said, 'Should be a scream, huh?'

Strange how it then happened. Hazel and the girls in green stopped abruptly. Ziggy sallied on into the middle of the road and turning from the hip he called back, 'You'll be the one that's screaming, man.'

At that precise moment a red car came round the corner very fast and smashed straight into Ziggy. He was up on the bonnet for a few seconds. The screech was the last sound before a cod-like slap as Ziggy rolled off on to the deck. Sound fell away like science fiction: the city suddenly frozen, veiled like a room awaiting decoration. A low-pitched zinging in my ears seemed to affect my balance as I ran towards him, to where he lay.

I fell to my knees next to him in the puddles but I wasn't sure what to do. I was somehow afraid to touch. His eyes were closed, his head a little to one side. I gently lifted it, the blood beating in my arms and throbbing in my palms. With the weight of his neck in one hand, his head flopped back revealing bad razor-burn. 'Ziggy,' I breathed. I switched hands to wipe sweat from my palm and as I drew it into the open I realised that it wasn't sweat but blood that I'd begun wiping on my shirt. Sound returned, sound crashed in on me. As prophesied, we were indeed the ones who were screaming. Hazel had dropped to her knees beside me, the musculature of her face struggling to hold back hysterical sobbing like a dam about to give way. She began rocking, 'Ziggy, oh, Ziggy.'

I looked up. The driver was out of his car now, a dark cut-out against the sun.

'Uddy hell, did you see that? He wa'nt lookin, jus stepped owt infron' o' me.'

He began to address the gathering crowd. A monkey appeared at my shoulder. The organ grinder removed his comedy hat. I could hear the jangling of the chalky pavement artist's beads.

'Did you see tha . . .'

I let his voice trail off as the organ slurred to its untended end.

It was cold in the shadow of the car and I shivered as the Queen Anne's schoolgirls huddled in a worried scrum above me. Hazel was completely silent, staring at the blood on her hand. I lowered Ziggy's head on to my lap and brushed his dyed hair from his eyes.

'Ziggy?' I whispered croakily. 'Ziggy?'

A bustling voice came pushing through. 'Has he swallowed his tongue? Let me through, let me through there, I'm a nurse.' A plump lady bent down and grabbed his face with strong hands, turned it this way and that and put her fingers in his mouth examining him like a horse. 'Are these his own?' she said, agitating his front teeth.

'What?'

'He can swallow em,' she said. 'Are you his friend?'

'What?' I said again.

The organ gave one last groan, at which Ziggy's eyelashes fluttered and he blinked, once, and then again. He chimed in with a low moan of his own and began to rub his head from side to side against my tensed thigh. Then he opened his eyes.

'Ooooaahuw . . . wowhh.' He pulled himself upright, shooting his hand to the back of his cranium. He winced and his eyes clenched shut. 'Wowhh . . . wow . . . slow down, Arthur,' he flexed his shoulder blades, 'stick to thirty . . . oahhwow.'

It wasn't natural, I couldn't have heard him right. His eyes were open again and he was suddenly aware of the blood on his hand. I stood back, in awe of the extent of Ziggy's obsession. The Queen Anne's schoolgirls were spilling around him, all sympathy, helping him to his feet. My upper lip was throbbing gently where I'd been biting it.

He began a little shakily to dust himself down. The nurse was running through some fast checks. She stood up briskly. 'Seems fine.'

An American tourist who'd retrieved Ziggy's fedora from the road (but not before it had been flattened by a van) suddenly punched it out. 'Here y'ar, fella,' he said, dealing it a swift karate chop to the top. 'You OK, boy?'

'Yes,' said Ziggy, slightly dazed, 'thanks.' He took the hat from the American and was busy pinching it in at the front when the driver launched in.

'That were a bloody daft thing to do, you cud ave got yerself killed, y' daft cunt. Ere, jorwiz go bowt wi' yer eyes shut? Ere, are you listenin to me, you . . . you?' He stammered, giving Ziggy the once over, then, apparently satisfied with his appraisal, 'YOU FREAK!'

Ziggy, meanwhile, was crouching down by the wheel of the red Allegro trying to free his coat that was trapped beneath it.

'WEIRDO!' The driver bellowed. 'Are you listnin to me? Fifteen year I've been drivin and never s'much as a scrape in all that time.'

This, judging by the state of his auto, was hard to believe.

Ziggy looked up at him, squinting in the sun.

'Could you reverse please, Arthur. My coat's trapped under your wheel.'

'Arthur? Who the bloody hell's Arthur? I'm gunna get radged wi' you, son, see if am not. D'y' want mi to get radged wi' yer, d'yer? WELL, D'YER?'

In this shambles I'd advanced one or two thoughts of my own, a sense of déjà vu. The driver, the driver. Maybe it was the tear in his sheepskin, I couldn't be sure, but there was something familiar. The gravelly cough. Something put me in mind of that bloke in the dole office who'd wanted to twat Ziggy. No sooner had I conjured him into being than a battle cry went up behind me. I spun round to confront the bastard reality barrelling up Swinegate, a traffic cone on his head. His right fist was biffing the air, wheezing uppercuts. Oh fuck, I said under my breath.

'What's trouble, pal?' he asked the driver, panting heavily.

'This cunt ere.' The driver wagged his finger at Ziggy. 'Jus fuckin stepped owt in front o' me wi' out s' much 's lookin.'

'What?' He turned his head. 'You mean THAT!' Conehead's finger rose through a shower of spittle to stab at Ziggy. 'Is what 'e's tellin mi right?'

Ziggy went limp like a rag doll under his inquisition.

With gratuitous belligerence the fingers drilled out an Italian rhythm on his concave chest. 'Withart . . . s'much . . . as lukin.'

Ziggy attempted to wipe away some globules of spit that had landed on his chin. Coney slapped his hand.

'Eh, am talkin to you, puff'ouse. Silly 'ead.'

'Oh man,' groaned the hippie pavement artist as Coney stomped all over his chalky Madonna and Child.

Coney frowned, took a step back, and like a pugilist began to pace around. 'Someone say summat, eh! Thought not.' He turned back to Ziggy and let out a sorrowful howl. 'Aahhuu, whud y' jus LOOK at that.' He screwed up his eyes and shook his head as though he himself couldn't bear to. If you had to guess what he was looking at you'd imagine nothing less than wife or daughter in a gang-bang home movie. He dragged his limbs like a tragic pantomime ape. 'Prat neck. I'm fucking talkin to you,' he howled.

Ziggy bowed his head, his fedora falling neatly into his hand. Coney dropped the theatre at this and started getting really mad. The fluorescent orange of the traffic cone was clashing badly with his reddening face, textured like a slice of watermelon.

'Eh, prat neck, duz your mam know you've borrowed 'er hat? WELL? DUZ SHE?'

I could see something shaping up and I faltered, 'Look, mate, why don't y' jus forget . . .'

He looked round, moved fast. I saw his clothing crease then crumple as his boot found my knackers. He laced his fingers and cracked all his knuckles out in front of him, swivelling like a tank turret to face Ziggy.

During my decking, Ziggy had begun to raise his face to the

sky and turn it sideways, like a fey sunbather. Lifting up his eyepatch, he placed a finger under his bottom lid and pulled down the bruised skin, exposing the delicate socket and ball. With his free forefinger Ziggy was tapping at the taut skin under his eyeliner. Driver man and Coney were looking on nonplussed, as though the landlord had called time prematurely.

I was feeling pretty nauseous after that kick in the balls, notwithstanding the *mental* anguish connected with those soft ovals. It was as if pinpricks of light were exploding inside me and those two soft things were grinding across some raw membrane. The grey slabs of the pavement lay there impassively as I humped them in agony. All eyes were on Zig and, even in my pain, mine were too. Ziggy was still tapping his eye. I'd seen him do this before and I knew what was coming.

'Leave him alone, you big bully, can't you see he's in shock?' protested Hazel.

A clownish smile, befitting a man with a cone on his head, spread over Coney's wide-set features. The red Allegro driver looked slightly worried as though he thought Ziggy may have actually sustained some kind of brain damage in his fall. Zig tapped out the seconds before the pain began, his eyelashes quivering slightly. Oddly, I took pleasure in knowing that Ziggy would soon be in as much pain as me. Coney's clownish grin had vanished and I could see globules of spit, caught in his walrus tache, sparkling in the troubled sunlight.

'Are you cheeking me, cunt?' said Coney.

Ziggy tapped.

'EH, REETARD, IS THA . . . ?' He shuffled his shoulders and blew on his fists. Holding up the left one for Ziggy to see he said, simply, 'Hospital.' Then noisily kissing the right hand he introduced it as 'Cemetery.' 'Eeny meany miney mo, eh! thas me, int it? I'm the meany ere. Which one's it to be then, cunt, which . . .'

'Now hang on there, pal,' began the driver, 'this cunt's soft int head. You can't . . .'

But Coney palmed him off. 'Stay out of this, pal.' He snarled. 'This cunt needs teaching a LESSON, YEAHHHH.'

And without further ado he smashed his huge hospital fist into Ziggy's frail mascara'd face but, out of some passing courtesy, roughly in the spot indicated. The power of the punch knocked Zig back on to the bonnet for the second time that morning where, with a slow somersault, he fell off the far wing on to the road, pursued by Queen Anne schoolgirls.

'Taxi for David Bowie,' said Coneman, cupping his hand round his mouth. Then, grinning, he turned to the driver. 'Hey up, ah tell you what we've gorra do now, hold that freak down and stamp on his bollocks so's 'is sort can't fucking breed.'

'You can if y'want, pal, am fucking off. I ant got any insurance fir this.' He threw his car a huge nod. 'Und if scuffers see that . . .' he headed an invisible ball to where Ziggy was hauling himself up on to his knees, 'th'll do yer.'

I wrung my eyes as the last twinge of pain buckled my insides. The door of the red Allegro slammed shut and I opened my eyes just in time to see a brief and manly handshake through the open window as though some odd job had been taken care of. 'Dave's the name,' said Coney.

The driver's name was lost in the revving of the engine. Evidently it wasn't Arthur.

I helped myself up with the aid of a drainpipe. Ziggy was examining his face in the wing mirror of a parked car. I picked up his hat, which had once more been flattened. The scant crowd dispersed. No sign of the nurse. The pale-blue lining of Ziggy's coat was flapping in the wheel arch of the red Allegro. After a few yards it tore its way free, leaving a wisp of silk shivering in the mud flap. I imagined Driver Man later extricating it in disgust.

Cupping my crotch I staggered over to Ziggy. All that pain draining out of my knackers had left me feeling pretty spacey. I picked his coat off the road and wrapped it round him. More or less in silence, with the help of Ziggy's loyal fans, we bore him up, took his weight on our shoulders and made our way very slowly to the Theatre bar for a tea.

'Oh by jingo!' whispered Ziggy.

LOW RISK

Years after that cup of tea at the Theatre bar, five years, appropriately enough, after that awkward cup of tea at the Theatre bar, I often find myself trying to piece together his movements after I left him that afternoon, that afternoon being the last time I saw him.

I've pretty much lost touch with the old city of Eboracum. I've lost myself in the anonymous streets of the new capital now. But I often think of Ziggy, wonder what's become of him. It's as if he disappeared into thin air – no one's seen or heard of him. Occasionally, on a busy street I'll force my way though disgruntled shoppers to reach out, like Diana Ross, to someone 'who looks like you do'. Well, from behind he did anyway. One time, a thespian, outside the Royal Court, it was his hat and coat, I guess. One time, I even got up from a table at a crowded West End restaurant to examine a hat hanging on a coat peg, accosting the waiter, 'Scuse me, ju happen to know who came in wearing this hat?' and as I asked my eyes were already scanning the tables. And it was me who took the Halifax train over to Todmorden that time, where from his aunt I got only a slow shaking of the head on her doorstep. The dying light in her eyes as she answered the door to find only me had already answered my question. Being very roughly the same build as Ziggy I wondered if . . . for a moment . . . through the net curtains . . . she'd thought. But no, she'd forgotten I was coming. 'I'm sorry,' I said. 'I wrote to tell you, perhaps it got lost in the post.' The small passageway was lit by the glow from the TV. Peering over her shoulder, I could see, hanging on a coat peg above a shopping bag and football scarf, Ziggy's old fedora. I was wondering why she'd not been able to bring herself to chuck it when I found myself saying, 'He came back here then? I thought he probably had. And then he left again, did he? Didn't say where, no? But you would've heard if anything had happened . . . no . . . don't you think?' Had she tried the police, hmm.

Apparently, he was what they called a Low Risk, someone 'of age' with no mental problems and not requiring medication. The thinking was, such a person could look after themselves. She told me that the officer in charge of the 'miz puz' files had said if it wasn't for the fact that he'd left his possessions behind (Bowie memorabilia), if it wasn't for this, he'd continued, raising his eyerows at the B544 form as he jotted down 'Bow . . . ee mem . . . ora . . . beel . . . ia', he wouldn't even have run the usual checks: hospitals, ports, morgues.

Had she thought of hiring a private detective? I asked, as though I thought nothing of hiring private dicks, did it all the time. Her eyes widened. 'No, just a thought,' I said.

She had tried the spiritualist church, though. She smiled. No, she said, she didn't go in for that, it was a sister she was trying to contact, more of a day out really, tea and biscuits afterwards, you know. As I feigned interest, she said that as it happened she was going again tomorrow, did I want to go with her?

The mysteries of Ziggy's birth and his immediate family had all been explained away, made humdrum. Parents killed in a car crash, his sister, much older (he never knew her), emigrated to Australia, etc. 'Yes,' she said, 'all leads have been checked.' I smiled to hear this official lingo on her lips. 'Will you take a piece of cake for the journey?' I declined the Battenberg and closed the gate behind me, wishing I hadn't come.

No one else reported Ziggy missing. With Ziggy it was hard to explain, it would have just been uncool somehow, like . . . like interfering. What came to light was how little anyone really knew him. Hazel was giving out some really strange widow vibe, playing it in black. Baz and Purdcake just got on with their lives.

So it seemed to fall on me to make enquiries. Mind, what sparse information I gathered (scribbled on beer mats and torn napkins) was fairly worthless. I roughed it out thus in a spiral-bound notebook:

23 March 1981. Information relating to the disappearance
of Ziggy Low, aka Arthur Bannockburn:

1. He'd begun by coming through from Halifax way to the futurist nights at the Roxy – this was over a year ago (roughly the time I was on my way to Scotland).

2. At first he used to sleep in his car – and drive back next day.

3. Occasionally he got off with a girl and slept at her place. (These girls candidly remembered him as being great in bed but that was about all they did remember.)

4. He got a bedsit in the red-light district down by the river where no one ever visited him.

5. This is where he met Joby Schmidt. He heard him performing a set one night as he passed the Water Rat. The pub is a strange mix of prostitutes, jazz buffs and riverboat dwellers. Ziggy had sat in the corner and after the set had finished approached Joby about giving him some sax lessons. It was Joby who'd introduced him to the musicians he auditioned for his band. One of them, Sandy, a bass guitarist, had brought in Baz Barrel to take some publicity shots (one of which I later used for the poster). Through Baz he met Alex Purdey who let him my old bedroom above the shop to rehearse in. The various musicians Ziggy worked with or seemed to know, cared less than anyone. Instead, they talked a little bitterly of how he broke up the band to go solo just before the gig.

6. About the Ghost Rider routine: when he teamed up with

Lasher to become Inglewood – Lasher is altogether too gone to be of any use anyhow – he seemed to resemble for real the gothic horror he faked up in his working life.

7. About two days before we fly-posted the town, Ziggy had met that weird old sailor in a caravan near the disused carriage works. When I went back to the caravan site the sailor had moved on.

8. The waitress at the Theatre bar whom I'd seen taking his order from on top of the bus remembered him very well, but looked suspicious when I started asking her questions. Did anyone join him that you remembered? Did he say anything unusual? Did he say *anything*? She shrugged and began wiping a table. Before I left she turned round and said, 'Anyway, he was a weirdee,' as though that sort of wrapped it up.

SOMETHING FROM A DISTANCE

Ziggy had once said to me, 'I want you to think beyond this.' Something Mr Newton said maybe? Whatever, the next day at three p.m., I found myself on my way to meet his aunt outside the spiritualist church in Halifax.

Five Faversham Place was a grand old Victorian building in a part of town that had seen better days. I ducked in out of the rain and stood about in the hallway, at the foot of a wide majestic staircase. When Ziggy's aunt appeared, flapping the rain off her brolly, I paid for two tickets and followed her up to a first-floor room.

On the landing I got a brief low-down on what to expect from a white-haired lady whom Ziggy's aunt introduced as a friend of Arthur's. That made me smile and the woman smiled back, her translucent hands, adorned with amethysts, clasped under her powdered chin. 'This is your first time? Well, it's all very simple, dear. When he contacts someone – a spirit – he describes them, you see, and usually says he can feel their pain. Or he might say that he has a message for someone, and then he'll say, "Can anyone take this?" Which is the usual thing and if you think you know the person he's made contact with, and you want to hear the message, you put your hand up and say, "I can take it." Do you follow, dear?'

The room was set up like a lecture hall. I was surprised how full it was and there was even some delay getting started while more chairs were brought in from another room. We sat at the back and while we waited I noticed a man pacing up and down the aisle, his hands in a praying position, thoughtfully drubbing the tips of his fingers on his lips. There was a coach party of old women in from Todd. I thought because of his attire, he was very likely the driver. He was portly and his blazer and grey Farrar's Stay Prest were stretched at the seams. He had curly red hair, a large moustache and silver-rimmed Reactolites. Altogether, he reminded me a lot of Unreasonable Keith, the coach driver who'd splashed Ziggy that day outside the bus terminus – the day I returned from my uncle's funeral. My uncle William – Jeeesus! I'd forgotten about him. I hoped he wouldn't be contacting me.

As it turned out, this Unreasonable Keith lookalike was in fact the medium. I don't know why but I'd been expecting someone in a cloak. When everyone was seated he jumped up heavily on to the rostrum. A woman handed him up a glass of water, which he knocked back thirstily letting out a long 'Ahhh' of satisfaction that transformed into one of pain. He began immediately to heave his leg around as though he'd trapped a sciatic nerve or something and he had a hand up to his brow. 'Aghhh, I'm getting a pain, I'm getting a pain right here in my back, here! Oooh, I'm getting a pain. Can anyone take this.' There was some genuine urgency in his tone.

From the back we had a view of all the old women's heads.

None moved. He continued struggling up and down the stage. 'Anybody? No? Aghhh.' He let off an unfortunate fart. There were two large windows either side of the lectern, and as he limped in front of them he looked like a plump Bruce Forsyth – one hand on his brow, the other on his hip. There were no takers for his limping man, and after a few more times up and down the stage he sought to make it go away by closing his eyes, removing his spectacles and tightly pinching the bridge of his nose. He did this for thirty seconds or so, which seemed like a long time to be in spiritual pain. Then he looked up and made some crack about it probably just being to do with all the cream teas he'd had while on the spiritualist circuit down in Devon. I didn't know whether he meant the weighty limp or the fart. I didn't really get it at all. There was certainly no word from Ziggy.

It wasn't till later, back home in Eboracum, making my way across town, that something began to niggle. At the top of Swinegate, where Ziggy had been knocked down, I recalled his stricken figure and how – this was sort of freaky – how he'd held his back and winced as we'd helped him to the Theatre bar. His phantom limped on in my head. A car honked. I was standing at a pelican, which was pipping away for me to cross.

What it did, this sciatic memory, it took me right back to the Theatre bar and the last time I'd seen him.

THE LAST ORDER OF ZIGGY LOW

He was sitting sipping his tea, wrapped in his torn coat like a nearly drowned survivor. His eye was swelling up and turning an insipid yellow. One by one the Queen Anne's schoolgirls had all drifted away, Hazel leaving last. Then we were alone and he was staring at the tyre tracks on his fedora that he'd placed on the table in front of him. I'd badly wanted to leave with Hazel. She'd tried to comfort him but it was like an arm round a statue. So she'd finished up her ice cream and, smiling at me, said, 'I've got to go, Billy, I have to change for work. J'u wanna share a taxi with me?' She looked great with her wet hair and torn tights, but I thought someone should probably stay with Ziggy, he looked completely done in.

In all the time we'd sat there he'd neither stirred nor uttered a word. As Hazel let the door swing shut behind her, the draught caught the back of his neck and he collapsed fully inside his coat. I had the distinct impression that if I were to reach forward and gently loosen a button, cold ash would spill out of him on to the carpet. I breathed in deeply to indicate that when I breathed out I would be saying, I'm going now, Ziggy, are you sure you're OK? I held up five fingers in front of him and he winced as my chair scraped backwards. His left eye was almost closed now, like the cleft in an unripe plum, and the swelling was being threatened by all sorts of colours. I had a feeling he'd gone too far this time and pictured the expressions of the doctors and nurses at out-patients.

'What?' I said. He'd spoken.

'I can't explain but –' He lifted his hand in front of his face and murmured something I didn't catch.

Outside the Theatre, I jumped on a bus and from the top deck I pressed my face against the glass to get a last glimpse of him. He was studying himself up close in the back of the spoon Hazel had been using for her ice cream. With one hand shielding his good eye, he brought the smeared spoon as close to the raw plum as possible. Then, as the bus started moving, he began to slowly draw the spoon away until it was at arm's length. He didn't see the waitress standing over him in analyst pose, pad and pen at the ready. The bus lurched forward into the stream of traffic and the last I could see of him was his hand in his coat nursing his ribs, the bosom of the waitress heaving an impatient sigh.

'Henna more fares, please?'

I twisted round to face the conductor. 'What?' I said.

He looked at me blankly, then said again, 'Henna more fares?'

'Sorry, I thought you said something else.'

'You want to clear your ears out,' he joked, handing me a ticket. I rolled it up like a cigarette and drew on it heavily. Something he'd said as I was leaving. He'd said something else. I smoked on absently, blowing out my ruminations.

There was a complex pattern of grease on the window, left by someone's hair resting there. For a few moments I examined it with disdain, imagining the dejected citizen who'd left it, and then, tentatively, I lowered my head to where his had been. I had a queer vibrating feeling in my stomach as the bus once more got snagged in traffic.

COSMIC RISK

Ziggy's occultation took the form of growing speculation, and with every day that went by that speculation grew.

He was supposed to be playing a gig on Joby's barge on Saturday the thirty-first. On the Friday morning I went along to see him. The river was in flood and coffee-coloured, raging along in torrent mode, and I felt giddy crossing the gangplank.

Old Joby was down below, drinking a beer. He hadn't shaved and seemed to be on his nerves about it all. I was surprised to find he hadn't yet cancelled the gig – he was convinced Ziggy wouldn't let him down, that he'd show. In the dark V of the prow, the stage area where Ziggy was to perform, candles were burning, guttering in the breeze from the raised forward hatch. It was a kind of shrine, I realised. Between the candles was a saxophone in its stand and propped up against it a picture of Ziggy that Baz had taken. In front of that, like mince pies left out for Santa, Ziggy's favourite brand of cigarettes. They were opened with the filters sticking out like the pipes on a church organ, the way cute waitresses bring them to you in smart restaurants. Once Ziggy had said, Why arrive when you can really turn up? and Joby had read much into this. He was always misquoting it, 'Vy come ven you can really arrive?' I think he thought at any moment Ziggy would simply appear shinning down a rope or something, through a porthole or a trapdoor. 'Anyone aboard? Suffragettes . . . Don't be suspicious . . . Why arrive . . . ?' And as if to illustrate this point he picked up the book he was reading, *Cities of the Red Night* by William Burroughs. He stabbed at a page and read some lines to me in his crazy German accent: 'Zer chic clients make zer entrances through trapdoors in zer floor and ceiling, or through disguised side entrances, and even now zey are popping up sroow zer floor in green drag screaming like mandrakes dropping down through zer ceiling in gauzy parachutes.' I think he was losing his hold, old Joby.

'This is kind of important to you, isn't it?' I said.

'Important, ah, I fuckin sink so,' he said, trying to look relaxed. He was rolling a joint and his tongue darted like a reptile's at the gum arabic of the Rizla. He went over to Ziggy's shrine and before I could tell him it was bad luck he'd used one of the candles to light his joint. 'Oh, ya, real April showers,' he said gruffly. 'Gutt, *fuckin* gutt.'

He was wearing a rainbow sweater with knitted crotchets and quavers. I couldn't take his depression seriously. His jumper wouldn't let me.

SAIL AT DAWN

I had my own theory as to the whereabouts of Z. Low: far away somewhere, propping up a bar on a Greek island. There was a reason for this, some vague mention, half heard, half remembered, that only in hindsight made sense. I imagined him a little sloshed, slurring with the hint of a Sean Connery inflection that he was soon to play a gig. 'No, notch here.' I'm imagining him then glancing at his watch. Everyone would be expecting him to show . . .

The next night some of us did. CANCELLED had been pasted like a suffragette's sash over the Forthcoming Attraction poster – the smoking silhouette, the raked fedora.

I recall the Low clones drifting aimlessly away through the Prossies with their bare legs and umbrellas.

SAILOR GOSSIP

The beginning of May was unseasonably cold. No sign of spring. We would feed the fire splinters of Purdcake's wardrobe, Purds prodding the coals and prodding for gossip. Although he was trying to get over his Anthony Blanche phase, his eyelids couldn't help fluttering whenever he wanted to hear scandal.

'We just snogged,' I said.

He looked away like a bored bovine chewing, pointing with a veneered splinter to his spare room. 'Whu-ot, in there, dihr boy?'

My old room, Ziggy's room, where he'd slept with Hazel on the mattress from the shove-me-up. Hazel was still holed up there, sleeping on that fucking mattress, a raft in a sea of Ziggy's stuff, all his amps and everything. She'd left school at Easter and was doing more waitressing at Plunkets.

It was on one of her nights off I'd gone round to Grimshaws's on the off-chance, and thrown gravel at the window. Hazel had opened the first-floor sash.

'Oh, hi,' she'd called down. 'You've just missed them, they've gone to the pub.'

'Ah! Are you coming?'

'I don't know, wait there.'

She'd come down to the door cinched in a 1940s-style Prussian-blue backless and I'd had the feeling I'd interrupted something. She'd taken me inside and for a while I'd watched her gazing into the fire. She had make-up on, lots. The dress had a repeated sugar cube design that glistened in the firelight. It was warm to the touch too, like fresh tarmac.

'Are we alone?' I'd asked, but not too suavely, more speculative and nervy.

She'd looked up at me, unclasping her arms from her knees. Then, placing them behind her, palms down, she'd leant back and stretched out her long legs. 'They won't be back for ages,' she'd said.

'Maybe . . .' I'd looked out the window at the bad weather and back at Hazel pulling a fifties-style pin-up pose on the rug. 'Maybe I'll just stay for a bit?'

I didn't really feel like talking about what happened next with Purdcake and co. They were pressing me for details. 'Use your imagination, can't you. Yu've gotta good imagination. You should be writing scripts for Twentieth Century-*Fox* with your imagination.'

Purdcake nodded. 'As a matter of fact I'm working 'n a script. It all takes place in a mental hospital.' I began to tune out when he began talking about Ziggy appearing on a 'wuh-hite Arabian charger, dihr boy'. Most nights someone would ask for any new word on the Zigster but tonight Purdcake had picked up on my indifference.

'She was never his girlfriend,' I said.

'No no,' he said, 'no, of course not. Anyway, it's been weeks.'

'Months actually, two and a bit.' I got up to break more wood off his wardrobe, not because the fire needed it, I just felt like it.

'Just shows you how time flies,' said Purdey into the fire, 'even when you're not enjoying yourself.'

The strangest thing was, up until I'd snogged Hazel, there'd been no definitive acknowledgement of his departure. Now I quite wanted it to be fully established. Some voiced doubts about his return but the popularly held belief was that he'd soon be making a heroic comeback. Fragments of an *NME* interview tolled through my head – He's back, rested, relaxed, tanned.

Purdcake had intuited that I was in love with Hazel. At least that's what I thought. Mostly, though, I was in awe of her beauty. In our backwater she was too tall, too skinny, white as a sheet and in need of a good pie rammed down her neck. These were the kind of remarks she had to put up with. No wonder she wanted to do The Elmer. Quietly, she'd pursued this model idea – a portfolio and all those insufferable hand movements of Baz from behind the lens.

VIENNA

It was maybe two, three weeks after I snogged her that she got her first break modelling, quit Plunks and moved to London. In that time we'd been meeting up for walks, holding hands, sheltering from showers, going to the pictures and that type of thing. We even took a rowboat on the river. She was quite into dropping acid. I held up my hands. Maybe later, I'd said, and told her a bit about my breakdown and all. I thought she was listening but I'm not sure now, perhaps it was all just so much more Vienna to her. We kissed a lot but never fucked. Doncaster – I didn't even feel her cunt. Just feeling up on the outside of clothing, titting up on Purdey's rug before that gay Geordie twat Footsick would come in and disturb us. But I was pretty happy on that slow chuffer. Hazel, though, had other ideas. She wanted King's Cross, the real King's Cross, on an Intercity 125. I imagined her lugging her case down the platform, some cad offering to lend a hand – 'Allow me, bew-di-full.'

It was Mugeen, the Irish waitress with the strange name, who told me.

'I'm sorry, luvee, she's ghaaan.'

'Left already?'

'Uhmm, yes.'

'When will she be back?'

'No, she's ghaan to Lahndun, darlun.'

'To London! Oh, uhm, well, d'you know when she'll be back?'

I was looking around as though half expecting to see her emerge from the kitchens. I tilted my head reading the Stones' signatures on the wall, absently mouthing Brian Jones, Charlie Watts . . .

'Are you all right, dear? D'you wan a drink?'

'Wha?'

'D'you wan a drink?'

'Oh, yeah, please.'

I sat at the bar, hot and flushed, firing questions at the waitresses as they rushed about. Going a little wholesale with the booze, I suggested, amid bubbles of false laughter, that, She'll, ho ho, no doubt call me in a few days . . . you know, when she gets settled. I shaded my eyes and began to sort of shake with laughter. 'Model you say, thas top. Don't have an address, no? She's gonna write . . . yes . . . let you all know . . . ho ho, thas great.' I finished my drink, pissed up now. 'If she gez in tush, asg her zu call me, wurt you.'

Out on the street I was, as I'd anticipated, unsteady on my feet. An appalling wave of Joy Division-style self-pity came over me. What I fancied was taking some drugs and I knew what to get and where to get them. I had the credit, too.

WHERE IS MY OAR?

When, a few days later, I asked Purdcake if he'd known Hazel was planning to leave, he didn't answer me straight, but made some veiled suggestion that, anyway, what I really wanted was to fuck Ziggy, and as I couldn't square that with my dreary sexuality I wanted to fuck his girlfriend instead. He started making some fucking comparison between me and Charles Ryder fucking Sebastian Flyte's sister.

'Amazing,' I said, shaking my head. 'Is that what you told her?'

'No.'

'But you told her I was mad?'

'No.'

'Insane?'

'No.'

'Oh yes, I think so.'

PART III

IN THE TIME OF THE STANDPIPE

Records dating back to Roman times had shown this to be Eboracum's hottest ever July. Water rationing had come into effect. There was a hosepipe ban and car washes all over the city stood dry and empty. People began to fill baths, sinks, pans, bottles, any receptacle they could get their hands on, full to overflowing. When, eventually, the mains was turned off for long hours of the day, there'd be long queues at the standpipes at the end of each street. Not everyone was put out by this. At the local hardware shop there was a run on buckets and their price had soared.

I woke early at the Wigwam to find the thin curtains suffused with light streaming around their edges and laying itself in long strips across the ceiling. I tried going back to sleep but the sun was permeating my eyelids. Coming from the middle of my room was a gentle rubber-lipped snoring from Sumo, our new houseguest crashed out on a blue canvas camp bed. Sumo was a bisexual drifter who'd drunk himself into a strange likeness to a Japanese wrestler. Too hot for a sheet, he was completely bollocko, the line of his vest and pants delineated by raw sunburn. I turned over to face the wall so I wouldn't have to suffer the sight of him.

We'd got the bed for him from the Under a Tenner section in the back of the *Echo*:

For sale: Blue foldaway bed, ideal for overweight guests, friends and relatives. Nuh nuh nuh nuh nuh.
Fantastic bargain – Evenings after six.

'It's a misprint,' had come a sad man's weaselly voice on the other end of the phone. 'It's not overweight guests, it's over*night* guests.'

'Oh, I see,' I'd said. 'So, what, the ad should read: "Blue foldaway bed, ideal for overnight guests, friends and relatives who drop in unexpectedly. Never used." Is that right?'

'Yes,' had come the sad voice. 'Never used.'

'Well, we'll take it anyway.'

It was going to be another scorching day. This morning, then, would differ from no other of late, in that I'd wait for Si, Deeb and Ovo to leave for work before venturing downstairs. Sumo and Robin would sleep in till about eleven or twelve, so, for a few precious hours, I'd have the house to myself. If either of them appeared to corrupt this calm time that had recently become essential for my sanity, I'd whistle up Jones, the bearded collie, and go for a long walk across Hob Moor. Si and I had found the dog abandoned on the Knavesmire, tied to Turpin's scaffold with a piece of scraggy rope. Some young skinheads were taunting it with a stick. Si saw them off and, wrapping its trembling body in his coat, he carried the grim-faced dog all the way to the Peckit Lane vet, where he was made well again. He was sleeping now at the end of the bed.

From somewhere over the way, Mrs Vipas-Colly's teenage daughter's baby was crying for its mother. I pictured Mrs V-C resting the iron a moment, her eyes closed and head hung, gripping the edge of the ironing board. 'SHERYLL!' she screamed.

All the doors and windows were open in the neighbourhood, to encourage some kind of through-draught, but nothing stirred the thin air into which Sheryll seemed to have disappeared. 'SHERYLL, WHERE THE FLAMIN HELL . . .'

From Hob Moor came the annoying buzz of a souped-up moped winging its way up and down like an angry mosquito. Somewhere close by, I became aware of Deeb rummaging around in my drawers. I cracked open my eyes and saw him hurdle the sleeping Sumo, landing nimbly and tiptoeing out of the room. This wasn't out of consideration for my sleep but because he'd made off with a pair of my clean pants. A spectrum of the sun's rays caught in my lashes, bedazzling me. This pants stealing *was* a bit much, but just one more thing to add to a long list of grievances. Should I get irate? I supposed not. It was too hot and I couldn't summon up the energy.

My head lolled to the side. The sunshine was streaming round Sumo's bulk, landscaping him. I really had to do something about him and soon. All these niggling matters – the pants stealing, the newly introduced chore rota on which my name seemed to appear disproportionately to everyone else's – all these irritations were knocked into a cocked hat by Sumo's continued presence at the Wigwam. Unfortunately, I'd been the one to offer him a floor and had thus forfeited my right to complain about anything.

'When,' I'd be asked every day, 'is that fat cunt Sumo gonna fuck off?'

I'd argue his case for a brief extension – always just one more night – not because I felt sorry for him any longer, but because I lacked the guts to ask him to go. I didn't think I could stand the sad circus he'd make of packing and lumbering off down Barguist Lane with his rucksack. Off goes Sshumo – I can hear him saying it now, he seemed to be saying it in his sleep, 'Shoo mowww.' He had this sadness about him, a crass sense of self-deprecation. He would pronounce the letter S with an exaggerated pucker of his thick lips, a gentle hissing sound like a kettle just before it whistles, and would refer to himself in the third person. 'Ssss good enough for Shoo-mo,' he'd said gratefully, as I'd shown him a patch of floor he could have in the room I shared with Si. That had been about two or three months ago now. Just after Ziggy had disappeared.

I fell back into a semi-dream. Deeb was there again. There was a sombre light all around him. The pants shone out bright.

They were clean on, white, and he was wearing them on his head. He pranced past the fat wrestler in a clearing in the woods, reciting a few lines of verse. 'What is he doing the great god Pan down among the reeds by the river.' In a basement room lit by a dim blue bulb, a giant spider the size of a house had just been put to death, while in an adjoining room a pregnant woman's waters broke. Someone, Roger Moore in fact, telephoned for the midwife, explaining with a raised eyebrow, 'I should warn you, it's dirty here.' A child with a woman's head slithered from a hole in the ground. I pointed at her and said something. My voice echoed like thunder. She'd come to drink at my oasis? I stood my distance as her long tongue lapped at her face. Deep in the forest a shrill voice came. 'SHERYLL!' and the child disappeared back into her cool black hole.

I awoke fully as Deeb, examining the floor, realised he'd knocked over a beer bottle containing human piss.

'OAHH, FUCKIN SHIT, MAN.' Deeb was kicking the alloy frame of the camp bed. 'SUMO!' Roughly, Deeb shook his sunburnt shoulder. 'SUMO!'

Sumo rolled on to his back, his sleek black hair falling over his face which, scrunched up against the light, was pink like a newborn baby's.

'Ow menee times di I af to tell you. Piiiisssss – in – the – fuck – in – toi – let.'

Sumo groaned and turned over. Deeb straddled the bed waving the broken bottle first in his face then over at the patch of urine on the linoleum.

'Looka that – it's gunna smell like a fuckin brothel in ere now.' He shook his head. 'I've got some lasses comin over ere tonight. Hey, Sumo, you listnin? Ah sed I've got some lasses comin over ere tonight. When a get back I want that cleaned up and I want YOU,' he leant down and shouted into Sumo's ear, 'OUT. J'u ere me? OWE YOU TEA – OUT.'

Deeb gathered up an armful of the bottles to empty down the

pan but tripped on an ashtray, emptying a good measure of Sumo's piss down his bib and brace and on to the floor. He bent down to the rug, rubbed it, and then smelt his fingers. 'Oahh, bluddy ell – wha does that smell like, Gatsby. Gatsby, you listnin to me?'

I nodded with my eyes shut.

'Am holding you responsible t'see thah gets cleared up.'

I nodded again.

Gatsby was my new name at the Wigwam and although, unlike him, I didn't find it derogatory, I knew he only used it when he was genuinely hacked off with me. The name had come about last week after I'd been caught reading the book. It was snatched from me by Ovo who stumbled over the blurb while Deeb pinned me down.

'Story ov a man who – built – im-self an – illus-ion to – live by.' He tossed it away. 'FUCK OFF.'

Deeb got off me and opened *Back Door* at the centrefold: 'That's the only – built – illusion,' he stumbled over what he was trying to say, then prodded the centrefold. 'That's t' only fuckin illusion I wan to live by.' He seemed to realise what he'd said had come out wrong.

Coolly then, as I picked up *The Great Gatsby*, I said, 'Thas good, Deeb, cos thas the closest you're ever gonna get to it.'

Ziggy had given the book to me the night we'd broken down, a Penguin Classic, all tangerine and tatty. He'd handed it to me earnestly, saying, 'Read this while you wait, man, s'life-changer.' I felt bad now because every time I'd started to read 'No one ever rightly knew who Gatsby was', I kept thinking of Hazel pointing at herself saying, 'Me, I'm a prostitute, me!' I'd thought it would be pleasant to read the book in the back garden under the shade of the laburnum tree.

Later, when I got it back, Ovo had used a fair bit of the cover to create the illusion he wanted to live by – tell-tale inch-square tears. On the inside cover, Ziggy had dedicated the book to me like he was F. Scott himself. *To Billy*. And now, like Ziggy, the dedication was gone.

I slipped the book in my back pocket, intending to spend the day reading. Not in the garden though – I wanted to get away from the Wigwam for a bit. Down in the old ruins by the river. Before I left I scribbled a note.

SUMO, clean up piss.

This is serious – Kid.

I scooped up the second post off the coconut mat. A couple of bills and a postcard from The Elmer. Fuck. I slipped it into *The Great Gatsby*. I'd read it later.

A NEW DEPTH TO HERMITUDE

The last time I'd seen Baz he'd sliced the air in a southerly direction. 'I'm fuckin gone, dude, out of here,' he said.

We'd met in town. A tropical sweat was permeating his T-shirt. He fanned himself with a panama and told me of his plans to move to London. He'd got into Middlesex College to study fashion design. 'Purdey's packing up Grimshaws's and moving down with me.'

'Oh yeah?'

'Yeah, we're gonna share a flat.'

'You are?'

'Yeah, you two've fallen out, right?'

'Sort of.'

Baz shrugged. 'Yeah, well, we'll see how it goes. Either way,' he sliced the air again, and made a whistling sound, 'am gone, dude.'

We began walking in to town. 'Have you heard from Hazel?' I asked. He looked away.

'Yeah, once.' His mood pegged down. He began calling her

Miss World then Miss Fucked-up World. 'Sos, man,' he said. 'I know you've been slippin er a length 'n' that, since Ziggy left, and that's totally cool, man.' I didn't correct him, sadly, I was happy to let him think I'd fucked her. It actually made me think I actually *had* fucked her, just for a brief moment. 'But, you know, she seems to think it's something akin to being knighted, this being a model lark. Don't get me wrong or nowt, I fuckin luv models, dhone ah. It's just not the be all and end all, is it, dude?'

As he was telling me all this, I was trying to order it all into an acid-scape of boat rides, walks in the park, nights at the pictures, but it was hard to think in the heat. We passed a tramp lying drunk and smelling, his tattered clothes curling like sun-crisped leaves. What the hell good would it achieve to know what I thought? To hear how all the time I was so in love, she was just *filling* time.

'You know what she is,' said Baz decisively. 'She's a strategist, dude, she cun even trip strategically – cold bitch.' He did a mock shiver. 'Yeah.' I think in retrospect he was trying to paint a bad picture of her before admitting to me that he'd fucked her too. 'When she rang I was really pleased to hear from her an that. And you know what she wanted?'

'No.'

'She wanted me to send her the photos I took of her. Y'know, the sort of Roxy Music-type ones.'

'The porno ones.'

'Fuckin hell. You're as bad *as her*!' He began a hoity-toity impression of Hazel's affected outrage. 'She told me the woman at the agency had been appalled at my photos and said to her "What on earth are you thinking of, doing photos like this?" and that you didn't need to take your clothes off to be a model.'

'Oh,' I said. 'But, uhm, did she say where she was living?'

'Uh? Oh yeah, well, not really, in some models' apartments, sharing with other models. She didn't say where though.'

'And she didn't ask about . . .' I indicated myself standing at the bottom of Blossom Hill. Baz was shaking his head. The mood had sunk and it probably wasn't the best time to ask if he wanted to come and visit Paul with me, but suddenly I didn't fancy going on my own.

'That's where I'm heading now,' I said, aiming for a breezy blasé tone to disguise the pangs of misery. It came out, however, sounding a little neurotic. We hadn't spoken much about what had happened to Fizzy Paul and Baz threw up his arms at the mere mention of him.

'Oh, man, I can't hear about this now. I'll go before I leave. I *will*. Don't look at me like that.'

'Like what?'

'Like that!'

'I'm not, I'm not looking at you like anything.' It's true, I wasn't.

'Yes, you are.' He held up his hands. 'Look, *I'll go*,' he said, 'just not now – it's too bastud hot for the hospital.' He passed his hand over his sweating brow. 'J'u fancy a smoke?'

ICED GEMS

Stopping in at the station kiosk to buy Rizlas, we spied Purds. He was crouched down by a Photo Me booth, looking resentfully at a strip of head-and-shoulder shots drying in the slot. I hadn't seen him since I'd confronted him about spreading the madman rumours about me. Baz hailed him and he looked up a bit shocked and whipped the strip out and put it behind his back. Close up, we saw he had two black eyes and a cut cheek.

'Jus gettin my young dude's railcard,' he said, reaching for an impression of Baz. He was normally very good at impersonating

Baz, but not today. He wouldn't let us see the pics and shoved them down his pants.

Baz said, 'S'only a railcard, dude, s'not fuckin *Vogue*.'

'So, y'off t' London then, Alex,' I said stiffly.

'Uh-hu.' He seemed defensive. 'I'm going down with Baz.' He said it like a war bride.

'So he tells me,' I said, and lit a Sir Nige. I asked if he wanted to come and visit Paul with me. Parrot fashion, like a disagreeable old macaw, he sang, 'Visit Paul, visit Paul – that's a better fuckin name for him, isn it?'

Paul was another person in bad odour with Purdey, although that was of hardly any consequence now. Paul had begun working for Purdcake printing T-shirts but had freaked out one night and smashed the place up. Nothing personal, he'd just gone potty, though potty's probably not the right term. He'd been sectioned soon after.

'You look as rough as houses, pal,' said Baz, trying to disguise a touching concern. Purds, now gazing woefully at his Photo Me shots, swallowed and said, 'Yeah, I jus need to *doo* something – to *beee* doin somethin. Jus somethin so I don't have to go lookin for it in – tuh-hoilets and parks.' The musculature of his throat worked hard to constrain his self-pity.

They walked with me to the bus stop and behind the shelter we smoked a joint.

'Here we are,' sang Purds. 'The asylum express approacheth.'

He was suddenly breezy again, pleased as Punch that there was someone in more of a bad way than himself.

'One for Brayburn Park,' I said to the conductor.

They waved me off, Baz with the old GI salute, Purds hobbling knock-kneed alongside the bus as it drove away. Tongue out, he was tapping the back of one hand with the other. I wondered who it was aimed at, this mongi impression, Paul or me. Baz flicked the roach end at him like Harvey Keitel in *Taxi Driver*.

It was to be the last time I'd see them in that incarnation.

THE GO-AHEAD FOR THE STRAP ON

Since Paul's readmittance to 'the country club', as we called it, I'd already once made my way there on the Haxmill bus, my head vibrating against the window. The first time I'd arrived, visiting hours had finished. 'Ah,' I'd said to the receptionist, strangely relieved, 'I'll come back tomorrow.'

That was a week back. This time around I arrived early and wandered slowly towards the grounds. My conviction in coming was cooled by that Victorian edifice. Even in the baking sun it appeared icy and foreboding, you might say, even if you *weren't* that type of dramatic guy. Brayburn Park, in an arc of iron lettering on the ancestral gate, was burning hot to the touch. As the gate slid back on its silent hinges, the glorious grounds spread out before me, lush, green and immaculately tended. Conifers lined the path to reception and on the lawns rainbows were caught in the upward fan of the sprinklers. I guessed that hospitals didn't suffer from the same water restrictions as the rest of us.

Inside the relatively cool reception hall, I was aware that my mind had been softened by the sun and spliff. I began to wonder just what I'd have to talk to Paul about, especially when uppermost in my thoughts, as my flip-flops flapped down the ward, was exodus.

It was an average-sized ward, but overcrowded to my mind. Patients of both sexes were up and wandering around. One thin old stick was rabbiting away to herself in a full-length mirror attached to a pillar. Another man was rubbing gnarled knuckles into his eyes, a half-peeled banana curved obscenely from his mouth, the skin lying in a sallow starburst across his nose, cheeks and chin. He made no attempt to further eat the banana while I was there, and carried on rubbing his eyes the whole time.

At the far end of the ward I caught sight of Paul. He glanced up as I drew near, like the loner at the back of an underground train.

He was sitting up in bed, striped pyjamas buttoned up to the neck. Over them, despite the heat, he had on his black biker jacket. Hunkered forward from his plumped-up pillows, he'd pulled his right arm way up into the sleeve of the jacket, giving the impression that he didn't have a hand. Consequently, the left sleeve had ridden halfway up his other arm, twisting him as though he'd had a stroke.

Arriving bedside, he looked up and said, 'Look, Billy!' Poking out of the sleeve were two fingertips, deftly flipping a playing card over and back, over and back. 'Look,' he said, as if I'd never been away, as though I'd just nipped out. 'Av god it – look!'

He continued flipping the card over and back again. 'Hmmm,' I said. Next to the bed, on a flexi-back visitor's chair, was a lady's clutch bag. I picked it up and sat down, indicating to Paul that I was putting the bag on the floor. I wondered what significance, if any, this knave card had.

Paul gazed at me with a strange girlish glint in his eye, even though the rest of his face was that of an old woman. He was cleanly shaved with the odd missed whisker here and there. His hair was washed and tied back neatly.

'Nights in white satin,' he said, alluding to the incident that had led to his readmittance here.

'Wha's that, Paul?'

He set his face into a girlish suppression of a secret. 'Won't tell – *won't*.' I wondered just how long I'd have to watch him flip the jack of hearts over and over before I'd be able to respectfully leave.

It had occurred to me on the bus earlier that we'd talk about Ziggy, that I'd ask him if he'd seen him at all since his disappearance, and whether, if he had, if he could remember anything, anything at all. But, as I sat there now, Paul about a thousand miles away on the other side of the bed, I decided not to bother even asking.

I was on the point of leaving when a small woman with dyed

blonde hair, carrying a vase of daffodils, approached us. 'Hello,' she said from behind the flowers.

'Oh, hi.' I realised this must be who the handbag probably belonged to. I'd originally thought it was Paul's.

'Av you come to see ar Paul?'

She seemed to know me but I couldn't place her. She was somewhere in her late thirties, even though dark circles around mole-like eyes suggested she might be older. Her face was pale and famished and her eyes were a terrible contrast to the yellow blooms she was lightly and unconsciously nuzzling with her chin. Setting them down, she leant over to Paul and in a raised voice, like he was some old deaf bloke, said, 'Always a pleasure, Paul, never a chore.' She set the daffs down on the bedside table next to a card, not a Get Well card, it said Happy Birthday.

'You don't recognise me, do yer?'

Even as she was saying it, I'd begun to. She was Paul's sister. We'd met at their dad's funeral.

'J'u remember, you and yur friend – what was it? – Ziggy, you'd got ar Paul into a nice black suit. And a nice half-caste boy, uhmmm, don't tell me –'

'Baz – sorry.'

'Thas right, Baz! It war on tip u me tung, and he'd driven him there, ant he, mekin sure he got there 'n' all. And I came up and invited you all to the wake, dint I. J'u remember?'

'Thas right,' I said, recalling that very odd occasion back at the old house – Ziggy catching cake crumbs in his hand and Baz and I wolfing down sausage rolls. It was the day before the dole cheques and a gut-squeezing hunger had set in bad. We'd demolished the funeral spread and toasted Paul's old man with the rest of them, even though none of us had ever met him. We left furtively, with vol-au-vents hidden in Ziggy's fedora. Ziggy had walked up the street between Baz and me, passing the hat from left to right and back in silence, till all the vol-au-vents had gone, shaking out the pastry crumbs for some pigeons that came strutting across the road. I had the impression we were walking in the same strutty, scavenging way as the vermin birds.

'Ah know a muss look a sight now,' she said. A hand came up to her hair and touched at it, carefully, as though it was still possible to see in it some forgotten style.

'No, no,' I said quickly, 'you look fine.' I turned my attention to a trolley service of refreshments trundling past. 'Scuse a sec,' I said, and hailed the trolley. I bought two teas and some Peek Freans iced gems. Behind me, in the elongating reflection of the metal urn, I caught her reflection. She did, as she said, look a sight.

'Ta,' she said, carefully handling the hot styrofoam cup. 'Ma name's Carol, by the way.'

'Billy,' I said.

Indicating she wanted to talk, we left Paul flipping the jack and went outside into a walled patio where we sat on a bench opposite an uninspiring fishpond. She declined an iced gem so I let mine dissolve on my tongue, thinking it would be rude to crunch noisily while she talked about Paul.

'D'you know wha appened with Paul?' she asked, nuzzling her chin into her collarbone and running a crucifix back and forth under her lip.

'Uhm, well, it's uhh . . .' At that moment a doctor and an orderly came out on to the patio for a Sir Nige break. 'It's like they say, isn't it?' I nodded at them as they lit up. 'Diminished responsibility. All I know is some debt collector came round and Paul chased him down Scurriergate with a knife.'

'Ah know that,' she whined. 'What ah mean is wha . . . why . . .'

I shrugged, and crunched my way through the last memory I'd had of Paul. Shutting my eyes, I shook my head to blank it out. Carol seemed to intuit that I was holding something back. 'Please,' she said, laying a hand on my arm. 'Whatever you know, any little thing might help.' I felt kind of sorry for her so

I thought all right, here I go, and drew in a deep breath. 'OK, well, er, it's not much. But if it'll make you feel better . . .'

'It will.'

'OK, it was, uh, lemme see, a few months back now. It was a Sunday. I'd gone round to Grimshaws's, you know, Alex Purdey's place? Paul was working there . . . yeah. Anyway, before I even got there I could hear the music from streets away, Moody Blues it was. It was coming from Grimshaws's and I remember thinking to myself, that's bloody loud, especially fu this time on a Sunday. Ziggy used to rehearse there, d'you know Ziggy? Sorry, course you do, he came to the wake.'

She nodded impatiently.

'Well, anyway, he's disappeared somewhere now and he left all his PA system at Purdey's and what Paul had done, he'd gone and rigged it up to the normal record player and turned it right up to ten. Ten! That's like gig volume. In a tiny little room.'

She nodded.

''S really loud and he was blasting out this Moody Blues "Nights In White Satin".'

I paused to ask Carol if she thought there was any significance in this. She shook her head.

'No, oh, OK, just a thought. Well, anyway, I was feeling my way to the light switch when something whacked me on the knee. I bent over and it happened again, only this time it caught me in the head. I turned the lights on and, uh . . . well, there was Paul whizzing round like a mani . . . like ah, well, you know . . .' Carol's mole-like eyes were as wide as they could go. I tried to explain to her. 'Look, Paul had fastened himself to the circular printing machine, you see, and he was propelling himself round with his feet, like a . . . merry-go-round. The printer's actually called a carousel cos of the way it goes round, it's got these like flat boards on it which you put the T-shirts on, bit like ironing boards, and they spin round, gettin printed and . . . Sorry, it's a bit technical, but you have to picture it, y'see, Paul was lying on one of them, flat out on his back, with his feet on the floor, like a . . . like a limbo dancer.' I got up and bent backwards to demonstrate. 'Like this, ju see? And he was using his feet on the floor to propel himself round like a . . . like a crab.' I began some frenzied side-stepping, scuffing up spumes of gravel into the pond as I limboed around Carol.

A DRINK WITH THE NIGHTWATCHMAN

There was, I saw, as I limboed around Carol, a certain pertinence to the lyrics I was singing. Paul going round in circles, going round in the dark, never getting any place. On occasions I've degraded myself in pursuit of my fantasies, in private that is, I mean, stuff I wouldn't want people to see. Mindful of this, I absolved Paul of any shame or embarrassment us walking in on him like that might have caused him. Strangely, it didn't seem to embarrass him at all. All the same, I decided not to mention the women's clothing to Carol. I'd nearly blown it earlier when she asked where her handbag was and I handed it to her saying I'd thought it was, er, a nice, er, *colour*. So I kept schtum about the black stockings and suspenders, the pink mohair jumper, the delicate gold chains, the blood-red lipstick and dangling turquoise earrings. The hard-on poking out at me.

I was still limboing round and getting pretty dizzy when, out of the corner of my eye, I saw the white coat of the doctor approach.

'Everything all right here?' he asked briskly.

'Yeah, yeah,' I said, standing up straight. The sky, everything, took up the carousel and spun around me as I clutched my head.

Carol smiled at him and he nodded. 'Like to keep it down maybe?'

'Sorry,' I said, unsteady on my feet. I sat down. The sun, blitzing the patio doors, had crept over my feet. I wiggled my toes in the warmth.

'And what were he wearing?' asked Carol, after the doctor had left.

'Oh,' I said, 'you know about that, do you?'

'Oh,' she said, mimicking me aggressively, 'I do.' She seemed to have become a little hostile and I wondered if perhaps a choppy-changy psyche was a characteristic of Paul's whole family. As Carol began to talk, I started putting away the remainder of the iced gems, pitching them into the air and catching them in my mouth. I decided to give her till the end of the pack. As it was, however, long after the pack was finished, when it was all scrunched up and sweaty in my hands, I was still sitting there listening, my glazed eyes watching a cloud of midges hovering above the fishpond. Paul, she said, for all his talk, had occasionally been Paula. She went on to tell me that he used to dress up in her clothes when they were kids, and used to . . . *relieve* himself into them, and then put them back in her drawer. That he'd been tried for lewd conduct and served time, that their father had hanged himself and after the wake she'd found him in her old room up to his tricks again, cutting jagged holes in the gusset of a pair of her old knickers with a pair of tiny curved nail scissors. 'I mean, it's not normal, is it?'

The fish I'd been watching flicked away under a large green leaf and, when the ripples broke on the side of the pond, I stood up and looked down at the mounting pile of Sir Nige stubs at my feet.

She paused and glanced down cross-eyed at her crucifix glinting in the sun.

'I don't know why I'm telling you all this,' she said, and then sadly, 'he's all av got.'

The flicks and turns of the fish muddled my mind. I looked up into the perfect blue sky and frowned. After a long silence she said brightly, 'I think you're really nice for coming, though.'

'Oh, yeah, well,' I said, a little automatically, 'I thought seein as it's his birthday.'

She looked at me a little strangely. ''S not his birthday.'

'Really? But the . . . er . . . the card you, er . . .?'

'Oh that! That was just one I ad. Din't seem sense in buying another, so I just crossed out Happy Birthday and wrote Get well soon.'

T-H-E Q-U-I-C-K B-R-O-W-N F-O-X

It was late in the evening when I got back to the Wigwam. Sumo was prostrate in the middle of the living-room floor, as though he hadn't moved all day and yet had somehow managed to levitate downwards through the ceiling.

'Y'all right down there, are you?' I said sarcastically, striding over his bulk, temporarily blocking his view of the telly.

''S gud enuf fur Shumo.'

'You cleaned up that piss, av you?' I asked. No response.

Robin appeared, holding a towel roughly fashioned into a turban round his head. He was scowling, his hand held over one eye. 'Hiya, Robin,' I called after him.

Robin was a half-caste kid we'd been at Hopwood with. He did a striptease act at the Wildman Inn halfway between here and Leeds, hen nights mainly. His stage name was Throbbing Robin. I liked him, though he was quite hard to reach – the brooding silent type. He slammed the door without answering.

'Fuck's up with him?'

'Si,' said Sumo.

'Why, wha's he dun to im?'

'Oh, he put yur . . . oh yeah – yer not gonna like this.'

'Why?'

'You know yur portable typewriter?'

'Yeah.'

'He put it on top of his door. It were a booby trap like, meant for Steve. Parantly he's bin nicking Si's clean pants – but anyrurd, Robin went int his room this affy to get something and . . .'

'Phuooooow.' I sucked in breath and likewise began rubbing my head. 'That could a killed im. Si's a mad bast . . . here, hang on!' Suddenly I saw my typewriter crashing off the top of the door. 'Whas happened to my typewrit . . . ?'

I didn't wait for an answer and ran through the wall and up the stairs. On the floor, just outside Si's door, the Underwood Noiseless lay on its side, roughly, I supposed, where it had landed. No one had even bothered to move it and there was still a sheet of paper curling off the roller. I sat down, right there on the old splintering floorboards, and read what what I'd typed. In upper case:

THINGS TO DO

And underneath:

Wake up

There was nothing else typed on the paper. I set the typewriter down straight and typed in T-h-e q-u-i-c-k b-r-o-w-n f-o-x j-u-m-p-e-d o-v-e-r t-h-e l-a-z-y d-o-g. Incredibly, all the characters worked. I sat there for a while staring at it, then went back downstairs, leaving the typewriter more or less where I'd found it.

'*The Virginian*'s on,' said Sumo.

'Uh-uh.' *The Virginian* always starts the same way – a prairie blown over with tumbleweed, here and there a cactus. In the foreground, always some rudimentary psychic crossroads, while off on the horizon a shimmering speck that comes slowly, slowly, slowly riding out of the heat haze – the Virginian. Just then the picture gave out with a horizontal flash and a predictable series of multicoloured chevrons juddering up the screen.

'It might work again later, if we turn it off for a while now,' I said. 'Give it a breather.'

'Ah, nah, ah'll jus lissen to it,' said Sumo.

'I suppose s'gud enuf fuh Shhumo,' I said. Around Sumo was scattered drug-taking gear, a melted Yorkie and a can of Lilt.

It was eight p.m. and still hot as hell. The sunset looked strange coming in through the triangles of fake snow we'd sprayed in the corners of the windows at Christmas. Every now and then Sumo pulled at a bit of the Yorkie, noisily licking the melted chocolate off his thumb and forefinger. He offered me some. I waved it away feeling nauseous and, leaning back, listened to the Virginian's horse approaching over the baked ground. *The Great Gatsby* was giving me a pain in my back pocket where I was sitting on it. I lifted my arse and took it out. Still inside was the postcard from The Elmer. Four views of Puerto Angel, in Mexico. Two at night.

'Dear all, having a great . . .'

I put it on the mantelpiece, slightly behind the clock.

AWAY DAY FOR EVER

Upstairs under the bed was my case, the one without the handle, the one there'd been no rush to bring back. I opened it up. A couple of silverfish were scurrying around in the bottom. I was too superstitious to kill them.

I sat on the edge of the bed with my head in my hands and drummed my fingers on my scalp. Every now and then my elbows fell off my thighs causing my head to jolt as though I were on a slow train to somewhere. I took out my sock drawer and lost my arm in the recess, feeling about with my fingers – always that heart-fluttering panic before my hand finally closed around the leather mouse with a zip up its back. Inside the mouse was nearly two hundred pounds savings. I folded it into a train timetable, which I slipped inside *The Great Gatsby*. Then I threw a few things into the case – keep, don't know, get rid. Downstairs, I could tell Sumo was still listening to *The Virginian*. Planet of the Mates were all on nights. Robin was on his way to out-patients. I slipped silently through the sheeted walls, stopping on the stair to type a farewell message on the old Underwood Noiseless. That took quite a while because I couldn't think what to put. I almost got a bit emotional and choked up. They were, after all, my mates.

I went out round the back way, up the side passage. I didn't want anyone to see me leave. I pushed through the hedge, very sparse and brittle from the heat. It left white scratches on my tanned arms.

The case was heavy, awkward to carry with no handle. I stopped by the disused petrol garage and rested on the wall a while. From out of the corner of my eye I saw one of the Cats approaching me. At the top of the snicket I saw the rest of the gang congregating around an alley post.

'Hiya, N.J.,' I said. She crept closer, squinting at my Sir Nige. 'You out causing mischief, are you?' The rest of the Cats appeared from the disused car wash, their faces peering round the big rollers that stood abandoned in the heat, like synthetic evergreens in a zapped-out Disneyland.

'S'av a fag,' she said.

I offered her the pack. 'How many of these d'you smoke a day?'

She shrugged.

'You know one's too many – it'll stunt yur growth.'

She shrugged again.

'Still the leader of the gang, are you?' I lit her cigarette. She gave me a quick smile.

N.J.'s mum was Indian; her dad was Irish, mad about Marilyn Monroe, hence Norma Jean.

'Hey N.J.,' I said. 'Here, take these for the rest of the Cats.' I gave her the rest of my cigarettes.

'Hey, you know . . . ?' I began, then I had a better idea and opened my case. I got out Valerian's embroidered *Aladdin Sane* jacket, won off him one night at cards. Her eyes lit up, N.J. was a big Bowie fan, she'd seen me wearing this jacket before. 'Hey,' I said again, 'you know my little sister Stacey?'

She nodded. 'Yeah.'

'Well, here, you look out for her while I'm away.' I gave her the jacket.

She was a cool kid, N.J., but she couldn't hide how excited she was with the gift. The rest of the Cats crowded round as she tried it on. It was massive on her of course, but she didn't care. I couldn't imagine ever wearing clothes again, it was that hot, so I gave away more of my stuff, all my New Wave T-shirts from Grimshaws's: The Cramps' 'Goo Goo Muck', The Velvets, The Fall, 'Gram Friday'. 'Hey, you carn have that.' I grabbed back my snowstorm.

At the end of Tangster Rise I spotted a station taxi and hailed it. From its rear window I saw the lightning strike on Norma Jean's back disappear down the alley.

The taxi took me back past the Wigwam and I caught a last glimpse of the GILBERT RATHBONE, HERE NOW, No. (?) THREE WEEKS before the cab turned left by the launderette on Foxglove Lane.

PART IV

CAMDEN TOWN, SUMMER 1987

My story is joined. Some months on from where I first began on this – this soliloquy of sorts inspired by the DHSS – I've signed off and got a job at the local blind school where I'm due shortly.

I return my cup to its saucer and once more pick up the wedding invitation that arrived in the second post. I pass my fingers, ridged and prune-like from their soak in the bath, across the raised silver bells: *Mr and Mrs Gregory would like to invite you to celebrate the marriage of their son Cecil to Hazel.* Hazel's mum is an alky and her dad fucked off when she was a kid so it is the groom's family who are organising everything.

Brushing away crumbs, I upset the salt cellar and watch a small white hill form from its spout. I take another sip of my cold tea and realise I've been off watching the salt for quite some time. I check my watch and rush to get ready.

YOU DIG THE TUNNEL, I'LL HIDE THE SOIL

It was a hectic day at the blind workshop, there was everything to sort out for the weekend profile event somewhere in Surrey, a kind of roadshow to Heighten Awareness, Raise Money. All the baskets and knitted things they make had to be priced, boxed up and packed into the transits. My only pleasure in all of this is Valerie, a colleague I fancy. But despite Val, I'm distracted. I glance at the time, six thirty, and we're still in chaos.

'Listen, Val,' I say, 'I've godda go. I have to meet some people.'

She's bending over a box of knitted bears. The way her natural blonde hair falls forward like that, a real 'on-top' style.

'Go?' she says enquiringly, straightening up. Then she seems to swoon a little. The back of her hand, the one with the teddy in it, comes up to her forehead. 'Oooh,' she murmurs, stepping back as though drunk, 'got up too quick.'

I sit her in a chair. My hand cups her warm neck under her hair and I kiss her cheek.

Val too has split from a long-term relationship and is living on her own. Like me, she says doesn't really know why she's doing this job. She smokes a lot, filterless French Sir Niges, and when she is talking she'll sometimes pause to pluck a fleck of tobacco from her lower lip. Sometimes she gets so distracted doing this she clean forgets what she's been talking about and sometimes it is just to stall you. Like when I asked her if she was happy in London, didn't she miss Plymouth and the Hoe and all that, and so saying I sort of bent forward and bowled the question towards her like old Sir Francis Drake. She didn't answer, just began this little spitting performance, like she had a grape pip on her tongue, and then looked at me and smiled. She has a homely smile, Val, that somehow suits the hot summer we're having.

'Oh, me neither,' I said, shrugging, 'I wanted to be a rock star.'

She laughed. 'You still can be.'

'Nah, I'd have to be dead in a couple of years. Besides, I knew this guy once, someone I really loved and he . . .'

'Maybe you can tell me about it some time,' she said.

'Yeah,' I said. 'I will.' I liked the way she'd said 'some time', a sort of subconscious Mae West vibe.

Looking at her now, with the evening sunshine falling about her tanned legs, this swoon still playing about her head and shoulders, I think there has never been a better time to kiss her. 'I'll see you tomorrow,' I say.

'Yeah,' she says without looking up, gently tugging at a green bow tie around the teddy bear's neck.

I get home around seven, thoroughly jaked. The wedding invitation is on the table where I left it, next to the breakfast pots. I light a Sir Nige, shut my eyes and run my fingers over those raised bells again like Braille.

I rush out of the shower when the phone rings and water drips from my face on to the yellow Post-it note as I scribble down a time and a place. The writing smudges, suggesting an altogether more romantic meeting place than Jimmy's. I smile at the irony which catches me by surprise – I have a feeling I'm pulling a strange face and register it like Mr Spock.

Since living with Susan I've become a different person, a London person, but in some Californian sense not my own person. That's why I'm kind of looking forward to this reunion at Jimmy's, with old friends from the north. Looking forward to looking back to a time not tainted (you might say, if you were that type of romantic guy) by Susan being part of it. That would be four, five years ago now. I never can remember.

Instead, when I look back my mind's eye gets all caught up in the thumbed-through pages of Susan's old 1985 Letts diary. I'd been looking for her work number when I came across my name. It came fourth in a list of other guys' names, each with a score beside it, mine the same as some cunt who was a one-night stand. The dates of all these infidelities roughly spanned our entire relationship. I pulled the dartboard off the door and threw it at the hall mirror which smashed all over the floor. I left her just about everything, designer clothes, all those matt-black and chrome objects from Harvey Nicks – bottle opener, Parmesan grater, CD holders, all that stuff. All I took was a drawer full of pre-Susan things, deemed too unfashionable to share the light of day with her 1980s chrome and black fantasy.

It was the night of the Elvis shades. I'd already nearly run over a mother and child and been sick on a grass verge next to some aged albino dog shit. The cops pulled me over and it was only then, when one of them flicked the price tag dangling from the shades, that I realised what it was the petrol attendant, wielding a pair of scissors, had shouted after me: 'Cut, cut!'

There was a half-empty Thunderbird on the passenger seat. The breathalyser was a formality – banned for a year. My Renault's now beached on the outskirts of the estate, jacked up on bricks. Every day I pass it and notice some new piece of vandalism. Wedged under the wipers is a flyer for a nightclub I'll never go to and some official-looking notice I won't even read. The back seat where I slept for so many nights is covered in shattered glass.

Under the sobriquet Nick Barrel, things are getting better – sort of. All day Nick helps blind people make things, but come the end of the day he has to unmake everything. There's already a backlog of stock that no one wants to buy, so he unpicks, he unravels, he disassembles so it can be made again tomorrow. He hates this. And he hates helping the blind package up aeroplane knives and forks into those hermetically sealed cellophane wrappings, sheer exploitation by the airlines. When, as sometimes happens, a passenger finds himself with two spoons and no knife, or two salts but no pepper, the stewardess never says in her bright way, 'I'm so sorry but they're packed by blindees, you see.' Still, there you go.

INTERNATIONAL LONELY GUY

Since I've been waged I've taken to eating out. Dining alone, as I do, I seem to often get seated near fish tanks. In their murky depths, after a while, I'll find my own reflection shoaling this way and that. I use the glass to observe the other diners, and have come to know some of the different types – black mollies with their efflorescent fins, lonely secretaries in organza layers; red-tailed sharks, travelling salesmen; silver shoaling sharks, those looking for a mate. I'm the omnipresent plastic skull sunk in the gravel. In and out my eyes they weave. How indifferent the fishes are, how easily provided for. Once or twice I've witnessed feeding time. A pinch or two of confetti-type stuff, dispensed by an impatient waiter, just a dismissive rub of the fingers. It breaks my mood.

I'm coming round, I'm joining the land of the living. In accordance with my old friend Alex Purdey's definition of an optimist, I have actually got out of the bath to answer the phone. And soon I'll be taking part in this reunion, stepping out into the blow-dried air of Saturday night.

Nick, the new me, Baz's supposed brother, doesn't know these people in the blanched-out photograph. To me, the timely change of name came as an opportunity to make a new start, and that's what I'm attempting to do. Every now and then, though, Nick needs info about his past, about Kid Glover. So I'll get dressed in front of the mirror, give him the run down on who's who.

Let me see, Nicko, I say, buttoning my shirt in a distinctly jovial way. Tonight you're gunna meet Baz, yeah, he's like a successful fashion designer now, kind of obsessed with America. He'll probably turn up in a backwards baseball cap, a tracksuit and some gold chains or crotchless leather chaps or something. He'll be with his girlfriend, Maria, the Dutch beauty. She looks a lot like Amanda Lear. Then . . . then there'll be Hazel.

I pause to scoop out some Brylcreem and watch Nick rub it briskly between his hands before plastering down his hair.

Yeah, I continue, Hazel's a successful model, who I once went to Peterborough with, now it seems she's marrying into the aristo scene. Used to think we had a chance there, Nick. Ha! Whada fucking joke.

I fit a Sir Nige to the corner of my mouth and search for a light.

Still, I hope some last-minute thing won't prevent her from showing, I tell Nick, pausing to look for a match . . . like last time, when the empty seat next to me was sat in by Purdcake. In the mirror Nick lights his cigarette and shakes out the match. I wait for him to exhale. Yeah, Purds . . . seems too easy to call Purds an alky, but that's what he is these days. The Lady Esquire shoe dye type. Works in a clothes shop in Covent Garden, least he did till he got sacked. Apparently had some scam on the go, whispering to customers that he'd buy them the item they were trying on with his fifty per cent staff discount and bring it round later, right to their apartment if they wanted. Only he'd have stolen the garment in the first place, so he'd be making a hundred per cent. He's got a court appearance next week; he may even wind up inside.

I blow out smoke.

The changes are a lot more evident, Nicko, a lot more evident.

JIMMY THE GREEK'S

At Jimmy the Greek's in Soho, over retsina, we spill our news. Hazel's effervescent, talking about herself, and when the conversation's not about her, she says annoying stuff like, 'Oh, cut to the chase, willya.' I feel like the old man.

'Oh, God, where do I begin?' She's super-affected now, talking about her marriage. 'We met in Paris. That's where Cessy's livin –'

Before I can help it, I've choked on his name. '*Cessy?*'

'Ce-*cil*,' she corrects me, shaking her head in a patronising, puzzled way that shifts into a practised look of pity. Still, I can see I've hit home – she becomes vague and distracted, moving her lips as though her face is constrained by a clay mask. It's as though I've pointed out something really terrible, like he's a bigamist or something. Eventually she says, 'His father's one of the richest men in the world, you know?' and looks genuinely relieved at this re-discovery.

Most of us have got a few lines in our faces now, but Hazel's brow is smooth, untroubled. I begin paring back a cuticle with a toothpick when she breaks off to touch my arm.

'You are coming though, aren't you, Billy? To the wedding?'

'Sure.'

'Alex? Baz?' She goes round the table, ignoring Maria.

'Oh, for deffers,' says Baz, putting an arm round Maria.

DIGNIFIED DON

Baz is wearing lots of gold jewellery, big rings, bracelets. A chunky chain with dollar signs on hangs just above his soup. His high-tongue trainers and even his red tracksuit are trimmed with gold braid. 'From NY,' he says.

'North Yorkshire?' I say with mock innocence.

Baz snorts. 'Fuck off, man. The Big Apple, dude, *New* York, not *old* Eee-bor-a-cum.'

'Yeah, I know,' I say, smiling at him, 'but you know rap fashion – b.boy style, that is – the whole hip-hop tracksuits, trainers and gold thing' – I indicate his get-up with a sweep of my Sir Nige – 'started in North Yorkshire.'

'You what?' He's laughing now, and turning to the others. 'Ere we go, 'nother fuckin theory according to the great Kid Glover: rap dint start in Brooklyn, after all – started in North fuckin Yorkshire.' He grins at me.

'Yeah, thas right,' I say. 'You know, with Jimmy Savile.'

Baz's grin falters. 'Jimmy *Savile*?'

Nonchalantly I light another Sir Nige, wafting the match. 'Yeah, I think yu'll find I'm right in this, I just got his auto-biography, he was the very first person to wear tracksuits and trainers and always with, you know, loads of gold on his wrists and those medals round his neck.'

Purdcake does a passable Savile impersonation, shaking his wrist. 'Jewellery jewellery.'

'Yeah,' I continue, 'it was his style statement, totally unique back in nineteen seventy-whatever it was.' Baz is frowning now, searching his mind; he knows I'm right, but he hates to lose an argument especially about style matters. 'He was *totally* rap man, he drove a Rolls, smoked cigars, and when he signs his name, the J for Jimmy is a pound sign, and the S for Savile is a dollar sign.'

'Fu-kin ell,' mutters Baz, 'you might be right, you bastard.'

'No might about it, Baz, as it 'appens. Check out the cover of his book, *Love is an Uphill Thing*. If you painted out his face, could be the Run DMC.'

'Yeah, you got me,' says Baz. 'Yu're absolutely right, dude.'

During all this Purdcake says nothing. He's yet to take his glass away from his lips, it's like it's glued there. Tilting back in his chair he rocks back and forth, gentle waves of retsina slapping against his upper lip. He leans his head right back against a Cretan landscape and a waiter tut-tuts at him. I guess Purdcake's in a state about the pending court case. I smile as I remember an incident from, what, five, maybe six years ago. I was at a party, twenty minutes into another great joke, about to deliver the punchline. Purds had suddenly begun to sniff the air theatrically, gaining everyone's attention, then he'd looked at me and enquired loudly, 'Oh, is someone wearing the new fragrance by TCP?' The liquid I'd applied lavishly to my spots earlier that night seemed to pulsate by way of answer. Try that in the clink, I thought, see how you get on.

'No!' bursts out Hazel, swivelling the peak of Baz's baseball cap round and over his eyes, 'I would never do *Playboy*. Well, no, not unless they pay me a *serious* load of money,' she adds, more to herself than to Baz.

The phantom issue flicks past me. I temper my desire with thoughts of the accompanying text. Nick would probably go out and buy this magazine, bring it home and jerk off over Hazel in a cheerleader's outfit. When days later a sparrow's tear is all that can be wrung from another wank, I'll sadly address my already bowed head to the racy text. *Eee by gum, fellas, Hazel creates a weeee-urd ambience! This young lass hails from Yorkshire, famous for great fish 'n' chips. And like the down-to-earth northern lass she is, Hazel wants nothing more than to meet Mr Right and settle down. But she's single. Why? Maybe because all the guys she meets are jealous of Hunter. Hunter? Yeah, Hunter! For this lovely lady has an interesting pet. Beware, guys! Hunter is a fully grown tarantula called after the great Leeds United half back, Norman 'bites yer legs'.* 'Hunter,' I blurt out.

'Pardon, Billy?'

'Does Cessy like tarantulas?' I ask.

'Luuuuurvs them,' she says, narrowing her eyes at me.

Bollocks, I think, does he fuck. Hazel's gothic enigma is really waitress-based, and all that mystery she hides behind is no more than a morbid fear of going back, back there to Plunky's Burger and Chips. She wasn't as glamorous back then, just taller than everyone else, so she would stoop, her face always hidden behind that returning sweep of long black hair. *A tarantula, with free rein among the bedclothes, fellas! Lets it crawl all over her – yup,* all *over her,* and I see Hunter in her white sheets, creeping up her inner thigh, melding with the black hair on her pubic bone. Hazel simply puts down her book and watches. The glossy sheen of the phantom *Playboy* would eventually repel me. Although Nick may pin the centrefold up in his locker at work, I may touch the page, finding it cold and flat. Her proximity to sachets of cup-a-soup highlighting just how far apart we really now are.

Looking at her now, nibbling an olive off a fork, I realise just how far apart we really are. I imagine her in Club Class and my blind packers sealing up aeroplane cutlery to be opened by her at five thousand feet. The thought depresses me and I'm grateful for the intrusion of our impatient waiter.

'Scusa, you lika to order now maybe, *yes*?'

'Oh, yeah, sure, uhm, lemme see here. I'll have taramasalada, then, uhm, kleftico!'

'Mas-ala-da – ef-ti-co.' He scribbles away under his breath. 'Hennything to drink?'

'Yeah, another bottle of retsina.'

'Thank you,' he says, withdrawing like a count.

I snap the menu shut. Baz, who's sitting next to me, reacts to the sound like a starting pistol and swivels his whole body round. 'Anyway, it's really good to see you, man. How's the old homestead?' He flashes his perfect teeth. 'I've bin tranna call you actually, you know, well, maybe y'don't. It's about this project I'm doin – could be something could be nothin. But I was wondering if you would write somethi . . .'

I fix my gaze at a speaker on the wall above Maria's head and begin nodding in absent consideration. Purds and Haze have fallen into a private conversation. Every so often the black gauze of the speaker vibrates, buzzing as though transmitting the death throes of some large bluebottle. I lapse into a kind of reverie, the wrong kind. Amid all the buzzing and nodding, and contrary to the best intentions of the evening, I find myself thinking about Susan and wondering what she's doing and who she's doing it with.

'Wha d'you think then? Will you do it?' Baz slaps his thigh like a triumphant auctioneer.

'S-sorry?'

Baz slaps his thigh again, as though it was already sold to the man with the faraway expression, and I take a long sip of retsina. I've hardly heard a word he's said but am shaping an answer anyway when Hazel suddenly lets out a startled scream. In a tradition usually reserved for family weddings, the speaker, that had been gently crackling away, suddenly blasts out at some horribly distorted volume. We all jump up with such force that all the candles are blown out. The volume is quickly turned down. Baz sparks up a match and the relit candles seem to reveal a better night. Everyone's sort of laughing, everyone except Purdey who's thrown red wine all over himself and is busy dabbing at a large stain spreading across his crotch, reminding me of the blood on the night we stole all those light bulbs. The musical outburst I'd taken to be heavy rock turns out to be some Greek folk song. More retsina arrives. A shepherd pipes away and by the time coffee is dished out we're entrenched in reminiscence.

Ziggy's mentioned, but with none of the reverence of old, more as a joke figure, all used up, reduced to anecdote. I glimpse him like some worn-out sherpa among the foothills of the Cretan mountainscape, wistfully doffing his fedora, regretting that this is as far as he goes.

'What the hell d'you think happened to him anyway?'

'Has anyone seen him?'

'It's a mystery of our time. Get James Burke.'

Purds tells us about the last time he saw him. A long story about a car crash they'd witnessed on a country road just outside Eboracum, how they'd tried to help by flagging down a car that by fluke had a nurse in it, who'd just got married, was still in her wedding dress, and how they'd carried her down the overgrown embankment to the crashed car, holding her above their heads so she wouldn't rip her dress. Purds always forgets this story is in fact a real downer. The passengers were dead or completely fucked, severed limbs everywhere. He's describing how, 'Anyway, the bride's dress ended up looking like a bloodied butcher's apron and . . .'

I wonder if Hazel remembers the last time she saw him – the last time *we* saw him – in the Theatre bar just after he was run over and punched in the face. If she does, she doesn't say. I down what's left of the retsina. Things are starting to blur.

We decide to head off up Berwick Street to an after-hours drag club and carry on drinking.

Outside, in the warm night air, the market street seems to do just as much, if not more, business than during the day. There's a balmy tang of leftover fruit and vegetables which makes me want to throw up. It's impossible to stroll five abreast through the busy throng, so we pair down, Baz and Maria melding into a shape with four legs in front, me following behind Hazel and Purdcake. I hunch over and thrust my hands deep into my pockets. Alcohol regurgitates in my throat as I'm jostled on and off the kerb. I let my eyes close a moment and feel the ghostly darts of electric signs speed across my retinas.

In this slow strobe of alcoholic saturation, if I'd blinked I'd have missed him – a lean and serious figure in a dark-brown suit emerging from a phone box on the other side of the street. My fingers claw at the fluff in the lining of my pockets as I keep pace with the solitary man walking now on the other side of the street. I think how I might let him fade off into the crowd, mention later in the nightclub that I could have sworn blind I saw . . .

'ZIGGY! ZIGGY! HEY, ZIGGY!' I find myself calling.

Baz and Maria look back but I'm already crossing the street. A car honks, someone shouts. When I reach him he's standing motionless, caught in the doorway of a peep show. He is startled but his eyes show no sign of recognition, but it is Ziggy, it's definitely him. I stretch out an arm and fix him in my sight until I feel his fingers in mine.

'Ziggy,' I pant, 'don't you recognise me?'

He's smiling lopsidedly, chewing a toothpick, nodding as though he's been caught out.

'Sure I do,' he says slowly. The toothpick slips to the other side of his mouth. 'Sure, it's justa, hmm, well, it's bin a while, since . . .'

'Yeah, yeah,' I broke in, 'bout, what, five, mebbe six . . .
Christ, I thought you were dead. Yu've really changed, man, I
nearly din't see you.'

'No, no,' says Ziggy, taking the toothpick out of his mouth. 'I
mean, it's been a long time since anyone called me . . .' He
replaced the piece of splintered wood.

'ZIGGY! Baz, Maria, Hazel and Purdcake have crossed the
road now. 'ZIGG – HEYYYA! Hey, Ziggy, is it really you?
Fuck! Jeez, I can't believe it.'

I stand back as the greetings play out. Ziggy's having trouble
with his toothpick which prevents him from saying more than a
few words at a time without having to spit a splinter of damp
wood from his lip.

He answers most of the questions with marked reticence. No,
he says, he's not into Bowie impersonation too much these days
and he visibly winces when Purds elbows him in the ribs saying,
'What's all the hubbub, Bub?' I'm taking in the changes. Gone
is the 'Low' bouffant, his hair's brown now, cut in no particular
style, his suit the same.

'So, Ziggy,' Maria says, puzzled at his insistence on being
called Arthur, 'vy haff you changed your name?'

Ziggy spits out what remains of the toothpick and there is an
uncomfortable silence. Hazel steps through it, linking her arm
with his. 'Come for a drink with us,' she says. She takes hold of
his arm with both hands and, sensing his reluctance, as though
Ziggy was a catamaran, she leans out into the sea of passing
traffic. 'C'mon, it's just up here.' She pulls on him some more
and he finally gives in, stumbling into step behind her. He's
either lost or is covering up what's left of his Yorkshire accent
with some strange drawl.

On the way up Berwick Street, he answers more questions,
patting himself up and down, presumably for a toothpick or a
match. He noses each question up in the air like a seal, as if
looking for the answers in the first-floor windows. Squinting, as

though trying to remember exactly where it was we'd all grown up, he tells us how, about five years ago, his aunt had died. He'd got a little money and developed a bit of a taste for travelling. So, when the money ran out, he'd got a job on the *QE2* as a croupier.

His arm rears forward like a conjuror's before fanning the pack. 'Calling cards isn't really where I'm at,' he says. 'It's just my cover.'

'Cover?' says Hazel, still hanging on his arm.

'Yeah, cover,' says Ziggy.

'What cover?' says Purds, meaning what cover could *you* possibly need.

Ziggy produces what are in fact five white calling cards, and hands them round to each of us in turn.

'Cover,' he says, ''s a must in my profession.'

'Away,' says Baz, stumbling drunkenly.

'A – Way,' says Ziggy.

'Phwat?' says Purds incredulous, staring at the card in his hand:

A. Way
Private Investigator
549003

'Arthur Way,' I murmur.

Ziggy isn't giving much away but, from what we can work out, there'd been some incident on board the *QE2* – particularly unpleasant for the Germans. He didn't really want to go into details but, being privy to careless talk at the card table, he'd discovered . . .

We reach the door of the club and Hazel disengages from Ziggy to talk to the doorman. He unclips the red cord for her to pass through then, letting his tongue loll out in concentration, draws a line through a name on a clipboard, nodding blankly to us all in turn, letting the full weight of his stare fall on Ziggy before allowing him to pass. Ziggy clears his throat and adjusts the knot of his tie. I concentrate on a vein at his temple that's pulsating as though he were chewing gum and I imagine the voiceover in Ziggy's head audible only to dogs and cats. His manner is Marlowesque. I'm reminded of the last time I'd seen him at the Theatre bar, the waitress standing over him like an analyst, taking down the last order of Ziggy Low.

A VERY CLASSY JOINT

'And I can't emphasise the word classy enough, luv,' says the proprietor, looking pointedly at Ziggy.

The club is small and intimate, red lighting and dark corners, the crowd a real mix. Drag is a great leveller. I make my way to the bar with a list of drinks to remember, and one new one, vodka Martini. Waiting to be served, I turn to face the crowd, resting my elbow in the sticky interlocking Olympic circles on the bar. I feel my sleeve getting soaked but I'm now packed in too tight to move. There is the smell of strong cologne. Next to me a tall Swede is talking to a tranny about his underwear fetish, telling her what he likes. 'Suspender belts,' he says, swallowing, 'black ones – in rubb . . .' A rocker type to their left dives in on them enthusiastically. 'Oh yeah – straps – all of it, I love it, that's me! I'm there.' On the stage, there's a man performing a heartfelt rendition of 'I Am What I Am' and a few people are swaying on the dance floor. The singer's head is bald and he's wearing tight jeans and a grey T-shirt with a map of sweat on the front that resembles Canada. I find myself drunkenly mouthing the lyrics: '*I am what I am and what I am nee –*'

'And *who* am *I*?'

I turn sharply and lock eyes with a huge black drag queen.

'Epiphany,' she says, 'Eh-piph-an-ee,' drawing out the syllables. She cups a huge hand over her mouth and inhales on a black Sobranie as though it were emergency breathing apparatus.

I introduce myself and she toys with my name a while – 'Hmm, Kid, Kid *Glover* the *lover*, hmmm.' Then, in quick spurts, 'Andwhoareyou, darling – youhaveinteresting eyes – whatdo*you*do?' She comes even closer, putting an arm around me.

'I dunno,' I say.

'You don't know?'

'Well, I mean, I – er – I – er. Lemme see. You know when you travel on aeroplanes –'

'Yeassss.' She seems interested, bending her head to hear.

'And you get a meal given to you –'

'Yeassss.'

'And you get these knives and forks all wrapped up in cellophane –'

'Yeassss.'

'Well, I supervise the people who do that, who pack them, blind people.'

'Excuse me?' She cups her ear and leans further towards me. 'BLIND PEOPLE!'

A few queens turn and give me filthy looks.

'Oh,' she says, disappointed. 'And who have you come here with tonight?' She brushes a strand of hair out of my eyes. 'It's not an outing, I hope.'

Jostling at the bar forces me to lay a sudden and steadying hand on her. It glides up the smooth satin of her dress, on to her clammy back and then her shoulder. On tiptoes, I periscope round and spy Ziggy's pale face peering anxiously out of a dimly lit alcove. He seems ill at ease and keeps glancing around him. Clearing his throat, he adjusts his thin brown tie again, hooking a finger between the collar and his thin neck, running it back and forth like a man in the Tropics. He's still chain-smoking, although I notice the brand has changed. I squeeze Epiphany's shoulder. 'See over there, that guy lighting a cigarette in the alcove, the one in the brown suit, see him?'

'Where, sweetie?'

'Over there . . .' I raise my voice above the singer and the enthusiastic applause from his friends. '*IIIIII am what I AMMMMMMMMMMMMMmmmmmmmmm . . .*'

'Oh – I'm on – gotta go, sweetie,' says Epiphany, and suddenly she's picking her way through the crowd, nimbly waving her huge fingers at me. The bartender touches my elbow and I fumble for money.

I have to make two journeys with the drinks. As I set down the first cluster, Epiphany's putting her arm around the drying-map-of-Canada guy, retrieving the microphone, nestling it in her boa. 'Thank you, *Steeeve*,' she says, giving him a manly squeeze he looks uncomfy with. 'Ladies and Gentlemen . . .' A pause, then, over the bad bingo-sounding microphone that amplifies her breath, 'Boys and girls, let's hear it for Steve all the way from . . . GOOLE.'

She shoots him a look of reproach. Above the renewed applause Steve's trying to tell her something and she cups her ear. 'Sorry, Steve, sorry, darling, what d'you say, sweetie? POOLE!' She rears up, clutching her boa in mock horror.

'Ladies and Gentlemen, sorry, sorry, I'm getting my Ps and Gs all mixed up. It's *Steeeve*, and he's all the way from POOLE.' There is another much smaller smattering of applause as Steve climbs down from the stage, a little dejectedly now. Epiphany rolls her eyes towards the glittering ball above. Steve rejoins his boyfriend who frowns at the sweaty estuaries on his T-shirt and pulls a face at the guy next to him.

'Well now,' begins Epiphany, 'I hope you're all sitting, or standing, or doing whatever you're doing, I hope you're doing it comfortably. I'm going to sing a little song for you now I hope

you're all going to en . . .' she inhales from her cigarette '. . . joy.'
She blows out smoke. There's a stir, an expectant hum, the
beginnings of a surge of interest. As I said, the crowd here is a
real mix. Some of them come and arrange themselves at the
front. One or two fold their arms, shifting their weight on to one
leg. The trannies behind us sit up on the back of their fifties
convertible-style booth and look around them – at the ceiling,
the floor, the sheen on their nails, anywhere but the stage. There
are a few whistles and someone whoops. As I set down the
second cluster of drinks, Epiphany's snaking the microphone
wire and bending to whisper in the pianist's ear. He gives a
sombre nod, like a butler, and lays his fingers on the keys. Ziggy
looks even more uncomfortable than before. Watching his eyes
dart about, I imagine him standing at the roulette table on the
QE2, leaning forward to spin the wheel, pitching in the ball and
that rattle as it bobbles about, like a kid's stick along railings, the
wheel slowing to a standstill. Settling into the booth, we all raise
our glasses in a toast: 'To Ziggy.' But he's already downed his in
one and the light from the disco ball glints in the bottom of his
glass. We're all frozen, with our glasses in mid-air. There is a
kind of silent, Oh, right then.

'To Arthur,' I say.

Ziggy nods awkwardly. He stares into his empty glass and
knocks back the ice.

'Sorry – *Arthur*!' says Maria.

'*Way*,' says Purds, glaring at Maria.

Epiphany's singing a Jacques Brel song. Maria swivels round
to face the stage. I catch some of the words '. . . *dream of a Hell
where* . . .' One by one we all follow her gaze, all except Ziggy
who's on his feet indicating he's parched. '. . . *where bulls and
worn-out matadors still burn.*'

'Kid, Kid.' Someone is tapping my knee. I look around to find
Baz winking at me. 'Here,' he urges. I cup my hand under the
table and a pill is pressed into my sweaty palm. With a covert

movement of my arm, I yawn and take it down the red lane, as Purds says. I look and realise everyone is grinning – we've all been given one.

'What is it?' I ask Hazel above the *fortissimo* of Epiphany's song.

'Or perhaps with their last breath, did they pardon us their death . . .'

'What is it?' But she still doesn't hear me.

'Knowing what we did at Verdun, Stalingrad, Hiroshima.'

Ziggy returns and sets down the drinks which I soon realise are all for him. A lager, a double and something peppermint green with a red umbrella sticking out the top. He takes them down one after the other, stopping only to dump the red umbrella, which is poking him in the eye, in the ashtray. I can't remember which eye his patch covered and I notice how perhaps the left is more liquid than the right but then I think all this staring is making him nervous.

The crowd is 'Olé-ing' and clapping and stamping out of time. Ziggy's found a new piece of wood to chew, a cocktail stick, and he's making short work of turning it into soggy splinters. His eyes are still darting around, more violently now, like an heroic-type pinball game. I think it's only me that sees him this way and I wonder what everyone else is making of him, whether to them he's just shifty, out of place, Epiphany's prey. She gets them up on stage, makes monkeys of them and, if it turns ugly, well, she's protected by these big hams in dinner suits. You might find yourself physically ejected, put out on the street, jeered at by passers-by. Made to look a fool by a drag queen in a cheap cabaret, you alone with your failings. Right now, in this moment, I'm taking great gulps of air and I can feel my heart beat a little faster.

I'm thinking again about the day that red Allegro knocked him down in Swinegate. Epiphany is singing, '. . . *perhaps with their last breath, did they pardon us their death, knowing what we did at Verdun, Stalingrad, Hiroshima . . .'*

THOSE WHO INSIST ON THEIR OWN
ORIGINALITY HAVE NO SENSE OF HISTORY

The flare from Ziggy's match lights up two flame-grilled worry lines on his forehead as he eases into the shadows, draws back into himself. Whatever pills we're on, Ziggy didn't get one. My spine stiffens against the sticky PVC of the booth and my mind begins to wander. Ziggy's eyes glower at me suddenly, and I don't know why but I reach out to touch him and he's on his feet, my hand in the space where he's been. He disappears into the crowd.

'Who'd he say?' said Maria, frowning.

'The john,' says Baz.

'Pardon?' says Maria.

'I think he means he's going to the . . .'

'What?'

'Toilet!' Baz yells. I slump back.

'Hasn't he changed, though!' says Hazel who's been quiet for a while. I'd noticed she hadn't once talked to Ziggy about her marriage. I light Hazel's cigarette. It occurs to me that maybe she's still in love with him. I put my arm round her bare shoulders and when she slips her hand on my inside thigh I feel my cock stir. 'But I suppose we all have,' she says, blowing out smoke.

'No,' says Baz, firmly, 'we're just older. He's *really* changed.'

'Yeah,' says Purdcake, brandishing Ziggy's card. 'He's even got a new fuckin name, A. fuckin Way.'

I'm enjoying the sensation of my cock twisting against my thigh. I upend my glass somewhere near my mouth and ice showers down, hitting my nose. Vodka goes down my windpipe making me choke. I'm coughing and coughing and the ceiling flashes by, and then the floor. When I open my eyes they are full of water and I'm on the edge of the bench, bent double, staring at the carpet squares. Hazel's rubbing my back. 'Are you OK?' she shouts.

Epiphany reaches the climax of her song. '*SAI———*
————GON du du du du du———der du!'

I nod and croak and cough a few more times. When I finally regain my composure, Epiphany's stepping to the front of the stage, her sequinned dress twinkling like Christmas lights from behind some watery window-pane.

'Thank you, *darlings*!' She clutches at her boa. 'Thank you!'

The tired musicians have tumble-dryer eyes. They've seen it all before. Epiphany peers into the distance, beyond the spangled optics, and she holds up her hands, silencing the phantom masses. The light is streaming around her.

ARNOLD SCHWARZENEGGER'S NEW ENEMY

Epiphany will choose the next performer from the audience – I know this from previous visits here. Those who know this shrink away from the stage.

'What she'll do now, you'll see,' a Scottish queen is telling another, 'is pick on the most uncomfortable out-of-towner she can find – there always seems to be one. Mind you, a seasoned extrovert wouldnay fare much better. S'all about humiliation.' I start to feel self-conscious and slip down in my seat. 'Oh no, you're all right!' he continues. 'No, it's mostly businessmen she picks on, y'know, those types away from their families and veering off the beaten track, looking for fun, salesmen and the like.'

From my now almost prostrate position I'm staring up at the mirrored disco ball which is releasing pearly javelins of light.

'What . . . *what*?' Epiphany is rearing up frighteningly, ruffling her pink boa. 'What have we here, hmmmm? Don't be shy, darling.' Her hand cups an ear. 'Speak up, we can't hear you?'

As the applause dies away, heads turn to where Ziggy,

returning from the john, has come to an awkward standstill in his crumpled brown suit. He looks around.

'Yes, honey, we do mean you!'

She moves behind a stage lamp and lifting a thin metal flap isolates him in bright white light: Ziggy Hero, Ziggy Low, caught in a moon-age daydream, but not freaking out. It would seem that he has been making a bungled attempt to sober up in the john – his face is wet, hair spiked, his clothes damp and disarrayed. Epiphany is advancing towards him. He looks lost and disorientated, like that salesman from Crewe a week ago. With the back of her hands she wipes the feline stripes of kohl that frame her eyes. Ziggy's doing things with his arms, a window-cleaning mime, wafting smoke or something. 'He has to leave – catch a train – he'll be late if . . .' In his confusion his arm flails not at the exit but towards the door to the john which, on cue, wafts open. The sound of a toilet being flushed can clearly be heard.

'Ahh,' sighs Epiphany, coming ever closer, and Ziggy tries to slide away. But behind him, a loose and bitchy gaggle press him forward. Epiphany is talking softly into the microphone. Her breasts are sharply outlined, heaving and falling as she reaches down to him, wrapping him in her boa. He stumbles slightly, grazing his shin, but allows himself to be pulled on to the stage. Lifting my empty glass to my lips, a soggy piece of lemon slithers on to my cheek. With one eye I watch. There is a drum roll and a cymbal clash and Ziggy looks bemused.

Epiphany wraps the rest of the boa around his neck, turning him to face the audience like a ventriloquist's dummy, languorously stroking a crimson fingernail up and down his pale cheek. Ziggy looks stunned, the way he did that morning in the moment before the red Allegro smashed into him down Swinegate. The footlights bathe him in their eerie glow. The mirrored ball twinkles.

Purdcake makes a sucking noise through his teeth. A long cylinder of Sir Nigel ash falls into Hazel's lap.

Epiphany is commenting on the make of Ziggy's suit, pulling him this way and that. Ziggy just stands for it all, like a private on parade, his eyes on those optics behind the bar. His lips are puckering, converging to one side of his face like that old knot in the balloon, Ziggy Hero, Ziggy Low, the man in the brown suit, bending to his impulse again. He turns and whispers something in the pianist's ear. The pianist, still a long way from earth, raises his eyebrows and stands up. Ziggy sits down in his place. Epiphany inhales on her cigarette. A cocktail shaker is slowly shaken to a standstill.

I realise most of us round this table have been waiting for this moment for a long, long time. Since down on the barge at the end of Grape Lane, in fact.

He chucks the pink boa over his shoulder and I'm thinking how well it goes with his brown suit. He lights a cigarette and begins to play – Bowie of course. A few bars in I recognise it, one of my favourites of his, 'Lady Grinning Soul'. From the word off, you can tell his voice hasn't deserted him and the thing is he's not *trying* to sound like him at all. It's like incongruous to the extreme – they're all really shocked, all the trannies, cos you could tell they all thought he was a jerk, a real square, even those fucked-looking musicians are impressed. I think you can tell there is something about this – I mean, Christ, there is. On this night, in this dingy club with tinfoil ashtrays and dirty carpet squares, on this night Ziggy is giving the performance of his life. It's not, like, perfect sounding, indistinguishable from Bowie, it's more like Philip Marlowe, if you can imagine that. I know it's pretty hard. Anyway, I must remember not to drink like this.

As Ziggy reaches the climax of his song, I have a feeling he won't come back to us, and that we won't see him again. Sure enough, he gives us the slip, before the applause has even finished. They fucking love him, would that he'd let himself be carried aloft from the stage. He's making for the door, though. I get up to go after him.

Someone grabs my arm, Epiphany, she wants to know who he is and all.

'Who's your friend?' she says.

'What?'

'Who's your friend?'

'My friend?'

'Yes, yes, who is he?'

'What's his *name*, you mean?'

'Yes, what's his fucking name?'

I run my tongue over my lips.' His name . . . his name is . . .'

She lowers her head and I whisper in her ear and then she's scrambling back on stage. The taste of hairspray on her wig makes me retch. There's some feedback on the mike. I'm staring at the carpet thinking I'm gonna puke.

'Ladies and gentlemen, let's hear it – a really big round of applause now please for our friend . . .' she looks around to locate him, 'ARTHUR BANNOCKBURN!'

My tongue presses hard against the roof of my mouth to force back puke. Beneath the green exit sign on the tunnel side of the red greeting rope, I catch Ziggy's face and it's like slow whiplash. He turns for a moment, as though following the echo of some distant name, his name, round the room. Then he's gone. Vomit wells in my oesophagus and suddenly pours into my mouth. Bent double and dribbling, I charge to the john through the applauding crowd.

TILL THE COWS COME HOME

The woman at the launderette has washed his card that I'd left in my jeans. The name's gone, but the numbers are still partly legible. I've tried various permutations and international prefixes but have had no luck. The number, it seems, does not exist.

EPILOGUE

BONFIRE NIGHT, FINSBURY PARK, LONDON, 1987

Val is in a long line for the Ladies'. I smile and wave my toffee apple at her and she blows me a kiss. The apple is bad inside and I lob it into the fire.

Around me lots of kids are competing to see who can make the most racket. One of them, a girl, begins to shout 'Remember remember the fifth of Novemb . . .' but she's drowned out by her brothers mimicking her. Their shrieks, like rockets, rise in crescendos, before falling back into the darkness. Embers slowly float into the night sky. Some drift towards us and snag in the barbed wire above our heads where they glow on a while. Shh, I hear myself say. I bring a finger to my lips, touching off a memory of another bonfire night in what seems like a past life.

THE ANCIENT MARINER

Creeping closer to the old gypsy camp, Zig had become mesmerised by the huge flags hanging round it. Inside, there was a solitary caravan and a roaring bonfire.

'There's someone in there,' I hissed, 'in the caravan.' We lifted on to tiptoes over the crunching cinders, then, ducking down, waddled like Cossacks over to the flames. Crouching there, I felt my face begin to roast and a horrible stench filled my nostrils. I looked down – a binload of kitchen rubbish had been thrown on the fire. Sizzling by my foot was a tub of rancid margarine.

'I want that flag,' whispered Ziggy, pointing at a Zulu tricolour.

'What?' I said.

'I want it for the gig.'

I looked over to where he was pointing. The flag was billowing in the heat haze, just coloured vapours, some old colonial's memory, not something you could steal. Ziggy removed his fedora and stood up, smoothed a hand over his hair then ducked down again.

'Whazz ih?'

'Shh.' He pointed to the door of the caravan. It opened and in the yellow rectangle of light there came a melting man.

'Keep down, shh.'

The melting man bent forward, I couldn't see what he was doing at first. And then I realised he was untying a fucking great hell hound. The sound that I'd mistaken for the low whirring of Ziggy's portable cassette player was in fact the mastiff's growl.

'Yes, gents,' came his gruff voice. 'Can I do fu you?' He was peering about blindly in the darkness. He couldn't see us, but somehow sensed we were there. 'I know you're there.'

For some reason Ziggy stood up. 'Where you goin?' I hissed, then reluctantly followed him out from behind the flames. Our shadows shot up the side of the caravan. His mastiff sped towards us, its chain unravelling like a dropped anchor, snapping taut a couple of feet from where we stood. It strained and jumped in the air, barking like hell.

'Shaddap,' yelled the man, matching the mastiff's throaty growl. 'Arrrrh sed fak-iiiiiiiiin SHADDAP.'

The melting man stepped down on to an orange box that did as his step and flashed a torch across our faces. There was a wooden creak of the crate then a double click I recognised from my pest patrol days as the sound of a rifle being cocked.

I'd arranged to meet Ziggy at the Centurion café at three. He'd arrived at half past carrying his portable tape recorder, listening to 'Lodger'. Nine days to the gig and he'd been too restless to sit down so we'd got teas to take away.

It was cold out and we'd wrapped our hands round our styrofoam cups. The steam insulated us from the hubbub of the town.

I am a DJ, I am what I play, can't turn around no, can't turn around nooooo.

'How you doin?'

'Cool man, cool,' said Ziggy, lifting his cup to his lips.

And he could have had a Cadillac, if the school had taught him right.

As we'd walked, prompted by the Travelogue-type lyrics, I began talking about doing The Elmer, about the postcards piling up behind the mirror faster than Ovo could smoke them into surrogate destinations of his own. We came to a halt in front of Blue Lagoon Travel Agents. Like me, Ziggy often checked his reflection in shop windows. With me, it had become something of an obsession.

Shoppers in the street behind me were reflected among cardboard cut-out holidaymakers, stalked by a leopard in the long grass. I'd watched them enter from the Wimpy in front of the Taj Mahal and march dejectedly through sand dunes and blue azure lakes before disappearing through the solid wall into Woolworths. Ziggy and I stood out in our ex-army macs, delinquent and perverse, unsuitably dressed for the beach. A faded girl in a washed-out yellow bikini was splashing through the surf towards us.

Ziggy had begun to mumble the names of the destinations arranged crookedly in white plastic letters on the black peg-board. 'Malaga, Tunis, Benidorm, Barbados, Bahamas, Algarve . . . so,' he broke off, 'this Elmer man, he just took off, huh?'

I'd nodded as a flight booker appeared in the window, making an alteration to the international exchange rate. Each country was represented by a tiny flag and I wondered under which The

Elmer was now basking or banking. I thought of that dextrous trick he'd spent forever perfecting as a kid, the sunlight catching those silver heads of state as they flashed along the line of his knuckles.

His legend had begun with a group of friends, a fortnight in the sun in St somewhere-or-other. Assembling with their cases in the hotel lobby, someone had said, 'Hey, where's fuckin Dave?'

When the taxi had arrived to take them to the airport, there'd still been no sign of him. He wasn't in his room though all his stuff was still there and thinking about it nobody had seen him since the night before. The taxi driver was honking impatiently. They'd no choice but to go without him.

On an impulse someone had stopped the cab at the bar on the beach he'd like so much, Le Mistral, and there he was, just talking to the barmaid and sipping a cold beer.

'I arn't comin,' he said and, smiling at the barmaid, took another sip of cool beer. For a long while after that there'd been no word. Then came the postcards.

He'd gone to live with the girl from the Le Mistral bar.

He'd swum with dolphins.

He'd been to a party on Humphrey Bogart's yacht.

He'd saved someone from drowning.

He'd become a local celeb, a kind of guru from what he could make out.

He'd two-timed the Le Mistral girl.

They'd had a row.

He was sleeping on the beach.

He'd been mugged by some sailors from Marseilles.

He'd been feeling low and on the point of a whip-round to scrape his fare home when he'd overheard a couple of yachtsmen at the bar. A pal of theirs had been looking all morning for a deckhand and ... The Elmer interrupted to ask where he could find this bloke. They'd pointed beyond the bay. 'Seems like you're too late, I'm afraid, he's already . . . gone,' they said to an empty bar stool. They'd stood and stared as he'd hared off down the jetty, stripping as he ran. He'd dived off the pier and swam Olympically out to the yacht.

From the shore, all who'd witnessed it spoke of a brief exchange on the dripping deck, a welcoming handshake, and then the two silhouettes had disappeared below.

The cardboard cut-out girl in the yellow bikini was holding her hands out to catch a beach ball that her male companion was about to throw to her. She was laughing, carefree in the surf, and to me, just for a second, with her hands stretched out in front to catch the ball, she looked like she was applauding The Elmer. Oddly, her tan had *faded* from so many years in the sun. Behind her, a secretary was tidying brochures on the rack. I thought about the Le Mistral girl, wondered if, as the group who'd gathered to watch him leave dispersed, she'd been the last to turn away, walking slowly back along the jetty to where his clothes lay strewn around, the way they'd once been on the floor of her chalet.

Passing the last *Evening Echo* stand, I'd lit a joint and as the 'ECH-OO' died away, a silence fell between us. I offered the joint to Ziggy and our hands touched briefly as he took it from me. He held it abstractedly in front of him like a torch and then handed it back to me. Looking around I realised we'd strayed into an unfamiliar part of town. We were on an old terraced street of empty houses.

'Hey, Ziggy?'

'Mmm, yeah.'

'Where are we?'

'What?'

'I said where . . . turn that down a sec, willya. Where are we?'

He peered down the desolate street.

'Ziggy.'

'Yeah man?'

'Do you know where you are?'

'What?'

'Do – you – know – where – you – are?'

'Yeah . . . er, well, that is no.'

We'd carried on walking, under an old railway bridge with weeping walls. The pleasant effects of the weed had begun to rub off and paranoia was seeping in. There was the stench of piss and the movement of rats round my feet. 'Let's get a fuckin move on,' I'd said, increasing my pace.

Emerging from the tunnel, in front of us lay a stretch of wasteland and on the far side of it there was a strange something we couldn't quite make out.

'Looka that, what's that?' said Ziggy.

There were flags, lots of them, huge flags like I'd never seen before, all rippling like sail canvas against the wire-mesh fence of some old compound, a gypsy site. Under the night sky the flags had merged into one long train of nations. I didn't recognise any of the countries they represented though I imagined them flapping in troubled skies – breakaway republics, war-torn and bullet-ridden, burning Hiltons, armed peasants with rifles and dogs.

We came out from behind the fire with our hands up.

'We were just admiring your flags, pal,' I called out above his dog's fierce barking.

The gun he was pointing at us was an old gas cylinder repeater rifle, like Brother Ray used for shooting rats. I didn't really think he was going to use it and I was really more worried about the mastiff. Ziggy whispered something to me out of the corner of his mouth. I nodded to show him I'd heard and still with our hands up I shouted, 'Yeah, my mate here would like to borrow these flags here for his gig.'

I looked at Ziggy to check that that was right, and he nodded imperceptibly. (I was also thinking they'd make a nice wall at the Wigwam.)

'What gig? What y' gunna do wiv em?'

The man was a cockney. I'd only seen cockneys on telly, in sitcoms and documentaries about the Blitz and D-Day and stuff like that. Still holding up my hands, I looked about me, at the shabby flags flapping in the breeze, at the furniture and blackened tins and rancid margarine burning in the fire. It was like they'd held their party here among the bombed-out rubble of their homes. Left this one here to tidy up, keep the home fires burning, keep the flags flying.

Melting man gave a sudden shiver. He half turned to go back inside the caravan then paused and twisted around, as though pricked by the famous cockney welcome. 'Caaarm in den,' he said. 'Carm in ahrt the cowld then, if you wanna talk abart these flags, carm on, chop-chop, it's blady freeeeeezin' ahrt there. Carm on, arv made sam tea. Look, I'll put this darn, look see, arm putting it down.'

He put down his gun and whistled to the mastiff.

'Carm on, he won't urt ya.'

Inside, the caravan was brightly lit. There was a squelching lasagne of carpet laid over with flattened-out cardboard boxes covered in footprints.

'Sid dahn, go on, sid dahn.'

Flags brought tea and china cups and saucers from a tiny galley and set it down with a clink and tinkle between us on an upturned crate. The mastiff slumped heavily against the door and sighed.

'So,' he said, sitting down, 'whad you wanna do wiv deez flags den?'

Before Ziggy could speak, Flags said, 'Don't moind me,' and reached over for a magazine on which there was a familiar scatter of spliff-making material. 'This is for me ealth. I smoke cos I'm too fit uverwoise.'

He introduced himself through a series of stifling belches. Neither of us caught his name. 'Emp. Beg yer pardon. Hemp, y'see.' He cleared his throat. 'Withart it, y'know, where wid be daht yu? There'd be no fackin British Navy, ah nah.' He shook his head. 'No friggin riggin, no Empire.'

'Ummm,' mumbled Ziggy, 'so anyway . . .'

'Hemp, y'see – sorry you wuz saying summink. But hemp, y'see, is like yer worldwide thing. What I say to em . . . what I say to em is this – give hemp to everyone. Everyone! Make it legal, make it fackin legal. Ere I am, fit as fackin fiddle – without it there'd be no riggin – where wud the British Navy be without fackin riggin?'

My eyes must have betrayed the fact that I couldn't really follow what he was saying.

'Whas wrong wi you?' he asked fiercely, staring deep into my eyes. I held his stare till he leant back, nodding, satisfied it seemed. 'You're not roight, are you.' And then, in a cat-sat-on-the-mat-type way, 'LOOK! Plant, hemp, ROIGHT! Grow it, roight! That's employing thasands of pe-puwl. Perfec conditions.' He was carving karate blows through the air and winking.

I was getting a bit freaked. I'd heard about people who'd died on operating tables and found themselves looking down on their bodies from above. At the moment of death your soul can travel great distances in a matter of seconds, visit seemingly random places to which you have no particular attachment: a graveside in Australia, a restaurant in Madrid, a filling station in Arizona. You are whisked from one destination to another, weaving unseen vapour trails across the spirit plane, and then, with a jolt, you're pulled back into your body, leant over by panicky operating orderlies in their green masks and gowns.

'Disneyland – bring it here – I'll show em. I've got all the plans.' He roughly indicated the bare walls of his caravan with his tattooed arm. 'Sweeney Todd, Jack the Ripper, Mary Poppins – bring it to the East End ah Landan.'

He handed me the spliff and began pouring the tea.

'There's consi-crated land – graveyards all around.' He slopped the tea from cup to cup making it swill all over the tray. 'Land wot can't be touched. Make Disneyland in dee midduw ov it. It'll never change, always be der. Pearly kings and queens, *Chitty Chitty Bang Bang*, it's all up in dee air, have it in dee air, surraanded by Jewish cemeteries, Mary Poppins cammin dahn on her brolly.'

I passed the spliff to Ziggy who declined it. Steam from the teapot was condensing on the windows. Ziggy was responding to Flags with measured nods. Suddenly Flags stretched out an arm and said, 'Leser try it on then – y at, s'av it. I was into ats – uhh, scuse – when ah was yanger. Had a Davy Crockett at, din oi. Made it aht uh this old fur coat I farnd in a cabbud.' He toked on the joint. 'Only fing was, turned aht it wasn an owld fackin fur coat after all, but me ol gran's Sundee bleedin best. Wernt like goin out an killin a fackin bear like Crockett done, but if you knew my fackin grandmuver.'

Reluctantly, Ziggy handed over his fedora. Flags settled it on his head and pointed at the tape recorder.

'Whas that?'

'Oh, it's music – David Bowie.'

'Ooo?'

'David Bo –'

'Tarn it ap den. Les hav a listen.'

Ziggy turned the sound right up. 'Boys Keep Swinging' filled the caravan and for a while nobody spoke. *Boys keep swinging*. I sipped my tea – it had gone cold. *Boys always work it out*. Flags was following the music, nodding out of time to the next track, *I'm just a travelling man maybe it's just a trick of the mind.*

Ziggy tried a link-up. 'You seem like you've seen a bit of the world, Mr . . . er . . .'

'Action,' said Flags. 'Ah'll say.' His voice seemed in awe of his own past doings. 'Yhur, oh yhur lots! Used to be a sailor, din oi.' He rolled up his sleeves to show sailor's tattoos and smacked his lips at some past flavour of it all. 'Ah, yeah, India, America, Japan, Africa . . .' as he raged on I realised why the flags were so precious to him, '. . . Morocco, da souks. Oh, fack yeah, I've been in the thick of it, aw right. Handle meself ah can though, no facker can get near me. Ere!'

He put down his china cup and picked up a large ball-pane hammer that I hadn't noticed before. He blew on it then used it to tilt up the brim of Ziggy's fedora, same way a sheriff might. His manner had changed and he enlisted us now like fellow conspirators.

'People carm ap to me, y'know, all over du world – like this. Ere!'

He thrust the hammer at Ziggy.

'Ere . . . take it then.'

Hesitantly, Ziggy took hold of it.

'Now,' he cleared his throat, 'you stand ovur there.'

He pointed to where the dog was asleep. 'Go on den.'

Ziggy hesitated. 'Over there?'

'Mmm, thas roight.'

Ziggy got to his feet and manoeuvred himself past my knees. I was too out of it to move.

'Yeah, just there – jus there,' said Flags. 'Roight!' He got up flinching as his bad foot took his weight. 'Oooooh, yu barstud. Nah then, lift the ammer abav yer ead.'

Ziggy didn't move. His hair fell in his eye. The light in the caravan was showing up the unevenness of his fake tan again.

'Ovur yer ead, s'right, over yer head.'

The low ceiling in the caravan made it awkward but he lifted it as far as he could.

'Nah then.' Flags was shaking, beside himself with excitement.

'You say te me,' he dug himself in the chest, 'you say te me, roight.' He licked his lips. 'You say te me, I'm gonna kill yer.'

Ziggy looked aghast. 'Ha . . . hang on, man! Sorry! You want me to say . . .'

'Say, I'm gonna kill yer.' Flags was grinning insanely, like a dervish, stabbing viciously at his chest. 'Yer say to me I'M GONNA FACKIN KILL YER. Carm on, SAY it.'

The fedora trembled. The mastiff began a low growl.

Ziggy cleared his throat and with as much conviction as he could muster said, 'I'm going to kill you.'

'YOU WHAT?' Flags cupped his ear. 'AH carn ear yer.'

Ziggy cleared his throat some more and shouted, 'I'M GONNA KILL YOU.'

Flags looked like he was going to burst out laughing. With one hand on his stomach he pointed to the hammer above Ziggy's head. 'What, wiv that? Wiv that?'

Ziggy turned his head to look at the hammer in his hand, slightly puzzled, as though he thought it might have turned into a flower or something. And that, that was his mistake. He only took his eyes off him for a second but that's just what Flags had been waiting for him to do. While Ziggy stared at that hammer, Flags struck. Outside of films I don't think I've ever seen anyone move so fucking fast in all my life. I didn't even see what he did but suddenly Ziggy was lying on the floor.

Flags had got the hammer off him and was holding him down, straddling his chest, lifting the hammer high above his feverish head, screaming, 'SEE YER IN DISNEYLAND, ZIGGY.'

I was completely stunned, turned to stone yet jelly inside. But as the hammer reached the highest point of its upward arc it touched some impulse in me. I launched myself at Flags, landing awkwardly on Ziggy's legs and hitting my head on the edge of the table. From the corner of my eye I saw the hammer go down and heard a scream and a thud.

'There,' panted Flags. He struggled to his feet. 'See whad a mean,' he said, falling back into his seat as though he'd just come with an Amsterdam whore.

I tried to haul myself up but the pain in my head was too much. I put my hand up to my cranium. Behind my eyes a darkness began to close in and overwhelm me, I felt dizzy and vaguely sick, the electric lights grew dim, I was aware of blood on my hand and a warm jet of urine coming in spasms against my thigh. Then I blacked out.

At first I didn't know where I was and it was only slowly I began to remember. I was lying on flattened cardboard boxes, staring up at the ceiling of the crazy man's caravan. When I tried to move, I had agonising shooting pains in my head, so I lay still, waiting for things to become clear. I said to myself, You're OK, you're OK, you've hit your head, but you're OK. Slowly I sat up and looked around. I was alone. I began rubbing my head. No Ziggy, no man, no dog. Though oddly 'Boys Keep Swinging' was still playing on. I got up a bit shakily using the table to support me. That's weird, I thought, and instinctively lurched for the door.

The air outside was thick with smoke. I started to remember things like bits of a dream. I looked round the empty lot, slowly slowly turning my head and gripping my neck. And then I made out the Flagman. He was over by the fire, gazing into its flames with the black mastiff at his side. He heard me step on to the orange box and turned a cheek against the flames. He seemed incredibly calm.

'Feeling better nah?' he said. The mastiff growled.

I didn't answer immediately but took a few steps towards the fire.

'Where's Ziggy?' I said. 'Where's my friend?'

'Who?'

'My friend,' I said, 'the guy I was with – what's happened to him?'

'Oh yeah,' Flags nodded, 'your friend. Yeah, he had to go, he told me to tell you he'd see ya later.'

'But . . .' I paused. Flags had returned to face the fire. He was feeding it with a bag of rubbish, the way people feed the birds.

'But . . . but . . .'

Flags looked at me and carried on throwing bits into the fire.
'You . . . you hit him with – with that – hammer.'
He just shook his head. 'Nah . . . not me.'

He went like one that hath been stunned,
And is of sense forlorn:
A sadder and a wiser man,
He rose the morrow morn.

Samuel Taylor Coleridge
'The Rime of the Ancient Mariner'

ACKNOWLEDGEMENTS

In writing this novel I would like to thank all of the following for their help and inspiration, some of whom may not even remember me from what amounted to little more than fleeting meetings, much less guess that they had any lasting effect on me.

So, in no particular order I'd like to thank: Michael Warren – I was twelve when I first sneaked into the De Grey Rooms to watch you play, it became a strange turning point; Martin Barrel, for clothing me; Mark Elmer who once at the Old World disco stepped in to prevent two huge bastards from killing me, for which incidentally I've always been extremely grateful, and also, not least, for providing his own globe-trotting legend; Wayne Holmes for swapsies; Gordon Brown to whom not just me but a lot of people owe thanks for providing a great refuge from drudgery; John Wakefield, travelling companion and storyteller; Steve Dixon for tireless research; Mike Reid, again, a kind of inspirational figure; and old school friends Ando, Deano and Bow Wow.

More lately I'd like to thank my family, especially my mother. My wife Jane for her endless love and support. Di and Don for all they've done. My agent, Clare Conville, for her heroic patience, belief and, ultimately, for being who she is. Marian McCarthy at Bloomsbury. Same goes for Dave Huggins and Carl Hindmarch. A special thank you to Rankin and Jefferson at *Dazed and Confused*; Sophie Fiennes; J. Jopling for massive support; Sam Taylor-Wood for photography; Matthew Donaldson; Howard Sooley; Jarvis Cocker; J. C. Emin; Michael Clark; Malcolm McLaren; Ben, Pip, and Jo for lending me their flat to write in; Amanda Ooms for giving me, among other things, a computer; John Brooks, without whose technical troubleshooting this book would quite literally not exist; Max Wigram; Paul Fryer; Julian Broad; Lee Swillingham for his fantastic cover work; and last, but definitely not least, a Good Old Days medley of superlatives for his extreme caring, my editor Nicholas Pearson.